Brennan
CORNER
Dobson
Myers-
Pearse
KRUSS
Kennedy
Morgan
Granger
[illegible]

[illegible]
[illegible]
Thomas
[illegible]
HOWELL
[illegible]

Cold Lessons

Cold Lessons

Michael McCulloch

FIVE STAR
An imprint of Thomson Gale, a part of The Thomson Corporation

Detroit • New York • San Francisco • New Haven, Conn. • Waterville, Maine • London

This novel is a work of fiction. Names, characters, places, and incidents are either the product of the author's imagination, or, if real, used fictitiously.

Set in 11 pt. Plantin.

LIBRARY OF CONGRESS CATALOGING-IN-PUBLICATION DATA

McCulloch, Michael, 1969–
Cold lessons / Michael McCulloch. — 1st ed.
p. cm.
ISBN-13: 978-1-59414-524-7 (alk. paper)
ISBN-10: 1-59414-524-5 (alk. paper)
1. High school teachers—Fiction. 2. Students—Crimes against—Fiction. 3. Montana—Fiction. I. Title.
PS3613.C3864494C65 2007
813'.6—dc22 2006033095

First Edition. First Printing: January 2007.

Published in 2007 in conjunction with Tekno Books and Ed Gorman.

Printed in the United States of America on permanent paper
10 9 8 7 6 5 4 3 2 1

For my real-life English teachers, who did care:
Barry, Greg, Harry, John, Oliver, Robin, and Tom.

★ ★ ★ ★ ★

Garden City, Montana
1987

★ ★ ★ ★ ★

Chapter One: Wednesday

The average adult, thought Gil, probably assumed students only threw paper airplanes in TV shows and movies about high school. That same person might also reasonably believe spitballs were an anachronism that went out with boys dunking girls' pigtails in inkwells. They would be wrong. There were spitballs stuck to the walls of Gil Strickland's classroom, rubber bands in the chalk trays, and paper planes lying crashed in the corners, their blue-lined notebook paper yellowing with age.

Not that Gil gave a shit anymore. The little fuckers could sit quietly and pretend to listen if they wanted to, but they couldn't fool him. If, by chance, any of his hard-won insight seeped into their brains, it would disappear from memory as soon as they completed the next pop quiz.

There wasn't much he could do about it, given that he had no control over either the mating habits of the general population or the bylaws of the educational juggernaut. He wasn't a teacher, he was a babysitter with tenure, an annuity, and summers off. But as long as he kept showing up, he got paid. And, after twenty-three years in the trenches, he could recite *The Old Man and the Sea* in his sleep.

He was in his customary lecturing stance: seated, in a molded plastic chair at the front of the room, tilted precariously backward. As he spoke, his eyes roved from the tops of his students' heads to the small forest of pencils protruding from the acoustical ceiling tile.

"And who is Santiago's hero? Anyone?" No hands disturbed his field of vision. "Joe DiMaggio. And DiMaggio played for—?"

"The Los Angeles Dodgers," said a kid.

Gil didn't look. "I'm going to assume that's a joke. He of course played for the Yankees. Now, what's going on with DiMaggio? Anyone?"

A freckled, wispily red-haired arm shot up. Gil recognized it as Jerry Feinstein's. "Anyone?" he said again. "DiMaggio is injured, and the old man is following news of his recovery with great interest. It's significant because—"

The bell rang and the students bolted. Like so many stampeding bison, they thundered out the door, leaving in their wake twenty-four haphazardly strewn desks.

"Read the rest of the damn book!" Gil shouted after them as he brought all four legs of his chair finally to the floor.

"I finished it last week," said Jerry petulantly as he slouched toward the exit.

Gil ignored him and rose from the chair, wincing at a twinge in his back. He reached back and knuckled his lower spine ineffectually as he walked slowly back to his desk. As he stared at his paper-strewn desktop, he saw a cheerleader in crimson and gold approaching. He pretended not to see her and sat down, taking a swig from his cold cup of coffee. He winced genuinely at the taste, then feigned surprise at the girl as he lowered his mug.

She was leaning against the corner of the desk with her hip, holding her notebook to her breasts with both hands like a shield.

"Yes?" said Gil.

"Mr. Strickland, um, we have to go cheer at a game across town tonight, and I don't know if I'll have time to do the reading."

Gil contemplated the peeling lime green paint on the far

wall. "Read it after school."

"Um, we have practice, and then I have to do chores before I—"

"Have your mom put on a pot of coffee after the game. You'll be able to get all sorts of work done," said Gil.

"Mr. Strickland," she pouted. "It's a school-sponsored—"

"So's reading. Which do you think will serve you better when you graduate, stentorian lungs or the ability to read job applications?"

She bit her lip. "Um, I don't know what that one word means."

"Oh, what's the difference," Gil grumbled. "So you won't answer questions in class tomorrow. That'll be a change." He dismissed her with a wave.

Her face brightened, but she wasn't done yet. "And, Mr. Strickland? You know Kristen? Um, I know she's not like here today, but she's on the squad, too, and—"

"Let Kristen make her own excuses, Marla."

"It's Maria, Mr. Strickland."

"Maria."

She smiled and he pictured her practicing that smile in a mirror, wearing her little outfit. "Well, thanks, Mr. Strickland." She trotted toward the door.

He liked the way she said "across town," as if a ten-minute drive to the shitkicker school made all the difference. Forgetting, he took another mouthful of cold coffee and spit it back into the cup. He got up to erase the three things he'd bothered to write on the board. Lord, was he sick of Hemingway.

As if "Lord" was his cue, Vice Principal Tim Flannel, Jr. strode briskly through the door, his gait incongruous with his heavy, pear-shaped body. His earnest face close-shaved and scrubbed to a pink sheen, his hair blow-dried into a fluffy pompadour, he could have just stepped off the stage at a tent-show revival. Flannel's righteous radiance made students nervous; when he walked into a room, even honor-roll students shifted uncomfortably like pickpockets rousted for a police lineup. He made Gil, against his will, feel the same way.

"Gil, my good fellow," began Flannel with his customary over-formality. "Just your mid-week reminder that lesson plans are due Friday at noon."

"Thanks, but I haven't forgotten," said Gil.

"And I hope you won't take it amiss if I say it's my job to ensure you don't forget. Your performance does meet standards at the present time; however, I'm sure both of us want to avoid the unpleasantness that would be caused by a tardy submission of your lesson plans."

Gil sighed. "Not to worry, Tim." He drained the bitter dregs of his coffee, cursed silently, and swallowed.

Flannel eyed the mug. "You're hitting that stuff pretty hard."

"It's either that or put myself to sleep."

Flannel's big belly quivered with laughter. "You've always had a fine sense of humor, Gil."

"I need it."

Still chuckling, Flannel bid him good day and left.

As he walked away, Gil regarded the aft view. Despite his name, Flannel favored polyester suits from Big and Tall that seemed cut for a preacher, not an educator. If he was feeling somber, he wore navy; in a better mood, he chose white with a flamboyant striped tie. It was odd, Gil thought, that a proselytizer would choose polyester, but then again, Flannel was never betrayed by an unexpected wrinkle that could suggest, however vaguely, that all was not in accordance between mind and body.

Gil waited a minute and then peeked around the doorway to make sure Flannel wasn't still in the hall. He was gone, so Gil took a left and headed for the teachers' lounge, his empty cup in hand. The trip was short—just to the end of the hall—but never easy. To the left of the lounge door was a trophy case with dusty glass shelves. Wooden letters cut by some long-ago shop class proclaimed: *A+ EDUCATORS!* A few yellowed certificates curled forlornly or had fallen flat, but dead center was a large wooden plaque with an engraved bronze plate and a lacquered photo of a thirty-seven-year-old Gil. The plaque read:

For Exceptional Achievement
in High School Education
The Montana Educators' Association
Names
Gil Strickland
Teacher of the Year

Usually he flipped it the bird and kept walking, but this time he stopped. The halls were empty, quiet except for echoes of laughter and squeaking tennis shoes down on the second floor. The photo wasn't much, a headshot by the same hack who immortalized the students for the yearbook on the first school day each year. But Gil's smile was broad and confident, his hair dark and full, and his horn-rimmed glasses not yet bifocal. He looked barely older than the students he taught now. It was like looking at a photo of a cousin he'd never met: the features were familiar but he had no idea what the guy was thinking.

He jiggled the lock that kept the glass doors from sliding open, but the barrel stayed snug on its bend of jagged chrome teeth. The Teacher of the Year would continue to taunt him. He opened the lounge door and went in. The last cup of coffee was burning in the carafe. He sniffed it, dumped it, assembled a new pot, and stood over the appliance while it hissed and dripped. The windows of the lounge looked north on a fortress-like annex that had been built only a few years ago. The original building dated back nearly a hundred years, and was a massive, maze-like structure that Gil thought resembled a Victorian madhouse. The tall windows were darkening, pulling light out of the building and letting in the January cold.

Gil poured half a cup of coffee and walked back to his room. He shut the door. He sat down at his desk and opened his class planner. The next week was blank. His right hand found a bottle of Old Forester deep in a drawer and sat it down next to him. He spun the cap off with his thumb, poured a healthy brown dollop into his mug, and put the bottle away. He gave the cocktail a quick stir with his finger and then wiped his finger on a memo. He gulped coffee and pulled out a pen.

For Monday, under Period One, Freshman English, he wrote: *Reading day.*

It was fully dark by the time he got into his battered orange Datsun half an hour later. The ripped vinyl seat crinkled under his threadbare corduroy pants as he sat down, feeling every tear. The steering wheel was cold to the touch even through his wool mittens. His breath frosted the inside of the windshield like a chilled beer mug. He started the car, revved it hard, and turned the defroster all the way up. After a few minutes, little eyes of clear glass began to open at the bottom of the windshield, and he put the car in gear.

As he drove, he hunched over the steering wheel, peering as if through blinders at the road ahead of him. Mr. D's, where he drank, was only a mile away, one left turn and one right turn. Above him, streetlights etched naked tree branches out of the night sky, while oncoming headlights haloed his frosty windshield.

Sean had the bottle on the bar, next to a glass. When he saw Gil come through the door, he poured a generous amount. Gil took a stool opposite Sean, nodded hello, lifted the glass, and drank it down. Warmth coursed from his belly to his chilled extremities, making him shudder with pleasure. He set the glass down on the bar and Sean filled it again. Gil kept his hand cradled around it and looked up at his benefactor.

"Thank you, Sean."

"You're welcome, Gil." If young Sean O'Donnell had any idea he was the second most important person in Gil's life, he never let on. Around thirty years old, the son of "Mr. D," he shared his father's taste for a classic publican style: white shirt, black pants, white apron, black tie tucked in between the third and fourth buttons. His gentle manner and choirboy features contrasted sharply with those of his father, a Chicago Irishman who'd given and taken many beatings as a middleweight boxer before inheriting a bar in a place he'd never heard of, Garden City, Montana. The senior O'Donnell was seldom behind the bar these days, but Sean minded the store six days a week. Like clockwork, he opened the bar at ten, served sandwiches from noon to one, poured Gil's bourbon at four-thirty, and ceded to the relief bartender at seven.

A bartender's temperament was the key in selecting a place in which to drink, and Gil had been through a dozen men and women before he settled on Sean. He was dependent on Sean's regularity, his friendly demeanor that was neither subservient nor obtrusive, and his unfailing willingness to keep a tab for Gil. In return for these comforts, Gil paid his tab in full once a month, on payday, adding a fifty dollar tip for Sean. The bar itself was nothing special, burnt-umber vinyl seats and beer-company shamrocks, but the TVs were usually silent and the regulars refused to feed the jukebox. And it was out of the way, and no students ever screwed up their courage and tried to barge in with fake IDs.

"What's it like out there?" asked Sean. Mr. D's had no windows and a heavy metal door.

"Still cold," said Gil, sipping. "How's the pugilist publican?"

"Pretty well. He's planning a trip back to Sligo this summer."

"Are you going with him?"

Sean shook his head. "He doesn't trust anyone else to watch the bar. He says if he could wait sixty years to go home, I can wait a little longer. I guess he's right."

"I thought he'd never been," said Gil. "Home."

"You know. American Irish." A customer raised an empty glass and Sean said, "Excuse me."

As Sean glided off to pull a beer, Gil was revealed to himself in the long mirror behind the bar. Lit from the right, his face like a half-moon rested just atop the row of bottles lining the back bar. Green lights ringing the mirror cast an unpleasant pallor on his skin, and behind him the room was shadowed like a cave. The gray streaks in his hair and on his stubbled cheeks surprised him, as did the clefts running under his cheekbones, the filigree of squint lines fanning out from his eyes. It wasn't the first time he'd seen them—how did he ignore them so assiduously?

Gil lifted his glass of whiskey and paused before he drank. He could see a tiny, flickering reflection of himself down there. No gray, he chuckled.

Three drinks under his belt, the usual, he stood on the cold asphalt outside the green door to the bar. A lopsided moon glowed behind a tattered cloud. A children's park, kitty-corner, dreamed of warm days and sticky little hands.

Gil walked slowly to his car. The cold felt empty, antiseptic. He got into the car and backed out carefully. Driving home, back toward the school, he took a different route, residential streets only. When he had to cross an artery, he looked back and forth several times before pulling out.

Gil stamped his feet on the mat and then kicked them together to knock off the dry snow. His cheeks were flushed from the short drive in the cold car. The back door opened to humid warmth and the smell of cooking dinner. Probably casserole, not that he minded. Lo was a hell of a good cook. When they first married, he used to tease her that she could make afterbirth appealing—not that they'd had the chance to find out. He hung his parka on a hook and put his hat and mittens on a shelf above it. He rubbed his hands as he walked through the dark living room.

"Tuna," Lo called out.

"Sounds good," he said.

In the kitchen, Lolita Strickland was sweating a little, the stray wisps of hair from her braid hovering in the heat as she checked her casserole on the open oven door. Satisfied, she slid the dish back in. Gil crossed behind her and took a tumbler and a bottle from the cupboard. He squeezed out of the kitchen again and sat down in the dark on the outside of the breakfast bar. He poured.

"Ready?" he asked.

"Sure."

They both stuck out their fists, nodded, and then shook them three times. Gil chose rock; Lo beat him with paper.

"Please," he said.

She sighed, opened the fridge, and pulled a half-empty bottle of white wine off the door. "Well," she said as she poured, "*Arizona Highways* gave me a nice call, said, 'Thanks but we've run about eight different versions of that piece already.' They wanted to know if I had anything else."

"Which you do."

"I do but only on napkins. It'll take me a week or two to shape another pitch. I also got two mailed rejections on other pitches. One was a form letter and the other just returned my letter without a note. So, I assume that's a rejection. Norm at the *Garden City Gazette* called and asked me to cover German-fest this year."

"That's nice."

"And it's six months away and pays ten cents a word."

"You file the Glacier Park piece?" he asked.

"Yup."

"How about your column for *RV?*"

"I'm about three months ahead on that one. I keep hoping they'll pay me early, but they won't." She put the wine away.

"Well, that's all you can do," said Gil.

"I'm going to send the desert getaways pitch to about a dozen more places tomorrow."

Gil swallowed whiskey. He didn't care if Lo didn't earn a dime, but her new career was important to her.

"And there are a bunch of other half-formed things," she said. "I'll just have to clean them up, make some calls, send out some letters."

"I'm sure January is the worst time for travel writing."

"Your turn," said Lo. She picked up a wet brussels sprout and used a paring knife to score an *x* in the stem. She peeled off a wilted leaf and threw it in the sink.

"Flannel with the lesson plans. And the cheerleaders are asking to be excused from their homework. I feel like I have to make a show of caring."

"And you don't."

"Nope. We should bring back trade schools, stop trying to stuff literature down these kids' throats."

"Hm," said Lo.

"It doesn't matter what *I* do. These girls know they're going to get what they want—in school, anyway. The administration's going to side with them and their jock boyfriends over academics any day. I almost look forward to seeing them at the Bi-Lo checkout in ten years."

"They ought to take your teaching license."

"They may as well have," said Gil.

The lid of a saucepan on the stovetop began rattling, and Lo lifted it off. She scooped the green brussels sprouts in both hands and dumped them into the colander inside the pan. "Five minutes," she said. She wiped her forehead with a dish towel and took a stool.

"Is that necessary?" said Gil.

"Hot," she replied.

Gil got up and took the towel from her. "Your kitchen is always hot." He stepped into the back porch, leaving the door open, and threw the towel in a laundry basket. He knew Lo was rolling her eyes behind him.

"It's that stove," she called. "It's an antique."

He came back in and shut the door.

"Or maybe I'm acquiring more insulation." She looked down at her waist, pinched herself.

"We all are."

"You're not," she said pointedly. "You've lost twenty pounds since we got married."

"At least I don't have a beer belly."

"How you've managed that."

Gil drained his glass and poured another. Lo watched him.

"You're eager tonight."

"Thirsty," he said.

"Water's the answer."

He began gathering plates and silverware. Lo got up, lifted the lid on the saucepan, and poked a brussels sprout with a fork. She replaced the lid and took the casserole out of the oven. The slivered almonds on top were brown and crispy.

"Can't you just put the nuts on one half?" said Gil.

"This is the way I make it," said Lo.

Gil sat back down while Lo dished the food. She sat down

and they ate in silence. The phone rang.

They looked at each other.

"Sharon," said Gil.

"I know," said Lolita. "Do you want to get it?"

Gil looked at a soupy piece of tuna and a dangling noodle impaled on the end of his fork.

She exhaled slowly, slid off her stool, and went to the phone. " 'Lo? Hi, Sharon . . . Yeah, we just sat down . . . uh huh, I'll call you right after . . . Okay, bye." She hung up, resumed her seat. "The timing of that woman."

"We might miss her if she stopped," said Gil through a mouthful of food.

"Might," said Lo.

Gil washed up after dinner, feeling stupid and sleepy from drink. Steam from the hot sink fogged the window overlooking the side yard, reducing his reflection to an outline. Fishing around in the soapy water he lost his grip on a plate, cracked it, and stifled a curse so Lo wouldn't find out until the morning. He filled his empty tumbler with cool water and drank it down, then filled it again, his wrinkly fingertips numb against the glass.

In the living room Lo laughed sharply and Gil craned to look. He could see half her body through the doorway. She was sprawled on the floor in front of the TV, lying on her stomach and kicking one foot restlessly in the air like a little girl. She looked good, wearing gray stretch pants and an oversized T-shirt. Many of her friends had grown into matronly bodies, but Lo still had a figure. Her butt was a little less round, he thought, her hips and thighs a little thicker. But womanly. The little pillow at the front of her pelvis was just soft enough to be inviting.

He didn't wash a dish for several minutes, watching as she thumbed the remote control repeatedly. Her wiry curls were still thick and mostly dark, and the silver streaks that shot to the ends were elegant, not dowdy. She absentmindedly tugged on an earlobe, then wound a lock of hair around her finger. Then unwound it. She settled on a detective show, lifted herself on her elbows, gathered her feet under her, and sat back against the couch.

Eyes on the TV, she started to call to him. "Would you—" She turned as she spoke, saw him looking at her, and paused. "Oh." She lowered her voice. "Gil, would you bring my wine in?"

"Sure, honey." He dried his hands and brought her glass to her. The condensation on the outside of the glass felt slippery against his soggy fingertips.

She gave him a look as she took the glass. "What's with 'honey'?"

He knelt awkwardly beside her and kissed her ear, placing his hand on her belly. "Nothing." He got up to go but she grabbed his leg.

"Come back here."

"I'm not done with the dishes."

Playfully, she wrapped her arms around both his legs and leaned in with her shoulder, toppling him to the couch. Climbing up onto him, she pulled up his shirt and kissed his stomach. "You're getting thicker, too, you know."

She pressed her mouth onto his and slid her hand down the front of his pants. He felt a surge of warmth in his groin. He was suddenly excited. They hadn't made out in years; hadn't made love in how long? Awkwardly, he bit her nipple through the cotton of her shirt.

"Take it off," he whispered hoarsely.

She sat back, kicking over her wine glass. Ignoring the spill, she pulled her shirt off in a magnificent gesture that had mesmerized Gil ever since he first saw it as a seventeen-year-old: smoothly, forearms crossed, right over the head. Her breasts caught in the fabric, rose, and slipped free, bouncing gently. Her nipples were the size of silver dollars. Seeing them always surprised him. He felt his cock start to strain against his boxers as her fingers continued to gently knead his thighs, shaft, and balls. She unbuttoned his shirt and kissed his graying chest hairs, his too-pale stomach, and his belly button, nipping at the hairs just below. Then she unbuttoned and unzipped his fly and slid his pants down around his ankles.

She's as beautiful, thought Gil, as she was twenty years ago. He leaned forward and kissed the top of her head.

Sliding his boxers down, too, she took his nearly hard cock in her mouth and let her fingers wander over his thighs. Gil suddenly realized he was nervous. He noticed the TV. A local car salesman was blustering his way through a stupid skit. He closed his eyes and tried to concentrate, but the fever-pitched voices on the commercial needled into his ears. *But mama told me, never trust a used car salesman . . .* Like trying to grasp and hold back a receding wave, he felt his blood go flat.

"Ah, shit," said Gil.

She looked up, still expectant. "No?"

He dropped his head back against the couch and sighed.

"But I thought—"

"Sorry. So did I."

Lo pulled his shorts back up and rested her head in his lap. Her fingers gently plucked at the black hairs on his thigh. The softness of her hair against his skin almost made him groan. There was more gray than he had thought, the streaks fading the beautiful night of her raven locks.

"You know it's not you, Lo," he began. "It's—"

She cut him off. "Ssh. I know, Gil. Just, the way you looked at me, I almost forgot . . ."

"So did I."

She stretched her leg and used her toes to pick up the remote.

Bringing it to her hand, she lowered the sound and switched channels. The local news was starting.

"Your drinking doesn't *help*," she said.

"Chicken or the egg, Lo."

"I'd think an English teacher wouldn't turn to cliché."

He let it go. She slid back down to the floor and stood up straight, twisting her spine as if she had a sore spot. The blue glow from the set flickered on her milky skin. Her nipples were erect.

"I'm cold," she said, reaching for her shirt and pulling it on.

That night, as Gil fell asleep, memory drifted into dream. Their little blanket was spread neatly beside the stream, lumpy with little hillocks of grass. Shards of sunlight bounced off the bubbling water and glittered on the boughs above them. Ants explored the remains of their sandwiches, while brazen crows tossed a crust of bread. Gentle currents of air played on their naked bodies. Lo threw back her head and laughed joyfully and pulled him closer. Her foot knocked over the green glass wine bottle as they made love.

Chapter Two: Thursday

Morning hit him like a brick. After turning off the alarm in his sleep, Gil barely had time to dress and brush his teeth before driving the three blocks to Porte l'Enfer High School. The trip lasted just long enough for him to reflect on the aptness of the school's name. Just a mile or two west of the school, the Lewis Tongue River flowed out of Porte l'Enfer Canyon. A century and a half earlier, French trappers had noted hundreds of human bones on the ground and called the place, in their own tongue, "Hell Gate." The local Indians had found the steep mountain slopes above the narrow river trail an ideal vantage point from which to ambush unwary enemies. The school and various local businesses now carried the name, although only the skateboard shop and a record store used the English translation.

He parked on the street a block from school, the back half of his car blocking a driveway he hoped was little-used. Face-numbing wind gusted out of the canyon as he trudged toward the hallowed halls of hell. He entered through a back way, near the gym, and took a route through quiet halls that offered the least chance of running into Flannel. He dropped into his seat ten minutes before first period began. His coffee cup was empty and he was still rubbing the sleep out of his eyes when the first student arrived.

The freshmen, to his surprise, wanted to be talked to. He tried to give them an easy out, telling them either he could lecture, or they could use the time to work on their assignments. He placed subtle, suggestive emphasis on the latter option, but when one kid said, "Let's talk about the story," the rest of them jumped on it. Gil thought he should have suggested a pop quiz in place of the lecture. This group was still new to the high school game; in a year or two they'd know how to play this particular hand.

So, against his will and without coffee, Gil led a class discussion. It went surprisingly well. One kid even thought of something that had never occurred to Gil before. Still, when the bell rang, he was ready. Second period was his free period. There would be coffee in the pot in the lounge. But as soon as the last student made his exit, Flannel charged in and marched zealously up to Gil's desk.

"Good morning, Gil. Did you—?"

Gil handed him the folder.

Flannel looked serious. "Thank you. However, I actually didn't come here to retrieve your lesson plans. You know Kristen Swales."

"She's in my fourth period, junior English class."

"Was," said the vice principal soberly. "There was a party at a student's house last night, up toward Stone Creek. Kristen got drunk on root-beer schnapps and had an accident while she was driving home. It's not in the papers yet, but I'm sure word is spreading among the students."

"She was hurt?"

"Killed. She was the only one in the car, a small blessing I suppose."

Gil thought of Kristen. She was a quiet girl, very pretty, a member of the cheerleading squad but not, as far as he could tell, really one of the group. She'd never seemed to possess the social skills or drive to fully participate in the clique. He tried to remember when he'd last seen her and couldn't. Tuesday?

Monday? She'd hardly been in school lately and he didn't know why.

"Anyway," Flannel went on, "I'm sure you will have a few distraught students on your hands. Deal with them as you see fit, but I don't want anyone to go home if it's not absolutely necessary. Some of these youngsters are emotional blackmailers. They'll see an opening and exploit it to their own advantage. So be wary."

"What's Whitehead doing?"

"He's out today. But don't worry, I've got everything well under control. If any of your students need a guiding hand or a strong shoulder, I will be available."

"Glad to hear it," said Gil.

Flannel turned and strode briskly out.

Gil thought again of the dead girl. These accidents were a common part of life in Garden City, regular enough that the yearbook always had at least one page of memorials. Dead kids were commemorated by a soft-focus photo and a classmate's poem, the stridently rhymed words of anguish always hitting the same themes. The cumulative effect was more a testament to the inevitability of such losses than an inquiry into why, with such mind-numbing regularity, kids wrapped their parents' cars around telephone poles.

If there was anything unusual about this accident, it was that it had happened in the dead of winter, instead of fall or spring, when warmer weather allowed the kids to hold their parties outside, up in the mountains. Even at night, the winding gravel roads proved too tempting to would-be drag racers. One survivor had told Gil about a game called "Star Trek," where the driver killed the headlights and turned on the dome light, so the passengers rolled through a blackness as empty as space. The game was over when fear brought the lights back on—or the car crashed.

Gil felt sorry for Kristen, and wondered why he didn't feel sad. She just hadn't had that much going for her. When she had come to class, she'd sat quietly in the back, not talking to anyone, not doodling, not reading. If he called on her, she'd furrow her brow and pretend she was trying to remember the answer until he asked someone else. The tragedy was less that she died so young than that she'd done so little while she was alive. He couldn't really condemn her for driving drunk.

Dick Simonsen came in the door, bright-eyed, and tried to slap Gil five. Gil put his hands in his pockets. It was their little ritual. Stocky, short, and balding, Dick was a lifelong jock whose metabolism would have put a squirrel to shame. Before Gil knew what hit him, Dick had begun a recitation of his accomplishments so far that morning: waking at four-thirty, grading papers over oatmeal, then running eight miles down the old highway. Gil always showed just enough interest to avoid being rude, which Dick mistook for a vicarious thrill in his every activity.

"How's Sharon?" asked Gil.

"Fine—you know."

"Could you gently prod her not to call at mealtimes?"

Dick laughed. "I go to bed too early. I think she gets lonely."

"Well, I may have to start talking with my mouth full."

Dick thrust a piece of mimeographed paper at him. "I didn't know if you'd seen this gem yet."

Gil took it. "I haven't been to my box for a while."

"Yesterday's memo. Vintage Whitehead. Read it and stand in awe. Seriously. I gotta run. We on for basketball after school?"

"Basketball? Are you kidding?"

"Millman is sick. Come on, Gil, do me a favor. I'll come by and get you." He disappeared out the door.

Gil scanned the memo, realizing he hadn't mentioned the late Ms. Swales to Dick. Principal Ron Whitehead, an elderly veteran who spent many afternoons at the golf course, seemingly believed he was the head of a private school. His writing and mannerisms boasted a bygone formality that made it clear he'd found a kindred spirit when he hired Flannel five years ago. Gil wondered if, when he walked the halls, Whitehead imagined himself parting a sea of preppie kids in ties and blue blazers, rather than a motley mix of jocks, cowboys, metalheads, punks, and New Wavers. The full-page memo said very little: school morale was low and he wanted to see more *PEP.* Gil crumpled it and dropped it into the trash. How would Whitehead address morale in light of last night's tragedy?

Fourth period. Students drifted in, some plugged in to Walkmans, others describing the previous night's TV viewing. Jerry Feinstein approached Gil as Gil scrawled hieroglyphics on the board.

"Good morning, Mr. Strickland."

Gil paused a moment, looked at him, and resumed writing.

"I was kind of bored last night, and I was looking through my mom's books, and I noticed she had some other Hemingway stuff," continued Jerry. "So I read some of his short stories. In *In Our Time* and *The Nick Adams Stories.*"

"Great," said Gil.

"I really liked them," said Jerry, edging a little too far into what numerous pop psychology books referred to as Gil's *personal space.*

Gil underlined something he wasn't sure he could read and turned. "That makes you a proud member of an elite group of tens of millions, both living and living impaired. Still, objectivity is crucial. You may have noticed that an obsession with death—especially death as a part of the natural order—runs through his work. It might be argued that the author was making the ultimate critique of his own canon when he gripped a shotgun in his hands and leaned back against the wall of his cabin in Ketchum, Idaho."

Jerry blinked. "Can I take attendance, Mr. Strickland?"

"Quit sucking up, Jerry."

The kid's freckled face fell. The bell clattered and the students began to sit down. As Jerry trudged to his desk, Gil thought he overheard him say, "He sat with the gun on his knees. He was very fond of it." What was that? Something from *In Our Time?*

Gil scanned the room. The students didn't appear to be in mourning—except Maria, the girl who'd asked to be excused from homework yesterday. She sat at her desk, stoic but for the tears smearing eyeliner down her cheeks.

Gil called on Chester, a hayseed he knew was dropping out at the end of the semester. Chester, who wore a sheathed Buck knife on his hand-tooled, personalized leather belt, had spoken so rarely that Gil couldn't remember what his voice sounded like. The student certainly seemed surprised to hear his name.

"Chester, take roll, please," said Gil.

Chester looked right, then left, then reluctantly came up for the attendance cards while Gil quietly asked Maria out into the hall.

"Are you all right?" he asked, closing the door behind them.

"Yes," she said. Her lower lip quivered.

"Were you friends with Kristen?"

"Pretty much. She cheered, you know."

Gil put his hand on her shoulder. "I know."

She broke down and hugged Gil. Gil overcame his startledness and hugged her back. She cried for a few minutes, then stepped back.

"I'm sorry," she said, pulling a tissue from her purse. "I fucked up your shirt." She dabbed at his shoulder.

"It's okay." He took the tissue and cleaned up her face a little. "Were you at that party with Kristen last night?"

Something besides sadness passed over her eyes. Concern for herself? She hesitated, then shook her head.

"You can tell me if you were," Gil coaxed. "I'm not worried about the homework."

"No," she said. "I went home."

Gil straightened her shoulders. "Okay. Tell you what. You can go home for the day if you want to. Mr. Flannel's available if you'd prefer to talk, but . . ."

She smiled morosely.

"I know. Go home."

She shuffled away, a damp little cheerleader. Gil went back into the room and interrupted a game of crumpled-paper hoops.

"Does everyone know what happened last night?"

The silence of assent.

"Does anyone need to talk about it?"

"No," piped up Jerry. "We're fine."

"Shut up, Jerry. Anyone else?"

"Will there be a quiz today?"

Gil sighed. "No." He regarded the dispassionate faces before him. One of their classmates had blipped from the video monitor of life. "Chester, how many are we missing today?"

"Just Kristen."

"Thank you." Gil turned to the board, tried to remember what he had written there. "Right. Who can tell me how the book ends? Anyone?"

Silence.

Dick came by for him after school, before he could hide or think of a good excuse. As they drove to Gil's house for his sweatpants and sneakers, Gil wondered if the former had been cut into rags for some forgotten cleaning project.

Lolita was surprised to hear him come through the door two hours early.

"What are you doing here?" she called from her study.

"I'm going to play basketball with Dick," he called back as he headed for the stairs.

There was a stunned moment of silence.

"What have you done with my husband?"

"He's at the bottom of the Lewis Tongue River. I am his doppelganger, here to steal his prestigious job and beautiful, sweet-tempered wife."

Gil was winded after trotting up the stairs. His knees cracked alarmingly when he knelt on the floor in front of his closet. Under a pile of shoes and sandals, he found his college-era sweats rolled in a ball and secured with a red-white-and-blue sweatband. The leather on his tennis shoes was stiff with age.

When she heard him coming downstairs, Lo called again. "Don't have a heart attack!"

"Thanks," he chuckled.

"No, I mean it. This is how old drunks like you end up pushing up the daisies."

At the gym he lasted about twenty minutes. Playing one-on-one, Dick killed him—twenty to two. Gil's single basket came when Dick stopped guarding him and said, "I just want to see if you can hit the backboard." With his hands on his hips, he watched Gil shoot three times. The third shot was a lay-up that rolled lazily around the rim before finally falling in.

Gasping, his heart racing, Gil slumped on the bleachers and watched Dick shoot baskets, hustling after every rebound. Gil didn't like Dick very much, but they remained friends out of habit and proximity. At least, they went through the motions of friendship. Dick had traveled directly from graduate school to the room next to Gil's in 1970, his head full of the latest educational theory. When he saw that Gil had not only been successfully incorporating progressive thinking into his classes in conservative Montana, but had been rewarded for it, Dick took Gil as a mentor, even though Gil was only eight years older. Though they were nothing alike—Gil bookish and unathletic, Dick an avid outdoorsman—throughout the early 1970s they had lunched together nearly every day and discussed how they could better prepare their students to assume active roles in society. Back then, arranging the desks in a circle was a matter of small controversy. The guest speakers they brought to their classes—ragged environmentalists, angry women's rights activists, bushy-bearded poets—caused the administrators real concern.

But eventually, thought Gil, they both got tired. The administration never got any friendlier, like-minded teachers were few and far between, and most of the kids didn't care. There were a few, but eager minds were the fuel that kept Gil burning and after a few years of smouldering he fizzled out. Dick turned his energies inward, and Gil turned to a different kind of fuel. Dick didn't have many friends that could keep up with him, and neither did Gil.

Dick joined a more serious game at the far end of the court. The players were in their twenties and Dick was obviously conscious of it. He held his own, but he had to try harder than they did. Driving through to the basket, he charged a guy and they both tumbled to the floor. Dick practically leapt to his feet, shaking his head to clear it. "All right!" he shouted to no one in particular. He clapped his hands. "All right!"

Bored, his heartbeat closer to normal, Gil got back on the court and picked up a ball. He shot a few from the top of the key and completely missed the backboard. He tried a slow lay-up and sent the ball in a clean arc over the rim. He attempted a three-pointer that hit the top of the board and bounced to the side of the gym and up onto the stage of the middle school where they were playing. The ball disappeared under the curtain.

Gil looked to see if anyone was watching. No one was, so he limped back to the bleachers. Dick came over in a little while, breathing hard.

"Man," he said, digging in his duffel bag. "I showed those pups a few new tricks."

"Really?" asked Gil.

Dick drank from a water bottle and offered it to Gil. Dick's lips were flecked with dry saliva. Gil shook his head. Dick drank again. "What do you mean, 'really'?" he panted.

"Just that—really. Did you? I wasn't watching."

Dick looked at him suspiciously. "Yeah. It was a good game." He drank as if he had an unquenchable thirst.

They sat in silence for a moment, Gil annoyed at the acrid smell of Dick's sweat. He had an unpleasant image of Dick mounting Sharon athletically, monitoring his staying power on a plastic digital watch while sweat beaded on his large bald spot. Does Sharon like screwing him? he wondered.

"You know," said Dick, "you're really lucky—you and Lolita."

"What brought this on?" asked Gil.

"Nothing. I just, sometimes I think that. You've been married how long?"

Gil thought. "Thirty-two years. Three years longer than I've been teaching."

"It seems like you're really there for each other."

"That's because we're both too stubborn to leave," said Gil.

Dick wanted to be serious. "I know it's not easy. Anyone who's married knows it. But you seem to have it worked out. Thick and thin, I'll bet you'll always be there for each other. I'll bet you never even fight."

"Not with our fists," said Gil.

Dick shook his head, frustrated.

Gil shifted on the hard plank bleacher. "Are you having problems with Sharon?"

"No." Dick paused. "Well, sort of. I don't want to talk about it yet."

"Do you want to get drunk?"

Dick said yes.

They went to a bar downtown, the Cambridge, and Gil called Lolita from a pay phone. She was still working, and hadn't started cooking. Even if dinner had been on the stove, she probably wouldn't have minded much; they were long past the point of being annoyed with each other's quirks and no-shows.

She did jab him, though: "Dick tries to get you to do something healthy, and you manage to take him drinking. I wish I could say I'm surprised, Gil."

Dick didn't call his wife.

They ate hamburgers and got drunk quickly, drinking bourbon with beer chasers. Dick started slurring first, but Gil was feeling it, too. He wondered if the brief exercise was making the booze hit him harder. He had a rare feeling of fun and excitement, the way he had before drinking was a habit. Dick was surprisingly outgoing, making conversation with the bartender, random women, and a few gamblers who were pumping quarters into the beeping keno and poker machines.

"Ugly fucking things," said Gil. "They have no souls."

Dick shushed him. "Don't start anything."

"Those machines. They feed on the weak." Dick was already ignoring him, his attention fixed on a smiling woman in tight cowboy jeans. She walked over to Dick and began talking closely to him.

Gil looked around. The oldest bar in town, the Cambridge was a local institution and had survived holdups, grill fires, and re-zoning by zealous city council members. It had character—and characters. High up on the walls were hung paintings of legendary regulars; under them were framed magazine and newspaper clippings, mentions the Cambridge had received from journalists nostalgic for their collegiate days of slumming. The character studies were awful, making the rummies and winos look even worse than they did in real life. Gil was glad he frequented another bar and would not be immortalized by the broad, crude brushstrokes that might seal his fate, or at least his reputation.

Dick was still talking to the mystery woman. She was nearly as old as they were, well-traveled but with an interesting gleam in her eye. A poker machine bleated out a nursery school melody. Gil thought, What the hell.

He changed a dollar and pumped in four quarters. A pair. Nothing. Two pair. Nothing. Nothing.

Dick grabbed his shoulder, spilling beer on Gil's sleeve. "Can you believe it? That woman just propositioned me!"

"For how much?"

"No, not like that—get this," Dick slowed dramatically. *"She wanted her husband to watch."*

Gil swiveled on his stool. "Where is he?"

Dick pointed out a broad-shouldered cowboy in a black Stetson and a bullrider's shirt.

"You refused?"

"Yeah," said Dick, still excited.

Gil stood, clapped Dick's shoulder, and guided him back to the bar. "I think you made the right call." He drew a circle in the air with his finger and the bartender nodded.

"Would you have done it?" asked Dick.

"Are you ready to talk about what's bothering you?" asked Gil.

But now Dick's attention had been seized by a long-haired blonde who sat just around the corner of the bar, wearing only a bathrobe. A couple of construction workers flirted with her over bottles of Lucky Lager while a bouncer looked on, bored.

"Where's *she* from?" said Dick.

The bartender brought the round and Gil paid. He took a drink. "There's a strip bar attached."

Dick's eyebrows shot up. "Really?"

"What, you've never jogged past here in the morning?"

"I'm just surprised I didn't notice it before." Dick stared at the dancer. "What's it like?"

"I have no idea," said Gil. "I generally like to be drunk and aroused at separate times."

Dick took a quick look around, swallowed, and bit his lower lip. "Do you want to go in?"

Now it was Gil's turn to reconnoiter. He scanned the room to see if anyone might recognize him as Mr. Strickland, English teacher. Nope. Of course, if the parents of any of his students came here on week nights, they weren't the type to care.

"Sure," he said. "What the hell."

The entrance was in the very back, past a row of chittering machines and the doorway to the card room. They paid a skinny hunchback two dollars and pushed through a green plastic curtain that kept the bar patrons from seeing in. Nice update on the Green Door, thought Gil. His feet were moving so fluidly he had a hard time keeping up.

Heavy bass beats thudded into Gil's chest as electric guitars growled accompaniment. Dick's mouth formed words he couldn't hear, but he nodded anyway. They stumbled down a few steps into a large, dark, charmless room. To their right was a pool table; to their left, a raised stage with a bar top and stools on three sides. Tables were crowded together all around the stage to catch overflow, but there wasn't any. A handful of men sat, each alone, at the stage, their attention fixed on a naked woman swinging around a pole sunk into the middle of the stage. The music reverberated off the bare walls, hard floor, and high ceiling.

Directly ahead was a bar. Gil made for it while Dick straggled behind, gazing open-mouthed at the dancer. A man at the stage had put a dollar bill on the rail in front of him, and the dancer undulated over and dropped to her knees before him. She tossed her long, bleached hair over her shoulder and folded the note in half. He leaned forward eagerly, like a baby bird anticipating food. With a half-smile that was more polite than interested, she cupped her large breasts together and leaned over him, pillowing his stubbly face in her cleavage. She joggled her breasts for a moment and retreated, the dollar bill squeezed in her flesh, reddening a little where his cheeks had sandpapered her tender skin.

She let go of her breasts and the bill fluttered to the stage. She stood, turned around in front of the man and bent over, giving him a wink from between her knees. She slapped her own butt like a mule skinner and moved on to the next customer.

The burly bartender leaned against a beer cooler with his arms folded, watching the dancer uninterestedly. His biceps stretched the sleeves of a T-shirt that read: *BEEN THERE, DONE THAT.*

"Two Luckies," Gil shouted at him.

The man turned around, pulled two bottles from the cooler, uncapped them, and set them on the bar. Without changing expression, he held up five fingers.

Beers were half as much out front. "Inflation, huh?" grinned Gil.

No smile.

Gil handed a bottle to Dick, who took it without taking his eyes off the stage.

"Come on," Gil said in his ear, "you're so hot for this, let's sit up front."

They took seats at ringside. The dancer flashed a smile their way, welcoming the newcomers, and promptly turned her back.

Leaning her forearms against the wall, which was covered in fingerprinted mirror, she spread her legs slightly, arched her back, and wiggled her butt at them. Half of Gil's brain was taken aback at the primal obviousness of the exchange; the other half couldn't believe how round and firm that young, peach fuzz–covered ass was. He raised his eyes to the mirror and saw her watching his reflection. She laughed and Gil felt his face warm.

Another customer put a bill up, and she strolled over to him. She knelt before him and teasingly traced a line with her fingertip from her clavicle to her carefully trimmed pubic patch. She rolled onto her back, legs together and sticking straight up, then slowly opened her legs. Her fingers crept lower and then she did something that made the man's eyes goggle.

Dick put a dollar down in front of Gil just as the song was winding down. It fell onto the stage, unnoticed by the dancer. The song stopped and they clapped briefly, the hand slaps echoing in the momentary silence. The dancer walked around the stage collecting money and clothes, careful to give the men a view when she bent over to reach.

"Thanks, guys," she said. Green dollar bills and red lacy underwear bunched in her hands, she backed through a bead curtain and disappeared.

Another too-loud song started and a different young woman came out, wearing a black lace top and a leather miniskirt, her thick red curls cascading over her back and shoulders. She looked familiar. Gil squinted, raking his brain, trying to think where he'd seen her before. Dick mumbled something about going to the bathroom and walked off.

The girl shimmied around the outside of the stage. When her eyes passed over him, Gil thought he saw a glimmer of recognition. *Wishful thinking,* he told himself. A man across from him put down a dollar and she gyrated over there for a while. There was something about her face, but it didn't seem to go with the exuberant hair. The context fouled things. It was hard to think of someone he knew dancing naked in front of him in a bar.

Another song started and Dick still wasn't back. The redhead had shed her top and skirt and stripped down to a G-string. She pulled a chair into the center of the stage and writhed athletically on it, closing her eyes in a convincing simulation of ecstasy. It was just a regular bar chair with metal legs and black vinyl padding, but Gil thought every man there must have felt it had the better existence.

Although Gil hadn't put any money up, she dragged the chair over and squared it directly in front of him. She sat down and spread her legs, placing her feet on the railing, one on either side of him. She tossed her head back and lightly drew lines on her thighs with her lacquered fingernails. A little, heart-shaped gemstone twinkled from her G-string. Gil thought: *No way do I know her.*

When she lifted her head at the same time she pulled her G-string aside, revealing an extremely close job of shaving, Gil's eyes struggled with indecision. There was something awkward about examining a naked woman that could look back; and yet, looking away seemed even more inappropriate.

Hooking her toes over the rail, she wriggled the chair even closer. Gil met her eyes and smiled weakly.

She smiled back. "Hiya, Mr. Strickland." She snapped her gum and stood up to collect someone else's dollar.

Gil drained his beer and went for another, tossing back a shot at the bar. *Jesus me,* he thought.

He sat back down and gulped more beer. Looking toward the bathrooms, he saw no sign of Dick. The previous dancer was shooting pool, wearing a silk kimono that rode up her butt cheeks when she bent over to take a shot. Gil had an image of Dick, the great athlete, hunched over a toilet and thought it would be polite to at least check on him. He stayed seated and watched the girl onstage.

She came back and leaned over the rail, her breasts a few inches from Gil's nose. He could smell lilacs. Her breath was hot on his ear.

"Shouldn't you be grading papers?" she asked.

Gil laughed with her.

After the third song, she left the stage and came out at bar level, wearing a robe. She pointed at his beer. "All set?"

"Missy?" he asked.

She cracked her gum. "You just remembered? God, it was so funny seeing you here. I thought I was going to die."

"Well, I didn't remember you had so much . . . *hair,*" he protested weakly.

"It's a wig, duh."

"How long have you been doing this?"

"A while. You're not going to give me some morality trip, are you?"

"No, no—"

"After all, you're here."

Gil laughed. "Yes, I am."

She pulled a string of gum out of her mouth and sucked it back in. "Still at Porte?"

"Yes, I am. It's only been a few years, you know."

"Uh huh. Three. Then I dropped out." She looked over his shoulder toward the bar. "I gotta cocktail now. We're so *busy.* Let me know if you need anything."

Gil nodded.

She started to leave, stopped. "You know, you were one of my favorite teachers."

It took Gil by surprise. Halfway through a swallow of beer, he managed to choke out: "I'm flattered."

"If you say so." She flounced off to the bar.

Dick came back, looking a lot less chipper.

"Tired?" asked Gil.

"Yeah."

"Hey, see that girl in the bathrobe? Missy someone-or-other. I had her in class."

Dick flicked his eyes over, not really looking. "No shit. You ready to go? Let's roll." He had his coat on and was headed for the door before Gil could reply.

"Just a minute." Gil swayed over to Missy, who was at the bar getting a beer for a customer.

She saw him coming and turned.

"Bye Missy. I just wanted to say good luck."

She laughed and shrugged. "Whatever."

"No, I mean it. Just so you're happy, that's the thing."

"Bye, Mr. Strickland."

"Call me Gil. Bye."

"Bye."

He found Dick outside, walking carefully along the curb as if practicing for a DUI test.

"I thought you were the one who wanted to go in there, Dick," said Gil.

Dick fumbled out his car keys. "Well, I just realized how late it is. Running's gonna hurt."

They walked to the car. "You don't have to run every day of your life."

"If you say so."

Asshole, thought Gil. They got in the car in silence, then sat unmoving on the cold seats as Dick let it warm up.

"Attack of conscience?" asked Gil.

"Maybe."

Chapter Three: Friday

Gil felt like he'd just closed his eyes when the alarm clock began bleating like a garbage truck backing up. Groping for the snooze button, he knocked the plastic box off the nightstand. It clattered to the hardwood floor, sounding even louder, its insistent warning making Gil's adrenaline surge. He pushed the blankets off the bed in a heap, smothering the clock and almost muting it. Chilly air washing his bare chest, Gil pulled himself into a sitting position on the side of the bed like a jointed doll moved by three-year-old hands. The pulsing in his head made him feel like his skull was about to come apart; his tongue felt like he had licked his way up the driveway the night before.

When he arrived downstairs, buttoning a wrinkled shirt, Lolita was sitting at the dining room table, a half-dozen magazines spread out before her. She lifted her eyes only briefly as Gil passed through to the kitchen. There was a pan of oatmeal on the stove, but at an hour old, it would have served better as library paste than breakfast. Gil poured himself an oversized mug of coffee and joined Lo at the table.

He accidentally banged his mug on the table when he sat down. Lo looked up again, wearily this time.

"Morning," said Gil.

"You sounded like you were trying to blow a mouse out your nose last night," said Lolita, returning to her reading.

Gil gulped coffee. "I guess we tied one on. I had some idea about getting Dick drunk and getting him to talk, but nothing really happened."

"Get him to talk? About what?"

"Sharon. He seemed . . . down."

Lo was still half-focused on the article. "Well, she called and talked for a long time last night, but she seemed fine."

"I'm not even sure there's a problem. I don't really know how to read Dick anymore."

"Where'd you go?"

"The Cambridge. You mind?" He instantly regretted the question.

"Don't ask for my okay." There was a coldness in her voice.

Gil scanned the headlines of the *Gazette*. He turned over the front section to read below the fold. There was a story about Kristen at the bottom of the front page, along with a photo of her crumpled car. The headline: *FIRST CRASH OF THE YEAR.*

And he thought the kids were callous. He read the story:

The new year took a tragic turn early Thursday morning with Garden City County's first alcohol-related traffic fatality of 1987.

Kristen Swales, 17, was driving west on Interstate 90, several miles east of East Garden City, when the 1984 Chrysler she was driving left the road and collided with a large advertising billboard.

The wreck was discovered by a passing motorist, who in turn flagged down a tractor-trailer rig. The trucker used his CB radio to contact the highway patrol, although a unit of the Logville Police Department was first to arrive.

Swales, who was an active member of the Porte l'Enfer High School varsity cheerleading squad, was pronounced dead at the scene.

Police sources say the coroner has yet to issue an official ruling, but that alcohol is "strongly suspected" as the cause of the crash. The same source noted that the roadway was free of ice, and that a broken bottle of schnapps had been found under Swales' body.

The billboard, owned by Sky View Display Advertising, was

deemed structurally sound despite the collision.

A graveside service is planned for Tuesday at the Garden City Municipal Cemetery.

Gil thought it was odd that Flannel had known what Kristen was drinking, but then again, the man probably attended prayer meetings with the chief of police.

He was still getting his bearings when Flannel stormed into his room with a folder in his hand.

"Half the days say 'Reading day,' " he blustered. "I don't know what you were thinking, but these lesson plans are unacceptable!"

"We're reading a lot of books," said Gil. "I do teach English."

"Well, try speaking it for a change." Flannel tossed the folder onto his desk and raised a finger in warning. "Monday." He walked out.

At lunch, Gil went down to the principal's office. Whitehead was at the door, shrugging into a burly tweed overcoat.

"Ron, can I talk to you?" asked Gil. He squeezed by the older man into his office.

Whitehead smiled meaninglessly. "I was just going, Gil. How about tomorrow?"

"This will only take a minute."

Disappointed, Whitehead shut the door with a slightly shaking hand. He stuck his hands in his coat pockets, leaving the thumbs outside, and stood expectantly. "They're squeezing me in at the indoor driving range, so I would appreciate your brevity."

Gil leaned on a chair back. Whitehead's desk was spotless, his bookshelves nearly empty. The only personal touch in the room was a hinged photo frame on the desk, although Gil could only see the cardboard backs. At the window, a hissing radiator steamed the glass, misting the snowy grayness of Garden City.

"It's Tim Flannel, Ron. I think he's overstepping his bounds. Doing things that are really your jurisdiction."

"What sort of things?"

"Well, his attention to lesson plans is borderline pathological. I admit they're important, but just because every blank on a form is filled out, it doesn't mean the kids are learning anything. Some of the coaches assign nothing but busy work, but because they fill in their lesson plans with these idiotic assignments it's somehow assumed that they're teaching. I think it's all about control—"

Whitehead cut him off. "Tim does a good job, Gil. We appreciate your contributions, and we recognize your past"—he subtly emphasized *past*—"achievements, but teaching isn't just talk and theory. It's also about organization, accuracy, detail. How can we expect to train these young minds if we are not ourselves efficient? I'm sorry, but there are some details that just have to be attended to, and Tim's job is to crack the whip."

"I hope you're not going to give him a real one."

Whitehead's furrowed brow told Gil his joke had missed the mark.

"Okay," said Gil, "but can you at least get him to refrain from sharing Christian homilies? Separation of church and state, you know."

"If you've got a complaint about that, you'll have to go higher than me. Personally, I think it builds both the morale and spirit of these young people."

Strike two. "I see."

Looking pained, Whitehead cleared his throat. "Gil, forgive me for being indelicate, but a teacher in your position ought not to be too demanding. In fact, I would venture to say that it's the Christian spirit that has kept you employed among us." His watery blue eyes met Gil's for a moment, then uncomfortably searched the floor.

And three. Gil clenched his jaw. "Thanks for your time, Ron."

Whitehead opened the door for him unhappily. "Not at all, Gil. Nice talking to you. Stop by anytime."

Gil would have been more anxious for his retirement if Flannel weren't next in line for the job.

Explaining that he was providing an object lesson in democracy, Gil allowed each of the afternoon classes to vote on the day's activity. The choices were: a lecture, open discussion on the reading assignment, or a reading day. Fifth period voted unanimously for a reading day, and sixth followed with only a few dissenters. While the students read, chatted, or slept, Gil drank coffee and watched the clock. The slow sweep of the second hand could not have been more frustrating, or the reluctant ticks of the minute hand more aggravating, to the most restless student. Relentlessly his eyes roved the room, stopping again and again on the chipped black clock housing, the yellowed face, the old-fashioned black numbers. Gil visualized its hands spread at three, with the door shut and locked, the room dark and silent.

Seventh period shocked him and selected, by a narrow and hotly contested margin, open discussion. Reassuring himself that the freedom of the weekend lay only fifty minutes away, Gil gritted his teeth and dove in.

After school, Gil walked to the teachers' lounge for a final cup of coffee. The pot dregs were scorched and sludgy but he filled his mug anyway and went back to his room.

Tim Flannel was sitting in Gil's chair, his feet on the desk.

Gil stopped in the doorway. "Tim? Can I help you?"

Flannel pulled Gil's bottle out of the drawer and thumped it on the desk. Gil looked over his shoulder, where a few students were still drifting along the hall. He shut the door.

"Can I put a little of this in your coffee, Gil?" Flannel asked.

"It's a good luck totem," said Gil.

"I could almost believe you," said Flannel. "When the surgeon general issued his first warning as to the hazardous nature of cigarettes, my own father quit smoking. It was hard, but he managed to succeed by employing a peculiar stratagem: He kept an unopened pack in his shirt pocket. 'Doesn't that make it harder?' I asked, 'Knowing that all you have to do is reach in your own pocket to enjoy the thing you crave?' He replied that if he was going to smoke, he was going to smoke, and if he couldn't beat the nicotine demon when it was lying just above his heart, he couldn't beat it, period."

Flannel looked pleased with himself. "I could almost believe you, but you don't have my father's strength of character. And besides that, you've done more than break the seal on this bottle, you've half drained it."

Gil wondered how he should play this. Three years ago, he was draining a fifth of whiskey a day. He didn't know it at the time, but he stank, he slurred, and he staggered. Small-town etiquette allowed his colleagues to look the other way—until he passed out in class. The students had tried to revive him, he was told, before they called the nurse. The nurse roused him with smelling salts, then recruited Flannel to frog-march Gil out of the classroom. Halfway out the door, Gil vomited. He was too drunk to even think of an excuse, to claim he had food poisoning. He didn't remember much of the incident, just that his limbs had felt like lead and he hadn't wanted to move ever again.

Flannel had demanded his dismissal, of course, but Whitehead remembered that Gil had been useful once and opted for mercy. It was near the end of the school year, so they brought in a substitute and offered no explanation to the students. Gil dried out at the St. Ursula rehab unit and attended a few AA meetings. At a breakfast summons before the first day of school the next fall, the superintendent, Whitehead, and Flannel bought Gil waffles and black coffee and told him in no uncertain terms this would be his single second chance. His "mulligan," as Whitehead drolly called it. Gil had assured them coffee was his drink from now on.

Looking at Flannel lounging in his chair, Gil wasn't sure if he cared about his job any more now than he did the day he'd passed out at his desk. How to play this? Like Dick taking the ball to the hoop against a seventeen-year-old.

Gil walked forward. "Get out of my chair, Tim. What's this all about?"

Flannel looked surprised and took his feet off the desk. He remained seated. "Well, you know. Going to Whitehead about me. Nobody likes a tattletale, Gil."

"I just asked him to get you off my back about the damn lesson plans, for chrissake—"

"Don't use the savior's name in vain, Gil." He stood up. "Remember your place in this pack train. When I take over the reins, you'll find me even less sympathetic than kind Mr. Whitehead."

"Why not just turn me in now?"

Flannel thrust the bottle into the crook of Gil's arm. "I'm leading by example. It's the Christian thing to do. And businesslike. You may prove useful someday." Smiling, he patted Gil's cheek. "Goodnight, Gil. Good luck with those lesson plans." Leaving the door open, he stepped out into the hall and started whistling "Bringing in the Sheaves."

Gil closed the door and sat down heavily at his desk. After regarding the bottle for a moment, he put it away in the drawer. Across the room, the second hand dragged across the face of the clock. He could hear the slow grind of its motor, the insect hum of the fluorescent lights. He got the bottle out again and topped off his coffee.

"Bourbon sales were down yesterday," said Sean O'Donnell.

"I was abducted and forced to exercise," said Gil.

"I almost called your wife. I was worried."

"So was she."

Sean smiled. "This isn't the start of anything, is it?"

"He fears for his meal ticket." Gil held his glass to the light. "Well, don't adjust your purchasing just yet."

"If only I had some assurance." Sean tilted the bottle and poured.

"There are no sure things," said Gil. "But some reasonably safe bets."

The bartender began drying glasses with a white towel. "I can expect you Monday?"

"You can expect me Monday."

On the way home, a police car fell in behind Gil as he was crossing a main street. The speedometer needle fluttered, landing everywhere but the 30. He signaled each turn, and came to complete stops at stop signs. A half-block back, the headlights languidly followed him to his driveway, pausing in the street until he turned off the car. In the rearview, through partially defrosted bars on the back window, Gil saw his brake lights catch the reflective stripe of the cruiser as it glided on.

After dinner that night, Gil and Lolita went to a movie at the Sapphire, Garden City's art-house theater. It was their usual Friday routine. Lolita was a movie fanatic, capable of losing herself completely in the world onscreen. Her tastes were wide—she enjoyed foreign films and teen comedies with equal gusto—and hard to satisfy. On weekday evenings, Gil was sure he could tell when she'd snuck off to a matinee by her mellow mood and faraway eyes. Gil, on the other hand, had never enjoyed movies. It had started in the sixties with his dogmatic belief that Hollywood movies were like drugs that weakened the national character and diverted the people's attention from real problems. His grudge endured through the seventies, more out of stubbornness than anything else. And now, in the eighties, two hours was too long to sit without a drink.

He had negotiated a solution to the problem, however. They chose seats near the front, Gil taking the aisle. After thirty or forty minutes, or whenever Gil felt thirsty, he quietly made his way out the exit under the screen, making sure the fire door didn't latch behind him. Just across the alley was a drywall dive called Bumper's Casino. Half an hour later, Gil returned and watched the movie to its conclusion.

"Beginnings and endings are all that matter anyway," he'd said to Lo, more than once. "The middle part is just filler. Who cares how they get there—where are they going?"

Nonetheless, if he did actually take an interest in a movie, he made Lo fill in the blanks for him afterward.

This night's movie was based on an English novel, in which a teacher, haunted by his past, attempted to exorcize it by telling personal, historical stories to his students. Gil liked it pretty well, though not well enough to stay in his seat for the whole thing.

Afterward, they walked quickly to the car, shuddering in the cold. Lo didn't bite when he asked about the scenes he'd missed.

"It was good," she said. "Sad."

The street was quiet except for a barking dog a block away and the indistinct laughter of a knot of teenagers on the sidewalk ahead.

"How was work?" he asked.

"Okay. I got something out of left field that I'm not sure I want. My alumni magazine wants me to interview a woman who helped create the 'Just Say No' campaign. It's not like *I'd* be saying it, but I hate to give another forum to someone who mouths that mindless B.S. It just seems . . . I don't know. Distasteful."

"Hypocritical. 'We've had our fun, so you'd better not.' "

"I knew you'd find that angle."

Gil let it ride. "Well, it pays the rent."

"It will if I can get it done by Monday. I wish I could pass, but I'm still sort of building a base and I need clips."

"I know," said Gil as they reached the car. "Just say yes."

When they got home the phone was ringing. Walking hastily though the dark living room to the kitchen extension, Gil caught a toe against the coffee table and knocked it over. Stacks of papers and magazines avalanched off as he hobbled on, favoring the injured foot and trying not to lose his balance.

"It doesn't take any less time to turn on the lights," Lo called after him, illuminating the room with the flick of a switch.

"Yeah, yeah," he muttered, steadying himself against the kitchen counter. He reached for the hood light on the range, changed his mind, and picked up the phone. It was Dick, his voice thin and tired. "Dick? What's up? I didn't see you today."

"Yeah, I left early."

"Sick?"

"Can you talk?"

Lolita was stacking papers and magazines on the righted coffee table. "Sure. What's on your mind?"

"Lo there?"

"Uh huh."

Dick paused. "Well, maybe tomorrow we can—"

"Is it important?"

"Yeah."

Gil looked at the clock: nine-twenty. "Well, where do you

want to talk? The Cambridge?"

"No, not there again. How about the Castle Café?"

"Fine. Twenty minutes?"

"Okay."

They hung up. Lolita came into the kitchen and poured herself a glass of wine. "What did Dick want?"

Gil poured himself three fingers of bourbon. "Wants to talk. About what, I have no idea."

She left the room. "Well, I'm going upstairs to read. Please behave."

"I will. We're going to the Castle Café."

The Castle Café was a storefront café adjacent the Castle Casino. Castle Billiards was below, in the basement. It was a low-rent empire: In the café, morgue-like fluorescent lights glared around the clock at the motley assortment of regulars who came in from gaming to fuel their sleepless nights with coffee that sported the rainbow sheen of engine oil. Gil entered, shivering despite the short walk from the car. The hard light was dislocating after the soft incandescence of home. Dick hadn't arrived yet, so he stepped into the bar, which was darker.

Twinkling gaming machines circled the room like an electrified fence: To get out, a toll had to be paid. The bartender had a coffee cup behind the bar, and from the way he tilted it to his mouth, Gil could tell what was in it.

He had a shot and went back into the café. Dick was at a back table, wearing glasses instead of his contact lenses, stirring his coffee carefully. Gil sat down in front of another full mug. "So what's on your mind?" he asked.

Dick exhaled at length, then bought time, taking his glasses off and massaging the bridge of his nose with his thumb and forefinger. He put the glasses back on and looked past Gil to the street. "I know I'm acting strangely, but . . . you know, we've talked about a lot of important things, but we've probably never said one thing that really mattered."

Gil raised an eyebrow and waited. He had no idea where Dick was going.

"I feel like everything's falling apart, Gil. I've tried to keep so many things going at once, but I can't . . . I can't."

"Mid-life crisis?" asked Gil.

Dick laughed ruefully. "I wish. I'd buy myself a Camaro and get it over with. Well, maybe, shit." He looked Gil in the eye. "You know the girl who died, Kristen Swales?"

Gil nodded and felt his heart start to sink. His coffee cup stalled in midair.

"I was having an affair with her."

Coffee splashed as Gil set the cup down too hard. He felt a few warm drops land on his pants. He stared, thinking no one ever really knew anyone. "Jesus, Dick," he said. "What the hell were you thinking?"

Dick looked nervously around the room, but no one was listening. "Please don't condemn me, Gil. I've been hard enough on myself."

"Sharon might have something to say about that."

"It was bad before, but it was simple. No, it wasn't. But she's dead now, and I don't know what I'm supposed to feel. How to act. I'm not supposed to feel anything more than the concern of a teacher. But I feel a lot more than that. And I had to tell someone, Gil."

"Did you love her?"

Dick's hands trembled and he stilled them by wrapping them around his coffee cup. "What's love? I think I love Sharon, but do you cheat on someone you love? Does love take vacations? Did I stop loving Sharon a long time ago? If I don't know what I feel about my own wife, how can I know what I felt for this girl? I cared for her."

"For Kristen."

"Yes, Kristen." A note of irritation.

"Who is dead." Gil didn't know why, but suddenly he wanted to wound Dick. "You cared enough about her and her future that you were willing to fuck her. You selflessly risked your professional standing, your ethics—"

"Damn it, Gil, haven't you ever been in that situation? I mean, some of these girls' hormones are going crazy—"

"Not as much as some of the boys', apparently."

"—and haven't you ever—oh, I guess not. I'm sorry, but some of us mortals don't say no. *She* instigated it, and things haven't been so great with Sharon—"

"Don't blame either of them," said Gil.

"Okay," said Dick. "Okay. And I feel like a sick old man, or I did. Now I just feel old. Exhausted. She was a good kid, really. More adult than most of her peers, I suppose because they didn't accept her."

"Oh, I see, she wasn't a high school student, she was an adult."

"Damn it—"

"And since she was already out of the loop, what was the harm? It's just education of a different—"

"I know, I know, *I know.* Come on, Gil. Don't ride me on this. Not now."

"What do you expect, Dick? Look, in many ways—practically all—I'm a poor excuse for a teacher. You bring far more enthusiasm into the classroom than I have for years. But there are lines you don't cross."

"I need a friend," pleaded Dick.

"To lie to you?"

Dick closed his eyes and his face clenched. His chest heaved like he was holding in a series of coughs. "She's dead, Gil," he whispered.

The counter man came around with a pot of coffee and refilled their mugs. He looked curiously at Dick, whose eyes were still closed. When he had gone, Dick opened his eyes and dried them with the corner of a napkin.

"I'm sorry," said Gil.

Dick looked down at the table.

"Does Sharon know?"

"No. I don't think so. I was really careful."

"Anyone else?"

"Well . . . no." He shook his head as if to convince himself. "Just you, and I'm begging you to keep this a secret. Not even Lo."

Gil looked at him, a sturdy man suddenly grown small and desperate. It wasn't much of a choice. "All right," he said.

They finished their coffees quickly, in silence. They said goodbye at the table, after Gil said he had to use the bathroom. Dick hunched into his jacket and didn't look back as he walked out.

Gil walked into the bathroom and counted ten. When he came out, he went into the bar.

Chapter Four: Weekend

Saturday morning. Gil sat on the couch in his bathrobe, uncombed and unshaven, metronomically clicking the remote. Before noon the selection was dire. Cartoons. An early college basketball game on the East Coast. Infomercials with testimonials to the excellence of six-pans-in-one cookware. Even worse: golf. He couldn't stop clicking, and he couldn't look away. Click. Click. Click.

Lo entered the room from her study, glared at him, and walked over to the stereo. She shuffled records and selected one. Moments later, needle hiss gave way to Faure's *Requiem*. Loud. She stalked out.

"Thanks," called Gil.

Sighing, he clicked the TV off. On the coffee table was a pile of student papers, neatly stacked by Lo after Gil's collision the night before. He'd asked the kids to write reports on a film he'd shown about the Beats. He was a week late in returning the assignments, and he hadn't even looked at them yet.

"What the hell," said Gil, grabbing the stack. After searching a half-dozen drawers, he asked Lo for a red pen and was rewarded. He returned to the couch and started grading, spending five minutes on each paper. Most of the writing was filler, simple regurgitation seasoned with transparent attempts to feign interest in the subject matter. When there was original material, it was reaction, not critique. Jerry's was loaded with five-syllable words, of course, and would have delighted any other teacher.

His tone was steeped in an enthusiasm that belonged only to those who'd yet to see life grind the ideal out of the abstract. Gil hated ass-kissers, and wondered whether it was because he'd been such a good one when he was younger: Too bored to work, he had carelessly dashed off papers and bought insurance by sucking up to the teachers. Jerry would have been shocked at Gil's insight into his kind.

Gil flipped to the next paper in the stack, his pen at the ready. The name at the top made him falter: Kristen Swales. The hand that had scrawled this was cold now. He was surprised she'd even turned this one in, as she'd blown off most of the quarter's assignments—most of the classes, too. But she could have been there on film day, unnoticed in the darkened back of the room, perhaps even alert and listening. Some kids who slept through every lecture stayed rapt whenever movies were shown. Maybe she'd had a friend bring the paper to class, praying it would put her over the line from *F* to *D*.

He scanned the page. Loopy, girlish handwriting with a severe rightward slant, struggling to stay on the blue, wide-ruled line. Little circles dotted the *i*'s. Gil tried to imagine his colleague Dick Simonsen sweating and heaving atop this barely literate teenager. Fortunately, it was hard to picture.

Shaking his head, Gil tried to read the damn thing. Barely a third of the single page he'd asked for, Kristen's assignment also barely began to fulfill the requirements of the assignment. The film was mentioned just once, and its major subjects—Kerouac, Ginsberg, Burroughs—only in a passing, elliptical reference. What *was* interesting was the emphasis Kristen had placed on their drug use. This emphasis was decidedly lacking from the film itself, a toothless, thirty-minute documentary that had been approved to show teenagers in public school settings. And tame as that was, the film could only have gotten made in the liberal seventies.

The thing I thought, she had written, *was that it was bad the way the people in the movie seemed to think drugs were all good for you. Drugs are bad and people can't control them the way they think.*

"Okay, okay," chuckled Gil. She'd seen a few too many "Just Say No" commercials or taken the occasional classroom presentations by the police a little too seriously. Still, he shouldn't judge; he was reading the work of a dead girl. Maybe she'd had personal experience, a mother or a father who did something more than smoke the occasional joint. Should he grade it? Her grades, such as they were, might eventually be released to the family. Though it felt like sticking a band-aid on a severed artery, he wrote *A* across the top of the paper. Maybe it would bring her average up to a passing grade.

He put the paper face down on the completed stack and set the unread ones on the cushion beside him. Stretching out, he felt his muscles holding taut. His feet were almost numb and started tingling; his varicose veins slowed blood to a sluggish ebb when he sat for long. The front window framed the dark day. Sunlight barely passed through the leaden clouds. The big maple tree in the front yard waved its stick-like fingers vaguely in the winter wind. Powdery puffs of snow rose out of bushes or blew along, hugging the street.

Gil got up. He made a fire and poured himself a drink. He stood in the doorway to Lo's study, watching her work.

They went over to Dick and Sharon's on Sunday afternoon, supposedly to watch football, even though Dick was the only adult who ever paid any attention to the score. Gil had never seen the point in playing sports, much less watching them. He enjoyed an occasional game of pool, darts, or shuffleboard, but those were all easily performed in his preferred arena and would have been deadly if televised.

Dick's eleven-year-old, Tommy, was lying on the floor, mesmerized by the game. Fifteen-year-old Katie was out with friends, as usual. Gil made his standard joke, that he hadn't seen Katie since she was too old to keep grounded.

Everything seemed normal, although Lolita and Sharon went into a huddle and Gil realized that, given Lo's inquisitive nature, she would be probing for clues to Dick's recent behavior. And, though not an overly sentimental woman, Lo did have her protective instincts. Dick motioned Gil into the narrow kitchen of their trophy-cluttered house.

"Beer, Gil?"

"Sure." Gil knew something harder wouldn't be forthcoming.

Dick opened the fridge and pulled out a particularly repulsive brand of light beer.

"Are you kidding?" said Gil.

"It won't slow you down."

Gil took the beer. "The trips to the bathroom might." He looked into the living room. The women were talking. "How are you?" he asked quietly.

"I'm okay," said Dick. "I think it's best just to forget this whole thing. I mean, what am I going to do, go to her parents and tell them?"

"What about Sharon?"

Dick lowered his eyes.

"Are you going to the funeral?"

"I'd like to, but I don't know who else is. It might be awkward if other teachers don't show up."

"They will," said Gil, tasting the beer cautiously.

"You want to go with me?"

Gil swallowed hard, but the sour, carbonated liquid seemed to stick in his throat. "Uh . . ."

"Please, Gil. A favor to me. You had her in class, so you can talk to her parents. I could say a kind word if you did. That would be enough."

"When is it?"

"Tuesday. They're letting school out early so the kids can go."

"Sounds great," said Gil drily.

"You don't have to talk to the damn students, Gil," said Dick with a flash of anger.

Gil didn't want to get roped into Dick's troubles, but saying no was harder than saying yes. He said yes.

Dick smiled gratefully. "Thanks, buddy. If you ever need a favor—"

"I'm racking my brain, Dick."

They went into the living room and joined the women.

Chapter Five: Tuesday

They stopped by Mr. D's for a drink before driving out to the funeral. The bar was empty. Stepping out of the back room, Sean seemed puzzled to see Gil so early.

"I'm still gainfully employed, Sean," said Gil. "We're on our way to a funeral. A student."

"I heard about that," said the bartender. "Poor thing." He went away and returned with two brimming glasses of whiskey. Dick reached for his wallet but Sean dismissed him with a wave.

"I think that means it's on my tab," chuckled Gil.

Sean shook his head. "It's on the girl."

They sipped their drinks and Sean withdrew to the back room.

Gil watched as Dick sipped, grimaced, and set his glass down. Dick looked restlessly around the room, drumming his fingers on the bar top. He was clearly edgier than usual, but Gil was beginning to feel that this morbid pilgrimage might be a good idea after all. Dick could ponder the words of the preacher, watch the casket being lowered into the ground, and give the parents his condolences. Afterward, he would go home feeling he'd done all he could, given the circumstances. The roiled waters of his psyche would be still, and the whole, ill-conceived episode would be over.

Or would it? Would Dick return fully to Sharon, or would he lie awake in bed with a spectral cheerleader cartwheeling through his groggy brain? Would he visualize taut, young limbs and firm, girlish breasts as he obligatorily mounted his wife? Or, worse, would he find himself calling one of Kristen's friends to an afterschool conference, the subject of which would be a teacher's loneliness and the result of which would be another girl's premature passage to the trials of adulthood?

Dick turned to Gil, smiling weakly, and pointed at his watch. It was time. As Dick headed for the door ahead of him, Gil quickly downed Dick's half-finished drink.

He stepped out of darkness into bright sunlight. The clouds had lifted for the first time in weeks and the winter sun streamed down. It gave little warmth, though, and Gil was glad he'd worn thermal underwear.

The drive to the graveyard was pleasant. The wind had blown hard the night before, and with Garden City's stagnant winter murk temporarily banished, Gil felt he was seeing a new place. The chemical activity of his brain seemed more charged and his head felt lighter on his shoulders. The extra illumination cast the winter's accumulation of road sand and mud into stark relief against the white snow. The humpbacked hills north of town were pristine against blue-and-white crags beyond. He hadn't seen those tall mountains for a month.

They drove north over a severely arched railroad bridge, past the sawmill, and past the turnoff to the landfill. The road curved toward the railroad tracks and ran alongside. Idle boxcars stood between the sun and Dick's car, breaking the sun's low-horizon glare into a strident, flickering strobe. Gil closed his eyes briefly and was surprised at how sleepy the warm pulses made him.

Dick slowed the car and turned into the graveyard. They drove slowly through tree-lined avenues in the older part, where stern, craggy tombstones stood sentry over the bones of a century's worth of former Garden City citizens. Snowdrifts covered trees, bushes, and monuments like a sea encroaching upon the land. They crept on to the end of the trees, to the newer part, where tombstones became grave markers, and the graveyard became a cemetery.

They parked at the end of a long string of cars and trudged off through the snow. It was crowded ahead, a large group of dark-clad mourners huddled together amidst the white and brilliant snow. Here, in the modern portion of the burial ground, the flat headstones lay hidden beneath the snow and, save for the canopy over the grave, the people could have been congregating in a football field. Wreaths and bunches of flowers bursted in color, as did some of the kids, wearing their red-and-yellow letter jackets. Gil wondered if the young people were all there because they were going to miss Kristen, or if this was just another social event. Some of them stayed in their cars, smoking. Maybe they were drinking beer, too.

Gil led Dick up to the front. Dick greeted students in a subdued way; Gil spoke to the few he liked. Most of the kids didn't seem too broken up. A handful of girls were distraught—their boyfriends trying hard to look stalwart—but all of them looked self-conscious. They were too old to give themselves over to their grief, and too young to have mastered the adult expressions for it.

Gil made eye contact with Kristen's mother, whom he recognized from a fall parent-teacher conference. She smiled in a way that made him glad he had come. He saw Tim Flannel sitting near the family and almost wished he hadn't.

They shuffled their feet in the snow for a few minutes, Gil appreciating the small amount of warmth emanating from the bodies around him. The preacher was identified on a memorial card someone had thrust into Gil's hand as Ted Deal, pastor of the Foursquare Gospel Church. Deal was a frequent contributor to the op-ed pages of the *Garden City Gazette* with lengthy, poorly written attacks on secular humanism in the schools. Lo often read these to Gil, copyediting them for her own amusement, while he struggled to down his breakfast. As Deal began his introductory remarks, a light wind came up that further reddened the noses of Kristen's family, who were seated behind and to one side of Deal. The crowd seemed to shiver and slide closer together.

The sermon was trite and, perhaps in deference to the cold, brief. Deal mused on the tragedy of young life cut short, read from Ecclesiastes, and invited a short, plump woman to sing "Nearer to Thee, My Lord," which she did. The content of the sermon almost seemed designed not to provoke deep reflection, but Gil did take umbrage when Deal mixed his metaphors—referring to "poor little lambs who are so anxious to leave the nest"—in his warning against the perils of wanting to grow up too quickly. Flannel interjected frequent, ostentatious, *amen*s.

After about fifteen minutes, the young-looking eulogist closed with a call for silent prayer. Gil stood, head bowed, and prayed for a warming drink. He thought about praying for Flannel's disappearance but decided that would be pushing it. His ears were going numb.

Suddenly, a runny-nosed kid in a letterman's jacket jostled past him and into the open space by the casket. He looked wired, and Gil's first, frightened thought was that he was going to open fire on the crowd.

The boy screamed his words with startling abandon. "You're a bunch of fucking hypocrites! You never even fucking gave a shit about Kristen and now you're all standing around like you thought she was the greatest thing ever!"

He turned toward the family. Mrs. Swales looked like she was going to faint; Mr. Swales, rising from his chair, looked like he was going to wring the kid's neck. Pastor Deal stood frozen, a peculiar smile glazed on his face. The smile seemed to be an attempt to discredit the boy by condescension.

"Like she's some fucking saint!" the kid yelled. "Well, she

wasn't, and guess whose fault that is?" Wheeling in the clearing in front of the canopy, his rigid finger swept the crowd, bouncing like the needle on a polygraph.

Gil saw bewildered, ruddy faces and wondered if the accuser was pointing at random or with intent. He glanced at Dick, who was shivering and seemed about to collapse.

Flannel emerged from his seat, moving with surprising swiftness for his girth. Wearing a placid expression, he charged, with the funeral director and Mr. Swales several steps behind him. The wild-eyed kid backpedaled and looked for an escape route. Seeing none, he paused, wiped his nose on his sleeve, and jumped on the casket.

"No!" yelled the funeral director. Deal's smile slipped off and his mouth dropped open.

As the kid scrambled over the casket, Flannel grabbed the back of his Porte l'Enfer letter jacket.

"Fuck you!" screamed the kid, wriggling out of the jacket so violently Gil wondered if he'd dislocated his arm. He crawled to the other side of the burnished metal box, which began to list dangerously.

"You little punk!" hollered Mr. Swales, throwing a punch that missed by two feet.

Flannel jigged around the teetering casket, still trying to get a hand on the long-limbed teen. The metal hoist holding the casket over the grave buckled and swayed drunkenly, and one pole bent like a knee to the ground. The casket, with the boy astride, disappeared into the hole. Mr. Swales stumbled over a guy rope, pulling its peg from its indent in the hard turf. The black canvas awning sagged and deflated as the support poles clacked loosely inward.

There was a frozen moment, a heartbeat where nothing moved and Gil wondered if they had all seen what they just saw. A hundred mourners stood, utterly unsure of the proper etiquette for a violently interrupted funeral. Mrs. Swales fainted, crumpling into a folding chair and toppling backwards. She was quickly engulfed by a knot of family members in puffy winter parkas.

The funeral director called for help and most of the men moved forward. Gil found himself in a slow-moving surge of bodies that cleared aside the heavy canvas and moved poles out of harm's way, that embraced and seated the distraught family. Mr. Swales was sitting on the ground, pale as snow, holding a plaid scarf against his bloody forehead. His pupils pinpricks, he breathed shallowly and too fast. Help was called. Gil looked for Dick and didn't see him, then edged toward the grave, where groups of men were pulling on the long straps of webbing that looped under the prematurely sunken coffin. As he took his place in the tug-of-war, Gil caught a glimpse of the boy's unconscious face pressed against the frozen wall of earth. He was pinned by the vehicle he'd ridden down. The top half of the casket had fallen open like a Dutch door and Kristen slumped against the plush upholstery, looking beatifically unconcerned even with her fine blond hair in tangles. Far away, sirens began keening.

Half an hour later there was nothing left to do. Gil looked for Dick, then threaded his way through the dispersing group and found Dick's idling car. He got in. Dick didn't seem able to look at anything to the right of the rearview mirror. Gil didn't question him and they sat, trapped in the narrow avenues of the cemetery by cars that were penned in by emergency vehicles. Eventually, the police waved the halting cars on and they were free to go.

The sun still shone as they drove home in silence, but Gil felt considerably less bright about the new Garden City it showed him.

Chapter Six: Wednesday

Over coffee and toast, Gil read the story in the *Garden City Gazette:*

FRANTIC YOUTH FOULS FUNERAL

The funeral yesterday of Kristen Swales, 17, a Porte l'Enfer High School junior, was disrupted by Thad Chouck, 18, a senior at the same school.

According to bystanders, Chouck ran amok, shouting profanities and threatening the Swales family. Tim Flannel, vice principal at Porte l'Enfer, and Kent Swales, Kristen's father, tried to restrain Chouck. Seeking escape, the youth climbed onto the casket of the deceased Swales. The additional weight caused the casket hoist to collapse, in turn bringing down an awning provided by What-a-Party Party Rental.

Chouck was severely injured and had to be freed by rescue personnel. Police spokesman Lt. Roger Blanston confirmed that a small amount of cocaine was seized from Chouck, and it is suspected that Chouck was using cocaine at the time of the incident. Chouck remains in St. Ursula Hospital in serious but stable condition.

Lt. Blanston also confirmed that the City Prosecutor's office plans to bring assault charges against Chouck, as Mr. Swales received a concussion from a falling awning support. Other charges may be considered, he added, as the emotional toll on the Swales family was great. "We just have to figure out what we can nail the punk for,"

said the lieutenant.

Because of his age, Chouck will be tried as an adult.

Gil went to Dick's room before school. Dick was drawing pine trees on his blotter calendar when Gil dropped the article on it.

"Did you see this?" asked Gil. "I *thought* that kid was high on something—but what made him go into that tirade? I know coke is supposed to make you more self-confident, but getting in front of everyone like that and—"

"Kristen was doing coke," mumbled Dick.

Gil suddenly realized that, of all people, he should know that there were always new bottoms to grind against. "You're serious," he said.

"I wish I was kidding, Gil." Dick shifted in his chair. "I didn't buy it for her or anything."

"No?"

"No."

Gil leaned over the desk and put his face close to Dick's. Dick winced. "Who did?" asked Gil.

"Maybe that kid. Maybe he was going to make a public confession."

"For what? The attention?"

Dick blinked slowly. "Maybe."

"Maybe he was actually going to tell us," said Gil.

"Well, it would have been news to me, too," Dick retorted. "We didn't have time to share all the little details. And can we not talk about this right now? Someone could come in at any second. It's my career on the line, you know."

Gil backed off and headed for the door, unable to stop himself from adding, "Not your life," on the way out. He wished the awful revelations would just slow down. He really didn't expect the world to get better; he just didn't want it to deteriorate so quickly.

Flannel stopped him in the hall, but not to talk about the

funeral. "Gil, those course plans you gave me yesterday—"

Gil barked a defensive, "Yes?"

"—will do." Flannel chuckled, his odd-shaped belly quivering in counterpart.

"Great." Gil started walking, but Flannel caught his arm and leaned in close enough to sniff Gil's breath. Gil shook Flannel's hand off and stepped back.

"You will honor our bargain, I trust?"

Gil just looked at him.

"Good." The chubby vice principal clasped his hands in an oddly monastic fashion, nodded, and ambled off down the hall. "Keep up the good work," he called out, then began whistling.

Gil stormed through the choppy stream of students, ignoring the ones who greeted him. In his room, he shut the door and walked to the window. The radiator clanked and hissed its way up to a whistle, and warmth began seeping into his legs. Moving to his desk, he poured a shot into his coffee, then paused, holding the empty bottle. He looked at his bookcase, his file cabinets, his storage locker. Taking a key from his pocket, he unlocked an army-green, legal-size filing cabinet and put the bottle in the top drawer, behind the last hanging file folder. Rummaging in his desk, he found a full bottle and put it in the filing cabinet, too. He closed the drawer and locked it. Inconvenient, but better.

Coffee in hand, he returned to the window. It was gray and murky outside, and the cars on the icy street below moved like geriatrics unsure of their footing. The inversion above the Garden City Valley had settled again, a thick, murky blanket that obscured the mountains west of town. All he could see were the ragged lines of cars crawling back and forth on the street below and on Shield Avenue, an artery that intersected at an angle, bringing cars in from the Sweetstem Valley to the south.

Despite its idyllic setting in the Rockies of Western Montana, Garden City was cursed with pollution. In deep winter, fronts of cold arctic air blew over the mountaintops, trapping the town's warm smog in the valley, where it festered for weeks at a time. A few years back, local environmentalists had pushed for a crackdown on woodburning in homes, and the result was a city ordinance that allowed burning only when the air was good. Fireplaces and wood stoves had to meet strict regulations, and every day the newspaper printed a half-pie chart with air quality wedges labeled *good, moderate, bad,* and *alert.* Snow helped sweep the air, when it came, as did the fierce winds that sometimes blew from Porte l'Enfer Canyon.

Gil knew the real air-quality culprits were cars and the pulp mill west of town. Everybody drove, except for a few hardy hippies, and the town's decaying economy still depended on the timber industry. When the wind blew from the west, the smell of rotten eggs filled the air. When visibility was good, he could see the plume from the pulp mill chuffing high above the valley floor, ten or fifteen miles away.

Still, it had been worse. Back in the old days, around the turn of the century, there had been stories of women hanging out white laundry and taking it in black. They'd burned coal back then—coke, they called it.

Coke. The kid at the funeral. He'd had something to say, but what was it? Maybe he loved Kristen, maybe he knew she was having an affair with someone he couldn't compete with. That would explain why Dick was so nervous—he was afraid Chouck would scream out his name. But Chouck hadn't even pointed at Dick. Or did Chouck want to finger whoever had given Kristen drugs? But *Chouck* had had drugs.

Gil wished he could remember who the kid had pointed at. Had he been looking for someone and not seen them? Gil reminded himself that Dick could still be guilty on both counts.

Maybe Chouck just hadn't seen him. Maybe the kid was just high and none of it meant anything.

The bell rang, derailing his train of thought. Gil tested the handle of the file cabinet to make sure it was locked. A few kids came in, opening the closed door without knocking. Sitting behind his desk, Gil called to one of them, a girl who, despite freshman status, was part of the inner sanctum of the athletic crowd. It helped that she was dating a starter on the varsity basketball team.

"Jolene, come here a second."

Startled, she looked up from her notebook, then closed it and came over.

"Mr. Strickland, if it's about that assignment, I promise I'll have it in by—"

He shook his head. "That's fine. I have a question for you about something else." He paused, then plunged in. "Was this Chouck guy a friend of Kristen's? Were they dating?"

Relief, then confidence, lit her face. This was her strong subject. "No, they weren't going out. It's sort of weird, because none of these people that are saying they were Kristen's best friend really were, you know? I think everyone just likes to make a big, you know, deal out of it. Pretend they knew her the best. Like when that guy got shot last year, everyone was—"

Gil tried to bring it back. "But why would he be so upset?"

She seemed shocked. "That guy who got shot?"

"No. Chouck."

This was a poser. "Um . . . I don't know, Mr. Strickland. I mean, they partied together, 'cause, you know, they were part of the group."

"You wouldn't have seen them together at a party, would you?" asked Gil, smiling.

Jolene affected affront. "I'm not supposed to go to beer parties," she said.

"Of course," said Gil. "Well, thanks. I was just curious."

"You know," Jolene said. "Somebody did tell me that he has a crush on Kristen. I mean, had." She smiled and skipped back to her seat.

Gil leaned back and watched the room fill up, trying once more to understand Dick's attraction to Kristen. Sure, she was older than the freshman girls, but his own girl, Katie, was fifteen years old. Imagine making love to a girl barely older than your daughter.

A sullen office aide in a Clash T-shirt and a spiked wristband delivered a late memo, freshly mimeo'd. Whitehead's bloviating style was an odd read when filtered through his secretary's penchant for abbreviations, unorthodox spelling, and exclamation points.

GREETINGS SCHOLARS!!!

Item: Thespians, in their play preparations, have been macking too much racket and commotion during class hours. This must desist immed.!!

Item: Teachers who are harboring students for "intellectual" activities during pep rallies are warned that this contravenes Porte l'Enfer High policy. Also, as last week, all teachers must attend future pep rallies. This not only increases school harmony but school spirit as well. Let your school sprit soar!!!

Item: Students who have an interst in the field of Ham Radio Operation, come to this week's Ham Radio Club meeting, in Room 226 after school today, or see club advisor, Tim Flannel.

Item: Mr. Flannel offers his commendations to food service staff for this the latest round of excellent corn dogs.

Signed, Ronald Gerald Whitehead II

This day of our Lord, January 21, Anno Domini 1987.

Psalms 12:2.

"If anyone wants to see the afternoon memo, it's up here on my desk," Gil announced. All of the students remained seated.

He crumpled the sheet and dropped it into the battleship-gray trash can next to him.

Seventh period. What were these kids here for? The Mystery Novel. Gil hated mysteries. The only ones he'd read were the excruciating Hardy Boys tales, the only kids' books on the shelf during summers at his grandparents' lake house fifty years ago. He blacklisted Agatha Christie and Arthur Conan Doyle and selected the reading list each semester by ballot. Invariably, the students chose pulps that were more shotgun-happy than coolly deductive. That was fine with Gil. At least the students in this class tended to finish the assigned reading.

Gil stood up. "Who's the protagonist of the book you've supposedly been reading?"

A kid raised his hand. Gil nodded.

"Mack Bolan?" came the tentative response.

Gil turned and picked up the chalk, wrote: *BOLAN.*

After seventh period, Gil packed his thin plastic briefcase and put on his coat. The briefcase had been his father's and bore his initials: *C.S.* Curtis Strickland had been an insurance claims adjuster. Curtis was fond of telling Carmen, Gil's mother, that work should stay at the office; the skinny briefcase, he said, insured he wouldn't bring paperwork home. Traveling the town by day, Curtis returned to the office and worked until each thick manila file had been examined, judged, and passed along to the next bureaucratic waystation. When he could snap his slender attaché shut, it was time to turn out the lights and go home. Night after night, for years, Curtis returned home at seven, eight, or even nine o'clock, exhausted but—he claimed—fully focused on his family. Gil didn't recollect much playtime, just his father reclining stocking-footed in his chair, ice cracking in his scotch, while Carmen rubbed the stress from his tired shoulders.

One night, while Curtis unwound and Carmen kneaded, seven-year-old Gilbert amused himself by trying on his father's enormous black wingtips. He slipped his feet into them by the front door and flopped his way into the living room, drawing small smiles from his parents as he half-skated a figure-eight on the carpet. Returning to the entryway, he used an umbrella to lever Curtis' fedora off the hatstand and placed it like a bucket on his head. He needed a prop to complete the ensemble, and grabbed the briefcase from its spot against the wall. Traipsing near-blind back onto the stage in front of his parents, he slipped and fell headlong, springing the latch on the cheap case.

What fell out was not pens and paper but a pair of recently worn, French-cut panties and a rather explicit mash note signed with a lipstick kiss (he learned the finer details only years later). Gil was ushered into his room and missed the denouement, but when he awoke the next morning the house was missing many familiar furnishings and his father as well. Gil visited Curtis a few times over the next year, shadowed but not accompanied by Carmen, and then one day Gil received a postcard from California, his father's new home. He never saw the man again, though he received sporadic correspondence for years, usually containing a few small bills. One day when he was forty-four, Gil received from a lawyer a letter folded around a check for $7,332, his father's last gift. Carmen died only a few years later, having neither remarried nor spoken her husband's name again.

Gil knew some people might consider his attachment to the briefcase unhealthy if they knew the whole story, but it was the only thing his father had left behind, that and a powerful thirst. Gil certainly didn't admire his father's cheating, but he did share his disdain for bringing work home. He put only the most overdue papers in the case, leaving a healthy stack on his desk to be assessed later—by a layreader if he got lucky.

Stealthily, Gil looked out his door and down the hall. There were no faculty members to scold him for an early departure, and only a few students. He locked the door and headed downstairs, taking the steps two at a time. On the second floor he stopped inches short of smashing into Flannel, who was carrying a bulky apparatus with a microphone and headphones.

Flannel swung his cargo around so he could eyeball whoever was sprinting downstairs. "Oh, it's you. Leaving early, Strickland?"

Gil grabbed his jaw. "Dentist appointment. I think I've got a rotten tooth."

Flannel resumed his upward plod. "I'm surprised you can feel it."

Gil walked to his car. In the daylight it showed every one of its thirteen years. He let Lo drive the good car, determined to ride the Datsun into the grave. He felt loyal to the surprisingly dependable vehicle, which he'd bought new. He also felt it showed his humble character, though Lo said it just showed that he *was* a character. When it stopped sputtering and went into reverse without dying, he drove to St. Ursula-in-the-Field, which actually sat in the middle of one of Garden City's largest parking lots.

He asked at the desk for the room of Thad Chouck. The receptionist, a raw-boned pioneer type with a braid coiled on the back of her head, looked up the information.

"Mr. Chouck is under police guard. Access is restricted."

"I know," said Gil, raising his briefcase and tapping it. "I'm his lawyer."

She stood so she could see him over the high desk and dubiously looked him up and down. He was wearing faded tan cords, gray suede loafers, and an oft-mended parka. He refused to put goo in his thinning hair so he probably had flyaways.

The woman pushed her lower lip up with a pencil eraser and frowned.

"Public defender," said Gil.

The woman nodded and sat down. "Wing C, room 409. Take that elevator there." She pointed.

Gil thanked her and walked off swiftly.

It only took him twenty minutes to find the room. Afraid his cover would be blown, he didn't dare asking for directions a second time. At one point he tried a door and found himself in a room where an elderly patient was having trouble with her hospital gown.

Her back was to the door; hearing Gil, she beckoned him over. "I'm glad you came back, honey, I can't seem to get my fingers to work right."

Gil cleared his throat demurely and stepped forward. Clenching his briefcase between his knees, he knotted the gown as quickly as he could.

"Thank you so much!" exclaimed the woman. "I don't know how they think an older person could tie themselves into one of these, anyway."

As she moved toward the examination bed, Gil hastily slipped out the door.

Finally he found 409C. A policeman sat outside, reading *Field and Stream* and eating raspberry yogurt from a plastic cup. A black plastic name plate was pinned to his pocket flap: *BENTON.* Gil stopped in front of him.

"Excuse me, Officer Benton."

The man swallowed and looked up, the magazine spread open on his lap. "Can I help you?"

Gil attempted a charming smile; it felt like a grimace. "I'm Reverend, um, Bolan," he said. "Mr. and Mrs. Chouck asked me to come talk to the boy, offer him some guidance. Is he awake now?"

"Mr. Chouck asked you?"

"Well," Gil stumbled, searching Benton's face for clues. "Both he and his wife. His wife, really."

"I was going to say, you visited Mr. Chouck in the penitentiary?"

"Well, I do occasionally make prison visits, but I met Mr. Chouck before he, before he stumbled. He's a lost sheep from my flock. But his wife is quite strong in her belief."

"She swears like a sailor."

"A nasty habit," Gil agreed.

Benton cocked his jaw. He seemed to be trying to dislodge a raspberry seed from his gums with his tongue.

"So," said Gil. "Is young Thad awake?"

Benton took a seed off his tongue with his pinkie and smiled at it. "Oh, he's awake. But you'll have to keep it to about five minutes. Doctor's orders."

Gil smiled. "I understand." He put his hand on the doorknob.

The policeman touched his arm. "Hey, don't you wear those little white collars?"

"Unitarian, son," said Gil.

"Oh." Benton looked confused but pretended to start reading again.

Gil entered the room and pulled the door closed behind him. The blinds were drawn against the dim, gray day, but the bed was bathed in light from the blaring TV. Chouck was in a body cast, his right arm and right leg suspended in the air by cords, pulleys, and weights. The right side of his face was bruised purple, and his nose and mouth were covered with a clear plastic oxygen mask. A machine next to the bed emitted regular bleats. The hospital smell was stronger here than outside. Chouck's body may have been immobilized, but his eyes were not. The way they darted between the door and the TV, Gil thought they might start spinning like the wheels on a slot machine.

Gil approached the bed. "Thad? How are you feeling? You okay?"

Chouck rolled his eyes. "Yeah, I'm *great,*" he wheezed. He sounded like a teenaged Darth Vader.

"Okay, dumb question." Gil looked around the room, unsure where to begin. "Mind if I turn down the TV?"

"Who the fuck are you?"

Gil fumbled with the controls, adjusting the color before lowering the volume. "I'm sorry, Thad. I'm Mr. Strickland, from school. I teach English? I'm not here to hassle you or anything. I was at the funeral and I'm very interested in what you have to say."

Chouck rasped for a few moments, possibly working up his energy. "Gee, that's great."

"Well, I am," said Gil. "I'm very concerned about the death of Kristen, and about you. Are there any other kids who might be in trouble?"

Chouck laughed, coughed, and sprayed the inside of the oxygen mask with phlegm. He stared at the TV while Gil lifted the mask and wiped it out with wadded tissues. Gil looked nervously at the respirator and other machinery surrounding the bed, afraid it might erupt at any moment in a cacophony of sirens.

"I'm the one in trouble," Chouck said. "Ever go through withdrawal in the hospital?"

"Where did you and Kristen get your coke, Thad? I want to know."

Chouck concentrated on the TV, but it looked like his pupils were vibrating. He said nothing.

"Please, Thad," said Gil. "I'm not a cop. I'm not going to rat you out. Do you recognize me at all from school?"

Chouck glanced at him. "Yeah. Maybe."

"Okay, great," said Gil. "I know you've got problems of your own to think about, but if you can give me anything—a name, a place. If I can help you in any way, I promise I will."

Chouck looked toward the door, then turned his face away. "Okay," he muttered. "Farnsworth. Pishkun."

Pishkun was a mining town two hours' drive from Garden City. Farnsworth didn't ring a bell.

Gil leaned closer to Chouck's smashed ear. He could hear oxygen hissing into the mask. "Do you know a first name? Can you give me an address?"

"Asshole," said Chouck, still facing the curtained window.

"Me?" Gil asked. "Him?"

Chouck's eyes darted but he wouldn't turn toward Gil. Gil thought he heard grinding teeth. He picked up his briefcase and headed for the door. As he was leaving, Benton looked up.

"How is he, Reverend Father?

"It's just F—Rev, son. And that kid is going to be just fine. He's very sorry about what he's done, of course, but he promised to come to church as soon as he can."

The cop appeared surprised. "Well, I guess that's good news," he said.

Gil made the sign of the cross and left.

When he got to Mr. D's, he used the pay phone to call Dick's house. Sharon answered. Gil asked her if Dick was home from work yet.

"Uh, just a minute," said Sharon, and there was a rubbing sound as her hand covered the receiver. After a pause, she said, "Gil? I'm sorry. I thought I heard him come in, but I guess I was wrong. You want me to have him call you?"

"Yeah," said Gil. "Thanks." He hung up. He thought for a moment and then put another quarter in and dialed. When he reached Central Administration, he told them he would be taking a personal leave day tomorrow. For good measure, he also told Sean he might not be in.

★ ★ ★ ★ ★

At dinner he told Lolita his suspicions.

"Are you sure you don't just need a hobby?" she said.

"Come on, Lo. This is serious. Something strange is going on, and kids are getting hurt."

Lo took a drink of wine. "I appreciate your concern for the kids. I'm just surprised to find you playing the part of drug enforcer or whatever."

"This isn't pot, Lo. And it's not informed adults making a choice. I don't think anybody should mess with hard drugs, but kids are really just not prepared." He took a deep drink of bourbon.

"I'm not arguing against *that*," said Lo. "But don't you think the local oinkers are looking into it already? What makes you think you can do anything they can't?"

"The Garden City Police Department couldn't even arrest a litterbug quietly. Imagine what they'll do if they catch something as exciting as a drug dealer—everyone's names will be all over the papers." He hesitated before he continued, but it sounded good: "These kids need an advocate."

Lo arched an eyebrow, clearly keeping her mouth in check. It didn't matter. Gil knew what her acid riposte would have been.

"Well, what do you plan to do if you find this Farnham guy?" she asked breezily.

"Farnsworth," he corrected. "And I don't know. Try to talk to him, I guess. Tell him that dealing to kids at my school is not cool, that the word is out on him, and he'll be in trouble if he doesn't stop. He'll stop. He won't want to go to jail."

Lo chewed her last bite of food slowly and swallowed. "I hope he's the kind of guy you can talk to. Or she is—it could be a woman, you know."

"It's probably just some guy who works in a service station, a mechanic who buys from the bikers when they come through, then cuts it and sells it to teenagers. I'm just going to tell him to lay off. This isn't the Crips and the Bloods. It's not going to start a drug war."

Lo smirked. "I like the way you said, 'Cuts it.' It makes you sound *superbad.*"

Gil laughed. "Come on, we've both seen the movies. I'm sure that's where the drug dealers get their ideas about what's cool."

Chapter Seven: Thursday

In the morning, Gil kissed Lolita goodbye and got behind the wheel of the Datsun. His breath instantly began fogging the frozen windshield, so he lowered his window as he backed down the driveway. In a rare show of solidarity, Lo shivered on the porch in her bathrobe with a cup of coffee in her hand. Gil put the sputtering car in first and craned his neck to see Lo as he rolled away.

The freeway to Pishkun looked clear, though patches of black ice kept Gil from relaxing too much. Still, as the sun came up, it poked through the clouds in places and made him feel almost cheerful. He turned on the radio and sang along to "Take the Money and Run," by the Steve Miller Band. Steppenwolf's "The Pusher" came on and he laughed. The skies were much clearer outside of Garden City, and the change of scenery was nice, making Gil wish he hadn't waited for a crisis to give him an excuse for a road trip. Of course, he rarely had another reason.

Half an hour out, he pulled off the freeway to fill his plastic travel mug with gas-station coffee. When he got back in the car, he topped it off with a judicious amount of bourbon from the bottle in the glove compartment.

The freeway threaded a series of valleys, and when mountains began to rise directly ahead—where the road climbed to cross the continental divide at Stoner Pass—he'd reached Pishkun. It was midmorning, and the promise of the day evaporated as he gazed through his dirty windshield onto the mine-scarred walls of the natural amphitheater behind the city. Built on a hillside, city streets dead-ended against a huge earthen berm that marked the remains of Pishkun's long-gone economy. Behind the mound lay a pit thousands of feet deep. Though the town fathers had once possessed the "richest hill on earth," they'd chased the copper ore far below the water table. The hill became a hole, and when they turned off their pumps, it began steadily filling with water so acidic it was known to kill unwary waterfowl. High above it all, on a ridge overlooking the town, a huge white statue of the Virgin Mary blotched the rock. Known as "Our Lady of the Mining Industry," she had been carved too late to impart any blessing on the fading town. Tapped-out mine shafts still honeycombed the hills, threatening to reclaim the town's run-down buildings to the Rockies' cold bosom. As was the way with these things, while the descendants of the miners remained and hoped for renewed industry, the profit-takers had moved on to new locations and new enterprise.

Gil hadn't eaten breakfast, so when he left the freeway he pulled into a mom-n-pop coffee shop and ordered ham, eggs, hash browns with gravy, and toast. While he was waiting for the food, he looked through a phone book that hung chained in the vestibule. There were no listings for *Farnsworth* in the white pages. Following his original hunch, he checked the yellow pages under "Service Stations," and felt a smug sense of satisfaction to find a *Farnsworth Fill-er-Up.* Pulling the page out of the book, he sat down and ate breakfast.

He found Farnsworth Fill-er-Up easily. A sign in the window said: *CLOSED FOR SEASON.* Another sign declared *OPEN APRIL FOOL'S.* Gil parked and, zipping up his parka, ran up to the building. Peering in the window, he saw a solitary set of footprints tracking through a layer of dust on the floor. He knocked on the plate glass window but nothing stirred within.

Someone hollered, “What’s wrong? Can’t you read?”

Gil turned around and saw a man walking a pit bull. “Better than you,” he called back. “I don’t need gas. I’m looking for Farnsworth.”

The dog began barking and its master pulled back on the leash. He squinted suspiciously at Gil. “Why?” he demanded.

“Business matter,” explained Gil, hopping from one foot to the other in the blistering cold.

“Try the city cemetery,” said the dog man.

“He works there?”

“Lives there, has for the past twenty-odd years. Fillin’ station’s run by a man name of Del Mar now. Delbert Del Mar. He’s in Florida.”

Gil walked back to his car, wary of the dog’s vise-like jaws and sabre-sharp teeth. “Thanks.”

“My pleasure,” the man said cheerlessly. He dragged his dog onward.

Gil started the car and let it idle. He thought, *Now what?* He put it in gear and drove for a while, aimless loops up and around the hills of Pishkun, which were lined with turn-of-the-century brick buildings. Enterprising businesspeople had cheerily trimmed their shop windows with white lattice and fake ivy and carefully arranged last year’s fashions on mannequins in hopes of corraling wayward spenders, but standing next to dark storefronts and stolid but empty buildings, these spots of brightness were like the pink edge of a bruise.

Passing the Double W Café, Gil remembered hearing it had a reputation for attracting bums, bikers, and brawlers. For all he knew, drug dealers spent their time in fern bars, but he decided to check it out. It wasn’t as if he had actual leads to choose from.

Inside, the Double W was the Pishkun equivalent of the

Cambridge, which meant it was worse. Better, for connoisseurs of cigarette smog, sour beer, and three-time losers.

He sat down at the counter, ordered coffee and was handed what appeared to be hot water stirred with a brown crayon. Tasting it, he grimaced and felt he might be right. A bar on the other side of the room ran parallel to the food counter. He walked over and drank a shot of bourbon; when he returned to his coffee, he didn't mind it anymore. Down the counter sat an assemblage of dubious-looking ranchers, long-unemployed miners, hard-luck cases, and drifters. One anomaly, a man in a crisp suit and power tie, sat comfortably eating his breakfast while he read the *Pishkun Free Press.* Collectively, the crew looked like something Chas Addams might draw if he were suffering from delirium tremens. The staff was hardly a cut above the clientele: The cook had his beard tucked into his pants and the waitress carried four cups in one hand by plunking her fingers right into the water.

Gil turned to the young man next to him. The grease under his nails and in the creases of his skin identified him as a mechanic.

"Excuse me," said Gil. "Do you happen to know a Farnsworth?"

The man looked up from the countertop and raised an eyebrow. "From what?" he grunted.

"No," said Gil. "Do you know someone named Farnsworth?"

The man considered it, then nodded his head once, vigorously. He stood up and beckoned for Gil to follow. Gil looked around the café a little nervously, then followed the man toward the back. The grease monkey stopped in front of a booth with a pair of feet hanging over the edge of the seat. Kicking the feet, he turned to Gil.

"That's Farnsworth," he chuckled, and left.

Gil looked down. The feet were clad in blown-out, muddy

basketball shoes and were attached to a snoring man in a greasy goose-down parka whose feathers were bursting out of numerous rips and heading south. He shook the wino's pant leg gently, then firmly, then violently, and finally the man woke with a start. He sat up and looked at Gil with wild eyes.

"Is your name Farnsworth?" asked Gil.

"No," said the wino. "Maybe. Whattaya got for me?"

"Five bucks if you are."

"I am."

"Well, maybe five bucks if you're not."

"I ain't."

"Right," said Gil. "Do you have any idea who on earth Farnsworth is?"

"For five?"

"Yes," said Gil. "But I want proof."

The wino collected himself and slid out of the booth. A couple of feathers drifted up toward the ceiling. "Proof'll cost you ten."

Gil nodded.

"Okay, here's how I know. Guy you're lookin' for tall?"

"Maybe," said Gil.

"With a handlebar mustache?"

"Could have," said Gil.

"Wrong," said the wino. "He's average tall, clean shaven, and wears a camouflage parka with a furry hood. I know 'cause last fall I was sleepin' behind Super Big Save, in the weeds, and a car fulla kids drove up. They made a lot of racket for a minute, then they turned the radio off, and I hear 'em talkin'. Next thing one says, 'Where's Farnsworth?' and another one says, 'Shut up.' Then this big guy comes outta the weeds behind me like some sorta commando, puts his knife to my throat and asks if I seen anythin'. I pretend like I'm three sheets to, you know, full sail for port wine, and he lets me go but he kicks me once, real hard. I remembered that for sure. Now I see him all over town. You wait, he'll stop at the adult store by the bus depot."

"Adult store?" said Gil.

"Buys porno. Big porno fiend. It's disgusting."

Gil was tempted to dispute that he had received proof of any kind, but he noticed the wino was missing three front teeth and instead pressed a ten dollar bill into his hand and left. He walked outside into a whipping wind but it didn't make him any less dazed. He was up against a drug-dealing porno commando.

On the other hand, he had a solid lead. The wino's story had too many precise details to be an outright fabrication. It made no sense to turn back now.

The bus station was close to the Double W and easy to find; travelers who "rode the dog" probably made up a large portion of the W's clientele. As promised, there was an "Adult Bookstore" right across the street. The window displayed fur-lined handcuffs and panties made out of fruit leather, but large sheets of black construction paper prohibited any view into the store. Taking a deep breath, Gil tried to look very casual and strolled inside.

An electronic bleat announced his entrance. The room was unevenly lit and it took him a moment to get his bearings. Near the door were a few shelves of "amusing adult novelties" and a glass display case filled with simulated latex genitalia. The main part of the store consisted of racks and racks of magazines and oversized video boxes. Behind the counter, the clerk was eating a bag of Cheetos and watching a bootleg-quality tape on a black-and-white TV that flipped every fifteen seconds. A woman with a Brooklyn accent took on two men at once while proclaiming her love of semen at an excruciatingly loud volume. Gil read a sign on the wall: *WE ARE NOT A LENDING LIBRARY. FIVE MINUTES ONLY.* He assumed he could stay longer provided he didn't actually read the magazines, which was good—he was already unsettled by the vivid anatomical close-ups on the covers.

Customers came and went, roughly half of them fitting the description of Farnsworth. The clerk ignored him. Half an hour later, Gil had memorized the names of all the magazines and was singing them in his head to the tune of Bob Dylan's "Subterranean Homesick Blues." The woman on the tape had been joined by another, and it had turned out they were both cheerleaders for the Nude Football League, and they had wandered into the men's locker room, and Gil didn't care if he ever thought about sex again. When the eighth medium-height, clean-shaven customer had left the store—two of them had been wearing camouflage—Gil had an idea. He walked up to the counter.

The clerk was now reading a magazine called *Juggs*.

"Hi," said Gil. "You know a man named Farnsworth?"

"You mean Philo? Philo Farnsworth?"

"That's the one," said Gil.

"Just missed him. Didn't you see him?"

"Too busy reading," said Gil, heading for the door.

"You a lawyer?" called the man. "Alimony? 'Cause if you are, I'd warn you off right now."

"No," said Gil, opening the door. "I owe him money."

The clerk shook his head as if now he'd seen it all.

Out on the street, Gil zipped up his parka and looked both ways. To his right, the last man to leave the shop turned a corner and disappeared. Gil trotted after him and rounded the corner just in time to see him climb into an orange Blazer. Gil turned and ran the opposite way, gasping back to his car, and fumbled his key into the ignition just as the Blazer roared by on a cross street. His hands shaking and his legs rubbery from the hundred-yard sprint, Gil put the car in gear and followed. He hoped this would be the only track event of the day.

Farnsworth drove out of town, stopping for gas at the freeway on-ramp. Pulling over to wait, Gil eyed his own fuel needle, drooping below the halfway mark, and hoped they weren't going far. He didn't want to chance an encounter at the pumps. On the other hand, he didn't know what he was waiting for, either. He just hoped Farnsworth was leading him toward proof.

The weatherman on the radio said a storm was promised. Gil hoped Mother Nature would renege.

Taking the Interstate, Farnsworth headed west, back toward Garden City. Gil was relieved; climbing the pass, his puny Datsun would have been quickly left behind. On the flat, Gil followed at what he deemed a safe distance. They passed truck stops and industrial outskirts for about ten miles, and then Farnsworth left the freeway for a two-lane highway. Rooftops thinned out as trailer parks and tiny communities gave way to fringe dwellings, and, twenty miles on, Farnsworth veered onto an unmarked dirt road. Gil hung back, making the turn as soon as the Blazer disappeared from view.

The rutted, icy track wound aimlessly through trees and snow-crusted pasture, between and over gentle hills. Gil couldn't see the Blazer anywhere, though he noted a few turnoffs that looked more like driveways than logging roads. Suddenly, the road ended at a metal gate with a rusty-looking padlock. Gil turned the Datsun around, jouncing in the frozen ruts of the road. Thick-clustered lodgepole pines cast darkness on the road; overhead, the clouds were thickening.

Gil turned into a driveway and crept slowly along. When a metal-sided trailer home came into view, he stopped and peered at the dwelling. No orange Blazer. He backed up to the main road to try again.

On the third driveway, the first he'd passed coming in, Gil caught a glimpse of orange and backed up quickly. A plan formed. He'd come back after dark when he could see in without being seen.

As he drove back to town, the sky continued to darken, and little flurries of snow set down here and there like white geese exploding in a hail of buckshot. It was still early afternoon, though, so real darkness was more than a few hours off.

Gil found a quiet place and went in for lunch. He waited out the rest of the afternoon at the bar, drinking and searching for a strategy. When that failed, he watched the TV behind the bar. A rerun of *Columbo.*

At dusk, Gil filled up his car and headed back out of town. The roads were harder to identify in the darkness, but he managed to repeat the day's drive. When he found the turnoff to Farnsworth's place, he felt the chemical clench of fear seize his gut. Despite the cold, his armpits were damp. His forehead had a high, hazy feeling. Was this the right place? Was this guy even Farnsworth? Shooting trespassers wasn't just a cliché out here, it was a god-given right.

Shakily he pulled a U-turn and parked at the head of the drive, leaving the nose of the Datsun pointed toward town. After a generous gulp of heat from his glove-compartment bottle, he turned off the car. Bundled up in cap, scarf, and gloves, his parka hood up, he pushed the door open.

The cold hit him like a wave, but he got out and trundled down the road, feeling ludicrous, more like the Sta-Puff marshmallow man than a muscle man.

The house came into view, a large, modern log home with lacquered wood; rusticity without the outhouse. Gil left the drive and walked into the snow, which crunched under his feet like breaking Styrofoam. Stopping, he pulled down his hood to listen. No dogs barking, no angry voice—yet. He continued slowly, his footfalls sounding to him like sledgehammers in the quiet. The house loomed closer, bright lights in the high windows shining outward like searchlights. Gil crunched onward.

Ten yards away, he stopped by a tree and looked into the living room. He could see a table piled high with magazines, a chrome floor lamp, and a poster for a band he'd never heard of, but he couldn't see the floor. On the other side of the house, movement caught his eye, and he saw Farnsworth walk naked through a dim room. Gil grimaced. It was winter and suddenly he was seeing naked people everywhere. He hurried across the clearing in front of the house, dodging the bright rectangles on the snow, and flattened himself against the wall. He inched his head toward the window until he could just see in. With a better view of the table, he saw a gun barrel jutting off. He gulped. Farnsworth came back in, wearing pants now, then stepped out of view. A gentle thumping of bass told Gil he'd turned on the stereo. Gil breathed more deeply.

Farnsworth came back, stood at the table, reached down, and dipped his pinkie fingernail into something. He put his fingernail to one nostril and closed the other with the index finger of his opposite hand. Snorting deeply, he tossed his head back and rolled it on his shoulders. He sighed, then repeated the process with the other nostril. He was six feet from Gil's head.

Farnsworth looked down and said with a smirk, "Want some, baby?"

Who was lying on the floor? Gil inched closer to the window and stood on his tiptoes, his nose just over the sill.

Something smashed through the glass and Gil fell flat on his back, head buzzing. An enormous dog had pushed its head through the window and was woofing wildly. Farnsworth came to the window, mouth agape, and looked out. He saw Gil. Gil floundered backward in the snow, trying to get out of the light, afraid the dog would just shoulder its way through the hole in the glass and jump to the ground. Farnsworth grabbed his gun.

Gil ran blindly back toward his car. He heard the front door open. Farnsworth shouted something, then the gun cracked powerfully. A shard of bark whipped off a tree and hit Gil's gloved hand. His sphincter loosening, Gil tried to speed up but felt like his legs were made of rubber cement. Catching his foot on a concealed root, he tripped and went down in the snow again, skinning his cheek on the icy granules. Farnsworth fired again. Gil got up and willed himself forward.

The barking, which hadn't stopped, grew louder. The dog was loose and charging after him. The outline of his Datsun appeared, and Gil had a glimmer of hope that he would make it. The gun cracked again.

Gil reached the car, jumped in, and slammed the door. He didn't remember why he hadn't left the key in the ignition. Fumbling his mittens off, he dug his key ring out of his pocket, dropped it, found it, and finally jammed the right one into the ignition. Revving the motor, he floored it, counting three and flicking on the lights. Out of the darkness a tan streak leapt straight for the window. Gil ducked and heard a tremendous thump. Looking up, he swerved to avoid the ditch as the dog's body rolled across the roof of the car and hit the road. In the rearview, he saw it receding in the red taillights. He couldn't see it move.

A mile down the road, Gil tasted bile, pulled over and opened his door. He puked long and hard into the road, coughing and crying as the bitter stuff came out his nose. He wiped his face on an old Burger Bar napkin he found in the glove box, then shut the door and took off again.

In town, he stopped at a gas station to clean up. In the glaring bathroom mirror, his face was red and puffy. He had snow burn on one cheek and vomit on the front of his parka. He looked like he'd been in a fight: scared shitless.

Returning to his lunchtime spot, he had a few drinks to restore his balance. He was hungry but couldn't eat. One thing he was grateful for: The storm hadn't hit yet.

Of course, the storm did hit as soon as he started driving home. The howling winds pushed his aluminum-can car back and forth in the lane, and the blowing snow limited visibility to about ten yards. He kept going, more out of an inability to accommodate further variables than from an active decision. Drunk, he kept both hands crimped on the wheel, leaning forward and peering through the window for the elusive white lines. The radio crackled dimly, talk flitting in and out like the voices of the dead. A semi rolled by going seventy, and for a moment Gil thought it was a train. The roostertail of the big rig blinded him and forced him to stop in mid-lane for a frozen moment.

At his slowest, twenty miles per hour, Gil thought he had stopped and the landscape was roaring by him in a white blur. Somehow, hypnotized as he was, he failed to sleep.

The storm had died out by the time he rolled into the Garden City Valley. In its eastward sweep, it had hit there first and moved on toward Pishkun. It had also swept out the sky, sucking the air inversion along with it and leaving a clean, sparkling cold behind. Nearing dawn, the sky was a dark violet and only the brightest stars still twinkled as he rolled down the offramp and headed for home. The only other cars were delivery trucks, and a few older, boat-like American cruisers, driving slowly to unknown destinations.

Home, he crawled into bed with Lo, holding her and hungrily inhaling her sleepy warm smell. She woke, vaguely, asked him a few questions and slept before she'd heard the answers. Gil didn't sleep, just lay there with her until dawn broke, until the alarm buzzed and the day began.

Work, thought Gil. Fuck.

Chapter Eight: Friday

During his free period, Gil called the police from the teachers' lounge. It was time.

A laconic voice answered. "G.C.P.D."

"Who would I talk to if I had information regarding a specific crime?" asked Gil.

"Is this crime in progress?"

"No."

"Are you calling in response to an offered cash reward or as part of the Crimebusters program?"

"Um, no," said Gil.

"Hang on." The phone rattled on a desk, and the man called loudly: "Hey, Red, some citizen with a tip!"

Gil glanced around the empty lounge, hoping no one was thirsty for coffee. Over the copier was a sign Flannel had printed on his home computer, a dot-matrix needlepoint: WASTE NOT, WANT NOT.

The same voice returned. "Sorry about that. I guess you can talk to me. What's this about?"

"Cocaine, I guess."

"No kidding?" The man's surprise was genuine. He whistled. "Shoot, I'm sorry but I'm definitely gonna have to kick this upstairs. One sec."

Elevator Muzak droned pleasantly for a minute, and then a sterner voice came on. "Lieutenant Blanston speaking."

"Hello, Lieutenant. Listen, I feel a little weird about—"

"Just a moment, sir. From where are you calling?"

"Work," said Gil, suddenly annoyed.

"Work," Blanston repeated. Gil could hear a pencil scratching. "Name?"

"Gil Strickland."

"Please give me your real name," said Blanston wearily. "Don't make me trace the call."

"It's my real name," said Gil. "Look, Lieutenant, you know the recent incidents with Kristen Swales, her accident and then the disruption at her funeral?"

"Of course."

"One of my students told me that Swales and some of her friends were buying coke from a man named Farnsworth."

"The student specified the drug? She was not referring to the beverage?"

"It was clear."

Blanston paused. Gil could hear the pencil tapping.

"That is a pretty serious allegation, don't you think?" said Blanston.

"I do."

"What is the name of the student who told you this?"

"I can't tell you. I promised not to."

"I see. Well, thank you, Mr. Strickland."

"That's it?" said Gil. "That's all you want to know?"

"Mr. Strickland, you have accused a person named Farnsworth of a felony crime. You have done this secondhand, through the claims of someone—a high school student—who refuses to be named. This tip you offer might be completely bogus. And if it is true, how would you have me pursue it? Even if this mystery student were to come forward, high school students are not on any prosecutor's list of most desirable complainants or witnesses."

"But some of them can vote."

"Kristen Swales is dead. The coroner ruled it drunken driving. We are considering pressing charges against the parents of the kid who had the party. Though they were out of town, there is some precedent for prosecuting absentee parents of minors. And I'm sure the Swaleses are considering a civil suit."

"But Chouck was high on coke when he was ranting at her funeral—something about 'hypocrites.' Doesn't that make you suspicious?"

Blanston sighed. "Mr. Strickland, let me put this another way. I am suspicious about a lot of things. If my wife serves me dinner, I may have suspicions about its taste, which may lead me to believe she has poisoned it. But until I catch her in the act, or until I *am* poisoned, there is nothing I can do. Do you follow?"

"Enough," said Gil wearily.

"While I appreciate your concern, we are treating Chouck as an individual case. There is no point in putting the Swales family through any more grief than they've already suffered. When we can question Chouck more fully, we will find out if there is any substantiation to your student's claims."

"But—" Gil bit his tongue. It was useless.

"Yes?"

"Sorry."

"I would suggest you spend less time giving credulity to your students' fanciful claims and more time teaching them the value of empirical observation," said Blanston. "Goodbye."

The phone clicked dead and Gil hung up, grinding his teeth. Maybe Blanston was right. Gil was placing a lot of value on a mumble from an injured drug addict with a big chip on his shoulder. But something was crooked, even if Gil didn't know how to connect the dots. And Blanston was already putting away his pencil.

★ ★ ★ ★ ★

Before the freshman class began, he cornered Jolene by the window, away from the desks.

"Hi, Mr. Strickland. Geez, have you slept?" She cracked her gum, making Gil wince.

"Not much, actually," he admitted. "Listen, something's still bothering me. Do you think you can help?"

She looked toward the door like a prisoner afraid of being seen collaborating with the guards. Gil hoped it was just her discomfort with having a teacher approach her so informally.

"Well, I guess," she said. "I mean, if I know what you want, you know?"

"The night Kristen died, there was a party. Were you there?"

Jolene looked even more uncomfortable. "Like I said, I don't go to beer parties, you know?"

"Please, Jolene," he said. "Anything you tell me stops with me, all right?"

She looked at her feet and put one shoe over the other. "Um, I feel like you keep asking me questions, and there's not much in it for me."

Gil looked at the wall behind her, performing a quick mental equation. It didn't balance, but he swallowed and gave in. "You know that paper you owe me? It's an A. No matter what. Just write your name on a piece of paper and give it to me, it's an A."

She looked up. "Really? Okay, I was there."

"Great," said Gil. "Now: Kristen. What was she acting like when you saw her? I know she was drinking, but did it look like, well, like she was doing anything else?"

Jolene's eyes roved the ceiling and she frowned in recollection. "It's hard to say for certain, you know? I mean, I didn't really see her."

"But she was there," said Gil hopefully.

"Someone said she was there, but she came really late, and then . . ."

"And then what?"

"She went straight into the bathroom and stayed there for like half an hour. A bunch of seniors were going in there, but they wouldn't let anyone else in. I had to pee in the bathroom in the basement."

The classroom was filling up. Gil didn't think any revelations would be forthcoming, and he didn't want to drag it out in front of other students. He thanked Jolene and she turned to go, then turned back. "Mr. Strickland, everyone who came out of that bathroom was acting like they were having the best time of their life. So I don't think they were putting on makeup."

Gil returned to his desk. He had just bribed a student. Delving into this mystery was addictive.

In fourth period, Kristen's friend Maria was edgy and distracted. Gil noticed the change because usually Maria scratched her ear with her pen and stared out the window. Today she was chewing her lip, etching ballpoint doodles deep into her notebook cover, and tapping her foot like a jackhammer. He wondered if she was entering some new phase of the grieving process. He wanted to ask her a few questions after class, but Jerry beelined for his desk and kept Gil from catching her.

"Mr. Strickland, I have a huge favor to ask you."

"Something more than the free education I've been providing all year?"

"Well, it's related to that," said Jerry. He did look uncomfortable. "I totally messed up one of my college applications. It's for early acceptance, which my parents are making me do so they can figure out the financial stuff, and I thought the deadline for this one school was February fifteenth, but it's February first."

"Ah," said Gil. "A recommendation." Behind Jerry, Maria

stopped just outside the doorway to greet a friend.

"I'm *really* sorry, Mr. Strickland. I was kind of late asking you anyway, but now I'm really late. I'd have to have it a week from Monday so I could send it and get it there in time. Is that okay?"

"Sure," said Gil grudgingly, as Maria walked off.

Hangdog, Jerry removed a sheet of paper from his notebook and handed it to Gil. "These are their guidelines, but I'm sure whatever you write would be great."

Gil dropped the paper on his desk without looking at it. "I know the drill, Jerry."

"Sorry, I know," said Jerry. He walked off, looking very slightly relieved. "Thanks!"

Gil slogged up the steps of his house in the cold darkness, bone tired. When he opened the front door, Lolita trotted across the living room and gave him a hug.

"Welcome home," she said. She kissed his cheek, then unzipped his jacket and helped him out of it.

Gil stared at her. "We've finally inherited something, haven't we? We're going to move somewhere warm and live in a giant house on a private beach."

"Not exactly," she said. She led him to the breakfast bar, sat him down, and poured him a small drink. "I got a call out of the blue from *Travel Horizons.* A weird chain of referrals, and now they want me to go to California to do a piece."

Gil took a drink. "That's great. Where in California?"

"Bakersfield."

Gil coughed. "Is this a magazine for truck-stop enthusiasts?"

"No," said Lo, laughing. "I was just kidding. Actually, it's Big Sur, Carmel, Monterey—Highway One revisited. I think I get a tour of Clint Eastwood's house."

"Dirty Harry himself," said Gil. "I thought you called him a violence-monger."

"I'm writing about beaches, scenery, and houses," said Lo. "This isn't a think-piece for *Harper's.*"

"I'm happy for you. When do you go?"

"Nine-thirty tomorrow morning."

"That's sudden," said Gil, feeling abandoned already.

"I know you'll miss me, but I'll be back next Friday." She patted his hand. "There's a second surprise."

"What?"

"I've been so busy getting ready that I haven't had time to cook. You're buying dinner."

To celebrate, they ate at Lo's favorite restaurant, the Eggplant Stem. It was Gil's least favorite. He felt the choice should have been his, a consolation prize for being left behind, but he kept his thoughts to himself. It was a beer-and-wine place, so he made do with sake, the strongest stuff on the menu, and feigned interest in his plate of chewy brown rice and limp, bedraggled vegetables. Lo chattered happily about her surprise assignment, while Gil tried to nod, smile, and murmur in the appropriate places.

When they returned home, Gil locked the front door and turned off the porch light. Lo headed straight up to the bedroom to pack. Gil sat on the couch and counted a magazine's pages instead of reading it.

Lo came downstairs.

"Finished?" asked Gil.

"Uh huh." She sat down on the couch and put her arm around him.

Gil put his nose against her neck and breathed in deeply. "You always smell so good. When I got in this morning, I just lay there, smelling you."

"I know. I smelled *you,* and believe me I can't return the compliment." She smoothed his hair. "I'm just glad you're alive.

That was pretty dumb, what you did."

They had covered the events in the morning before Gil left for work. "I know," he said. "This morning I tried to tell the police what I know, but they weren't very helpful."

She looked at him with a clear, steady gaze. "Well, promise not to be dumb while I'm gone."

Her tone reminded Gil of a time when their love had been truly alive with concern for one another, when they gave frivolous favors and shared deeper fears. He kissed her and slipped his hand around her waist and up the back of her shirt, his fingers charting the bumps of her spine.

The phone rang. Gil slid back, groaning, while Lo went to answer it. "Hi, Sharon," he heard her say. He looked at the ceiling, tuning out of the conversation.

There was a noise out front. Not much, but something different: Not a creaking branch or a car shifting gears. A scrape. Gil sat up. Turning out the lamp on the end table, he walked stealthily over to the front window. Lo was still talking in the kitchen.

A dark shape flitted across the front yard. Gil heard a rasp of hinged metal and then a soft thump as something came through the mail slot. The something started hissing. Gil wanted to dive behind a chair but was rooted to the spot. He wanted to call to Lo but his lips only parted slightly. A great stinking cloud billowed out of the foyer. Gil recognized the smell from summer chores in the field behind his grandparents' lake house. He used to throw canisters of poison gas down rodent holes. They were called gopher gassers.

He ran to the door, thinking to open it and kick the thing out, but the cloud of smoke was too dense and he panicked before he got a hand on the doorknob. Coughing, his eyes watering, he ran back to Lo, who was covering the mouthpiece of the phone. Her eyes were wide with incomprehension.

"Grab a blanket," he yelled, running up the back stairs. Lo

hung up the phone. He shut the door to their bedroom and ran back down. Lo had retrieved an old green-wool army blanket from the linen closet.

"Gil, what on earth is—"

He grabbed the blanket, ran it under water in the tub, then carried it sopping to the front and dropped it on the still-smoking gasser. Though the plumes of smoke subsided quickly, they could still hear the gasser hissing under the blanket. They hurried throughout the house, opening windows. In minutes, a frigid wind was airing out the smoke and, less quickly, the stench. They put on coats. Gil had caught too many lungfuls of the toxic gas and was hacking raggedly.

"Gil," said Lo through chattering teeth, "I want very much to believe this has nothing to do with your trip to Pishkun."

"So do I," said Gil. He dialed the police.

A cruiser came quickly, but once the chubby policeman learned Gil was a teacher, he refused to believe the culprits could be anything other than disgruntled students.

"Maybe," said Gil. "But mention it to Blanston anyway. The timing is odd, given that I just phoned in some information that might be damaging to someone."

"I'll tell him," said the cop. "But there's just not an awful lot we can do. We don't have any undercover people in the high schools, so it would be hard to track down these kids."

"I'm suggesting," said Gil, stifling a cough, "that it might not be kids. And it might be more than a prank."

"Well, it's certainly more than we usually see." He chuckled. "I remember we went after a few teachers back in the day, but I don't think any of us had this much sand."

Gil put his hand on the doorknob. "Thanks, officer."

"You're welcome, Mr. Strangelove," was the sunny response. "If I were you, I'd invest in some air freshener and forget about it. Lilac Glade is on sale at Big Buy—three for $2.49."

Making a final hieroglyphic in his notebook, the cop touched his cap and walked out the door and down the steps.

"Pig," muttered Gil, turning up the heat.

Chapter Nine: Weekend

In the morning, the house smelled like a combination of spent fireworks, fecund mold, and, strangely, cooked asparagus. Their bedroom had been spared the worst, but in the other rooms the air was still hazy near the ceiling. Before they went to bed, Lo had suggested Gil visit the hospital, and she said the same thing in the morning. Gil did feel as if he'd run a marathon behind a diesel bus, but he didn't want to hear the medical terminology for whatever had damaged his lungs. He was sure the worst effects would wear off soon enough.

Now Lo sniffed her suitcase obsessively. "I hope the stuff inside is all right. It was closed, but I don't want them to quarantine me when I get off the plane."

"Just think what Mrs. Eastwood will say."

Lo stopped. "He's married?"

Gil shrugged. "I don't know."

Grabbing a notebook from her carry-on, Lo flipped pages and then made a note. "I can't believe I don't know that," she moaned. "I need to research these things. What's wrong with me?"

They drove to the airport. Lo sniffed her coat until she was lightheaded. Leaning back to catch her breath, she offered Gil cleaning tips between long, deep inhalations. The gopher gasser had left scorch marks on the parquet floor of their entryway, much to her chagrin. Gil assured her he'd take care of it.

At Lo's request, he dropped her at the curb of Garden City

International Airport—*International* owing to a daily flight to Canada.

He rolled down his window as she walked away. "Are you sure you can carry that?" he said.

"Yes!"

"When do I pick you up?"

"You'll be at work. I'll call the taxi." She slowed, then came back to the car. "I'm very worried about you. Please be careful."

"You, too."

"I'll wear sunscreen," she laughed. Turning, she lugged her bags across the pavement and disappeared behind two smoked-glass, sliding doors.

Gil tried unsuccessfully to clean the entryway floor, then wiped gray residue off the walls and some of the furniture. He put couch and chair cushions in the back porch to air out, then took all the drapes off the rods and piled them on the floor, planning to take them to the dry cleaner. But by eleven o'clock he'd had enough, and stalked the house looking for ways to occupy himself. He poured a drink, put on a record, and climbed in the bath. Dozing off, he woke in a tubful of cold water. He drained it and took a steaming hot shower to warm up. The ends of his fingers wrinkled, pink and raw. He put on his bathrobe and stacked a fire in the fireplace, but shook the match out before he lit it. He called Dick. There was no answer.

He got dressed again. He started up the Datsun and let it idle. After ten minutes he locked the house and got behind the wheel. He drove to the freeway and rolled up the on-ramp, heading east.

Making good time on clear roads, he arrived in Pishkun mid-afternoon. The sun looked like a cue ball behind ashy clouds.

He stopped at a bar, had two for courage, and drove back to Farnsworth's place. The orange Blazer sat in front and smoke billowed from the chimney. Gil parked behind the Blazer. Remembering his last departure, he left the key in the ignition.

When he knocked, no one answered, but he could hear movement inside. He knocked again. Farnsworth answered, wearing blue jeans and a dirty western shirt with pearl snaps and fraying collar points. His eyes were glassy.

"Help you?" He obviously didn't recognize Gil.

Gil wanted to sound friendly but not unctuous. "May I come in?"

Farnsworth regarded him suspiciously, but stood aside and waved vaguely toward the living room. "Okay."

Gil walked in and saw the rifle Farnsworth had used to shoot at him lying on the table. The hole in the window had been patched with cardboard from a twelve-pack of Lucky Lager. The dog, a German Shepherd, was lying by the open door of a wood stove. Staring at Gil, it growled but didn't get up. It had a dirty cloth bandage on its nose, and there was something awkward about its posture.

"Take it easy, baby," Farnsworth said to the dog. He turned to Gil. "She's just a baby, really. In human years."

"Nice dog," said Gil.

"She got hit by a car," said Farnsworth.

"What's her name?"

Farnsworth thought. "Well, the guy I got her from called her Marley, and I was gonna rename her 'cause that's a dumb name for a bitch, but I couldn't decide what to call her. So I guess technically her name is still Marley, but don't call her that."

Gil fiddled with a hood string on his parka, his nerves tightening. They couldn't exchange pleasantries forever; however stoned, Farnsworth was going to want to know why he was here. "Nice place you've got here," he said.

The man looked around the room as if it were the first time he'd realized he lived in a house. "Cool," he said.

"Look," said Gil. "You won't like what I'm here to say, so I'll just say it and then I'll go." *I hope,* he thought.

Farnsworth wrinkled his brow.

"Okay," said Gil. "I know you do coke, and—well, that's no business of mine."

"You a cop?" asked Farnsworth.

"If I was, I'd be arresting you. What I want to say is, don't sell it to kids, all right?"

Something passed over Farnsworth's eyes and his demeanor changed from stoned to stone-cold killer. It was like an eclipse. "Maybe I've sold once or twice," he said angrily. "What business is it of yours?"

"I'm a—parent."

"So?"

"Some of my—son's—friends have been getting coke from someone, and someone said your name."

"Who was it?" demanded Farnsworth, advancing and balling his fists.

Gil backed up, holding his shaking hands in front of him, palms out. "I can't tell you. I promise not to tell on you, either. Just knock it off and—"

Farnsworth pushed him against the door and slugged him. Gil gasped and tried to make words without any air. "Look," he wheezed. "I don't want any trouble, Farnsworth—"

"Well, you got trouble." He hit Gil in the face and for a moment all Gil could see was a nebula of winking stars. He raised his arms feebly as his attacker demanded, "Who told you my name was Farnsworth?"

"I can't tell you."

He pushed Gil against the door again and it banged open. Gil fell backward onto the planked porch. "Who are you really, old man?" He kicked Gil in the ribs.

"Jesus, Farnsworth, I'm only fifty-fi—"

"Shut up, you fuckin' freak! You don't know who I am." He shoved Gil with his booted toe and Gil tumbled down the half-dozen steps, landing on ice cratered with boot prints. Farnsworth slammed the door and yelled through it. "Get off my land or my dog's gonna chew your shriveled dick off!"

First she's going to have to walk over here, thought Gil with a trace of satisfaction.

His face numb and his gut throbbing, Gil climbed dizzily to his feet only by breaking the job down into smaller tasks. He hobbled to his car. Lifting the rear hatch, he examined his arsenal: paper towels, a tire iron, and a can of lighter fluid from a long-forgotten picnic. He glanced toward the house. He couldn't see Farnsworth, and Gil was partly shielded from the windows by several trees and the orange truck.

Wadding a handful of paper towels, he crimped the metal can in his hand and squeezed a thin, clear stream until the towels were saturated. He walked to the Blazer, unscrewed the gas cap, and stuffed the paper towels in as deep as he could. There was a matchbook in his glove box, a dull artifact from a previous geological era, four matches remaining. Standing at the back of the Blazer, he glanced at the house and then struck a match. He held the flame to the makeshift fuse but it didn't catch. Was it too cold for lighter fluid to burn?

He struck another match. It didn't light, and the red match head chipped off after three scrapes against the brown adhesive strip. The third match sparked, but the head stuck to his thumb while it flared. Cursing, he pressed his thumb against the icy glass of the truck to ease the pain.

He tried again. The fourth match lit and ignited the towels, and a streak of yellow flame climbed up the side of the orange Blazer. Gil dashed to his car and started it. As he backed up, he felt cold air flowing through the hatch he'd forgotten to close. He stopped, leapt out, and slammed it. He got back in the car just as the Blazer's gas tank exploded with a surprisingly quick report that folded the safety glass and sent debris high in the air. A fiery piece of upholstery landed on the hood of the Datsun. Gil sped backward, his eyes on the road in the rearview. When the Blazer's reserve tank blew, the brilliant orange flash illuminated the drab landscape around him like a sunrise.

Gil whooped and pounded the dashboard. He cackled all the way back to the Interstate, and smirked all the way home to Garden City.

It wasn't justice, but it sure felt good.

On Sunday, Gil woke wincing at a vicious banging in his head. He gulped water from a stale glass on the nightstand, then laid back on the bed and closed his eyes. His eyeballs were scratchy and his tongue felt like roadbed. He'd drunk far too much last night, draining the lower third of a liter bottle after he got home. The rhythmic pain matched his pulse—bang, bang, bang—until it missed a few beats. He pulled Lo's pillow over his head and muted the noise. It wasn't in his head.

His brain felt swollen as he pulled on his pants and crept downstairs. With each step it seemed to chafe against his skull, sending shock waves to his stomach, where they rippled into nausea. He was acutely conscious of the cold hardwood floor under his bare feet.

Gil opened the front door. A tall man in a burly overcoat stood on the porch, looking peeved. Cold streamed past him into the house. A white Dodge Diplomat stood at the curb.

"Gil Strickland?" asked the man.

"Yes?"

"Lieutenant Roger Blanston, Garden City Police Department."

"Come in," said Gil, standing aside.

Blanston entered, sniffing the air suspiciously.

"Thanks for coming down," said Gil. "I didn't think the patrolman who stopped by took our problem very seriously."

"Problem?" said Blanston.

"Friday evening," said Gil. "Somebody put a gopher gasser through our mail slot."

"Oh, that's right. Damn kids."

"I don't think—"

Blanston wheeled and cut him off. "Did you drive to Pishkun yesterday?"

Gil stammered, caught off guard. He couldn't think. It was as if there was cotton wool packed between his brain and his mouth.

"Don't lie," said Blanston sternly.

"Yes, I did," said Gil.

"A Pishkun citizen reported that his Blazer was destroyed by a man who drove away in an orange, mid-seventies Datsun with Garden City plates. We searched motor vehicles records and discovered that you are one of the few locals who put their trust in that particular make of automobile. And the Pishkun forensics team found a neatly preserved thumbprint on a piece of the Blazer's back window." Blanston grabbed Gil's right hand and examined his thumb, a small black burn neatly centered in the whorl. He nodded and let go. "We of course have your prints on record. And, finally, since you were recently on the phone making some fairly wild accusations about a cocaine dealer in Pishkun, I thought I would come by and arrest you."

Gil saw the floodwaters rising on his moral high ground. "Blanston, that man *is* a coke dealer! He admitted it!"

"He does have a record," said Blanston. "But so do you. When you called the station the other day, your name seemed familiar to me and so after our talk I checked you out. Two

DUIs, one drunk and disorderly, three public intoxications, and one charge of indecency for urinating in a public alleyway. Witnessed"—Blanston shook his head—"by a six-year-old girl. Your self-righteous attitude concerns me, Mr. Strickland. You of all people should appreciate what I am about to say."

"Those charges were years ago," countered Gil feebly.

Blanston ignored him. "You see, in the absence of evidence of actual wrongdoing, we are obliged to treat any citizen as law-abiding. If we are told that John Doe is, for example, dealing cocaine, we need to witness the exchange of said cocaine for cash or some item of material value. Just as, for instance, we have to catch you in the act of driving under the influence a third time before we can arrest you and take away your driver's license. An unsubstantiated complaint that you have been seen weaving all over the road is not enough, though I admit I would find that very credible. Now, if we had been able to catch the Pishkun complainant ourselves, we would have made sure to collect the necessary evidence to prosecute. And, under RICO laws we could have seized the Blazer. As matters stand now, the vehicle is of no use to anybody. Will you get dressed and come with me, please?"

"But you weren't going to do anything!" said Gil.

"I am under no obligation to reveal to you what we were planning to do, Mr. Strickland. It may chasten you to learn that we were planning to work in concert with the Pishkun authorities to investigate the man. After last night, if he is indeed dealing cocaine, I don't think he will be letting his guard down. Still, in the off chance that we are able to proceed, I need to know the following: Who told you this man was selling cocaine?"

Gil thought back to Chouck in the hospital room and the many problems facing him even after he got well. "I can't tell you," he said. "But I asked him where he got his coke and he clearly said, 'Farnsworth.' "

"The Pishkun citizen whose vehicle you destroyed was not named Farnsworth," snapped Blanston. "His name is Bill Potter. Vigilantism is not the answer, Mr. Strickland."

Feeling shell-shocked, Gil got dressed.

At the station, Blanston read him his rights and formally arrested him. Gil was fingerprinted, weighed, measured, and photographed. With no judge due until eight the following morning, there was no alternative to a day and night in jail. Before he was shown to his cell, Gil asked for his guaranteed phone call and was shown to a pay phone in an echoing cinderblock hallway. Using his calling card number, he had an operator search for a hotel he thought Lolita had mentioned. She was there. She had just gotten back from the swimming pool.

"Everyone looked at me like I was crazy," she said. "They think it's freezing. But sixty-eight degrees feels like summer."

Gil wanted to say something he would have said if he was at home on the couch instead of in jail. He said, "Nice work if you can get it."

"Don't be bitter," she chided. "You get your summers off. There are trade-offs."

Gil tried to ignore the bored guard who stood five feet away, staring at him. At the end of the tiled hall lit by buzzing tubes of pale fluorescent light there was a ten-inch-wide window. He saw black branches on a frozen tree jigsawing a pale sky.

"Are you okay, Gil?" Lo asked.

"I'm fine."

"It sounds weird. Are you in the bathroom?"

"I took the drapes down for cleaning, so it's kind of echoey in here."

"Oh, thanks," she said. "Well, I'd better get going. I've got a busy day ahead."

"Lunch with the Eastwoods?"

"I'm going there Tuesday. But I won't be meeting anybody

but the house staff. The writing will be a piece of cake, unless the editor expects me to know the brand names of the furniture. A photographer's been coming along with me: Dakota."

"His name's Dakota?"

She laughed. "I know. He's only about twenty."

"Keep an eye on him."

"I hardly think, Gil. Take care of yourself. I'll try to bring you something fun."

They exchanged goodbyes and hung up. Following the guard's directions, Gil was marched off to a sparsely populated holding cell. He wished he'd remembered to ask Lolita which day she was coming back. He'd already forgotten. And what was he going to tell her when she did return—that he had misinterpreted a drugged kid's mumblings so badly he had been assaulted, destroyed property, and been thrown in jail? There wasn't a delicate way to phrase *that.*

Chapter Ten: Monday

Jail was more annoying than scary. Gil had been in the holding cell several times before, though he had never spent the night. He wasn't afraid for his safety but his sanity: The three other prisoners would not shut up. One banged on the bars every fifteen minutes while repeating the same invective about the guard's mother's loose morals; another was intent on reciting—repeatedly—the inventory of the trailer home that his "bitch ex-wife" had wrongfully appropriated; and the third was certain Gil would find his checkered employment history deeply interesting. None of the men seemed to crave sleep. Every time Gil dozed off, he would be wakened by one of them. The third was the worst, with his whining insistence that "A workin' man just can't catch a break, bro."

Gil was fortunate to see a judge at eight o'clock sharp. Bail was set at fifteen hundred dollars, and Gil was allowed to pay by personal check after he phoned the bank and passed the receiver to the cashier at the city treasurer's office. The bailiff uncuffed him and he was free to go. On his way out of the courthouse, he saw Blanston waiting by the door, holding a Styrofoam coffee cup.

"Have you changed your mind about telling me where you got your information?" asked Blanston.

Gil stopped but said nothing.

Blanston shrugged. "I am looking forward to seeing Potter identify you at the trial. Unfortunately, he is busy and we can't set a date before February."

"Busy?" said Gil. "He spends his time high on drugs!"

"How do you know?"

Gil rolled his eyes.

"Can't say? It may not matter. If you had, for example, looked in his window and seen him snorting cocaine, it would still be inadmissable since you are not a member of law enforcement. So please do me a favor and keep your own nose clean. Isn't teaching exciting enough for you?"

Gil zipped his parka and looked longingly at the doors. "Why did a guy in the Double W Café tell me Potter was Farnsworth?"

Blanston chuckled. "Perhaps he had a grudge against Potter. Maybe it was an honest mistake, or a prank. Why would you expect a complete stranger to tell you the truth? What I would still like to know is how you became so fixated on the mythical Farnsworth."

Gil strode off. He wanted to know a few things, too. Was there still a real Farnsworth in Pishkun? Or had he misunderstood Chouck? Was the teen addled by withdrawal or playing a joke at Gil's expense? Gil needed to talk to Chouck again, but doubted he'd pass as a preacher or lawyer a second time. He was a criminal with an unprovable theory. He felt like Lee Harvey Oswald, who had screamed, "I'm just a patsy."

Hoofing it through downtown, stopping at a bar that sold package liquor, he crossed the bridge and reached his first-period class just over half an hour late. It wasn't a *Lord of the Flies* situation yet, but after another fifteen minutes, who knew what might have happened? He quieted the class, fabricated an excuse about a leaking water heater, and took it with good grace when half the students claimed not to believe him. He explained the purple bruise on his face by saying he'd clobbered himself with a wrench when a rusted bolt snapped. They couldn't see his aching ribs or the welts along his leg and buttocks—courtesy of Bill Potter's boot and front steps—but he knew he didn't have to make excuses for the way he hobbled around. As far as they were concerned, with or without injuries, he was an old man.

As soon as the bell rang and Gil had ushered the last straggler out the door, he opened the paper bag he'd carried in with him and took out the bottle. He was very thirsty.

By fourth period he was a little drunk. His aches had dulled, but he was feeling the effects of his sleepless night. He declared a reading day.

Maria was sniffling, wiping her nose distractedly. Gil read a *National Lampoon* that he'd confiscated from a student and tried not to make eye contact with Jerry.

Maria kept sniffling and Jerry cleared his throat.

Gil looked up. "Do you have a cold, Maria?"

"Yeah, I guess," she said.

"Help yourself to a tissue." He tapped a box on his desk.

"Yeah," said Jerry. "It's really hard to read."

"Lay off, Jerry," said Gil.

"Yes, Mr. Strickland."

Gil liked the fact that he held Jerry's fate in his hands. Students always snapped to attention when they were waiting for him to mail their recommendations.

Maria came up and pulled two tissues from the box. She seemed to close her fingers around them very carefully. Gil returned to his magazine and the class was quiet except for occasional whispers, flipping pages, the heavy breathing of a few sleepers, and Maria's now less-frequent sniffles. Gil finished the magazine without laughing—he had been concentrating too hard—and looked up. Maria wrinkled her nose and inhaled, preface to a sneeze.

"Ah—" she began.

"Gesundheit, Maria," said Gil.

"Tchoo!" Blood sprayed out of her nose and mouth, tie-dying her white blouse in vermillion. She looked down and screamed.

Jerry was transfixed. "Gross," he whispered.

Maria began crying and shaking, with strings of bloody phlegm dangling from her nose. Gil felt bourbon-calmed. He crossed the room and put his hands on her shoulders.

"It's going to be all right, Maria."

She wailed, almost convulsing.

Gil helped her out of her desk. He told the class to stay put and that he would be right back. He guided Maria out the door and into the hall. She stopped crying out loud, but shook as if she were burning with fever.

"Maria," said Gil softly. "We're going to get you help. But you have to tell me what you've been doing."

She whimpered, moving forward with little sliding steps. "Nothing," she mumbled.

They rounded the corner into a hallway lined with lockers.

"Maria," he repeated. "Is it coke? Tell me. What are you on?"

Her knees buckled and she fell to the ground, retching blood. Gil kneaded her shoulders and helped her up again.

"Keep moving, we're almost there. Talk to me."

"Yes," she coughed, her face and blouse smeared with red. "Coke . . . and other stuff sometimes. I have to stop, don't I?"

"Yes," said Gil. "Now tell me where you get it. Do you buy it from the same guy as Kristen?"

They reached the top of the stairs. The halls were quiet. Maria looked down the long flight of steps, frightened.

"Yes," she said.

"And from the same guy as Thad?"

"Uh-huh." Leaning on Gil, she took a tentative step down.

"Who do you buy from?"

"Mr. Flannel."

Gil nearly dropped her down the stairs. *"What?"*

"Mr. Flannel."

"You're not making a joke, are you? Or saying that just to get him in trouble?"

"Mr. Flannel!" she shrieked, her voice echoing down the stairwell and in the hall beyond.

Gil shushed her gently. "Okay," he said. "I believe you." They made their way to the nurse's office.

The gray-haired nurse gasped in surprise as Gil walked Maria in and helped her onto the bed. Then she sprang into action, checking Maria's pupils and pulse and covering her with a blanket. She called 911, then wiped Maria's face with a cool washcloth. Gil sat at his student's side until the ambulance came, holding her trembling hand and giving her encouragement. As the paramedics lifted the stretcher, Flannel poked his head into the office. "Am I needed here?" he said.

Maria locked eyes with Gil. She nodded.

Flannel saw Maria and said, "Lord save us!"

You'll need more help than that, thought Gil.

Eamon O'Donnell was making a rare appearance behind the bar at Mr. D's. He greeted Gil and they shook hands as Gil sat down.

"I can tell you what happened," said Eamon.

Gil looked at him quizzically.

"You dropped your left."

Gil caught sight of himself in the mirror behind Eamon, saw his bruised face, and felt it throb anew. "I don't think I ever got it up in the first place," he chuckled.

Eamon poured, his sparkling eyes attentive to the task. His own scarred features testified to his fighting experience. "My friend," he said. "There are three kinds of fighters. The first fella tries not to get hit. He won't get knocked out but he'll lose on points. The second fella keeps his guard up, moves his feet well, and lands punches when he can. He's in for a long, somewhat better-than-average career. The third fella"—he slid the glass to Gil—"the third fella doesn't even notice when he gets hit, he's trying so hard to knock the other guy off his feet. He won't have a very long career, but he's got the best odds of wearing one of those enormous belt buckles."

"What kind of fighter were you?" Gil asked.

Eamon looked over his shoulder, then poured himself a finger of Jamison's and knocked it back. "I was the second fella," he said. "But by god I wanted to be the third."

Sean was working in the back room, using the unaccustomed help as a chance to take inventory. He stuck his head out and waved, then returned to shifting boxes and counting. As Gil and Eamon talked, Gil could hear occasional thumps from the storeroom. Gil appreciated a chance to get his mind off recent events, and lost himself for a while in Eamon's stories of hard living in Chicago. The ex-fighter had a light brogue from growing up surrounded by newly immigrated Irish. He also had an uncomplicated worldview that allowed him to address problems head-on and shrug it off if he wasn't successful. He told Gil about being forced out of the ring after he ran afoul of a politically connected saloon owner in the Windy City, and of taking on Garden City's City Hall—over a perceived zoning infraction—and winning.

Eamon's stories seemed to belong to a simpler era. Gil wished the complications he faced were so cut-and-dried. After a few drinks, he wondered if maybe they were.

Home, Gil poured himself a drink with trembling fingers. He was cleaning his only gun, a K-Mart 20-gauge shotgun that had been left behind unnoticed when his father gathered his belongings to leave. Gil had never fired it, and it stayed zipped in its canvas bag on a dusty shelf in the basement. Like the briefcase, it was more a symbol of the things Curtis Strickland was not than the things he was. When Gil was a boy, during hunting season, his father would take him by the shoulder and say, "Next week, son, we'll load up the car and go shoot some grouse." But when he wasn't working those extraordinarily long hours, Curtis Strickland usually ended up in front of the TV set on weekends, killing a couple of six-packs instead.

Gil finished plumbing the muzzle with the long, wire-handled brush that looked like a bottle cleaner. He wiped the brush on a rag, then wiped down the whole gun. He loaded both barrels with lead #6 shells, the only loads he had. The paper hulls were old and brittle-looking; he hoped they would fire and not fizzle. Putting a handful of shells in his coat pocket, he started out the door. He stopped and came back. He took another drink straight from the bottle. He was about to terrorize the vice principal of the school where he taught. He was taking a gun, and guns had a way of going off. And he was again allowing the word of a drug-using teenager to prevail over common sense and the reputations of his peers. What if he were wrong again?

He remembered Maria's sad eyes, her nod when Flannel walked in, and knew he wasn't wrong this time. If the police weren't going to act, he would. Someone had to listen to the kids.

Gil checked the address in the phone book one more time and went outside.

It was dark and clear, too cold for snow. Drifts of dry powder collected in the western lee of houses, away from the Porte l'Enfer Canyon winds.

He drove north of town, up Copperhead Canyon, where on clear days the forests and peaks of the Copperhead Wilderness provided a majestic backdrop. Flannel lived far up the canyon, in an area populated by Garden City's small white-collar elite. Subdivisions set among the pines provided doctors and lawyers both privacy and room for large, boxy houses on baseball field-sized lawns. Too pricey for teachers, it was apparently market-rate for administrators. Of course, Flannel's position seemed to have paid some shady dividends.

Gil found the place, a white, split-level ranch-style on a cul-de-sac that dead-ended on a hillside. There was one other house, opposite Flannel's, and a half-dozen weedy lots waiting for backhoes to arrive. He turned his headlights off and pulled a U-turn, leaving his car pointed downhill across from the house, unlocked and with the keys in the ignition. He was getting better at planning getaways.

Only one car was in the driveway, the blue Jeep Wagoneer that Gil had seen Flannel driving around town. A few lights were on inside the house, and spotlights in the yard lit the exterior with a righteous glow.

On the porch, Gil pressed a doorbell under a small Methodist fish decal. The peephole in the door was set at the juncture of a wooden cross. Gil held the gun just behind his leg.

Heavy footfalls approached, paused, and the door flew open. Flannel had a napkin tucked into his collar and a fried chicken drumstick in his hand. "Gil!" he said heartily. "To what do I owe the pleasure?"

Gil brought the gun up and poked Flannel in the midriff. "Back up," he said.

Flannel's smile withered. He stepped backward and Gil followed him in, shutting the door behind them.

"What in God's name are you doing?" asked Flannel.

Gil listened for other voices. "Are you alone?"

"Yes."

"Hands on your head," said Gil. "Upstairs."

Still holding the chicken between a thumb and two fingers,

Flannel put his hands on his head and turned around, then climbed the six steps to the upper level. The living room was cheap and bland; the couch, chairs, coffee table, lamps, carpet, TV, and stereo could all have come from the JCPenney catalog. There were no framed photos, no knick-knacks or personal clutter to suggest anyone lived there. The room was dust-free and the air was hot and stuffy. It seemed designed to suggest a wholesome, tidy mind, and it felt like anything but.

Flannel stopped in the middle of the room. "You don't want to use that, you know."

"I don't," agreed Gil. "But the problem is, I'm a little drunk. My judgment is off and my physical responses are impaired. I might shoot you without even meaning to. So I guess we'd better make this quick. The longer it goes on, the greater the chance I'll fuck up."

Flannel stared at him, perhaps running calculations in his head. Gil's sudden arrival was one variable he couldn't have foreseen.

"Drop the chicken," said Gil.

Flannel lowered the half-eaten drumstick slowly and took a bite. He chewed it and took another. Gil raised the shotgun slightly and Flannel disdainfully let the bone drop on his brown, sculptured carpet. A crackle of static came down the hall.

"Ham radio?" asked Gil.

Flannel nodded. Gil prodded him backward through a doorway into the kitchen.

"Sit down," he said.

Flannel sat at the kitchen table, on a vinyl-upholstered chair in front of his half-eaten meal: a box of carry-out chicken, a plastic tub of cole slaw, and a can of pop. Gil leaned against the refrigerator and kept the gun trained on his hostage.

"Just yesterday I was questioning my sanity," said Gil. "But today I'm questioning yours. Tell me about Kristen and Maria and Thad."

Flannel was stone-faced. "Tell you what?"

"Why is Kristen dead? Why are Maria and Thad in the hospital?"

"You're upset, Gil—"

"Shut up unless you're going to answer my questions."

Flannel shrugged.

"You have a ham radio. Can you hear police frequencies on that, or do you have a police scanner?"

"It's not unusual around here," said the portly vice principal.

"You knew about Kristen's accident right after it happened. The trucker called the highway patrol and you heard it and got involved somehow."

Flannel said nothing.

"You knew they'd find cocaine on her or in her blood. Cocaine you sold her. You needed to keep it quiet."

Flannel stared at Gil in silence. Suddenly the gun felt very heavy. On the electric range behind Flannel, the white second-hand dragged across the clock face with a steady buzz.

"Someone hid the coke. Someone said Kristen was coming home from a party. Was she coming home from here?"

Flannel's expression was that of someone considering what to order for lunch. "Gil," he said. "You really need to reconsider what you're doing here."

"Maybe the kids never met you in person," said Gil. "Maybe you used a middleman, someone called 'Farnsworth.' Maybe you're Farnsworth."

Flannel smiled, a fleeting crease at the corners of his mouth that he quickly suppressed. But Gil saw it and knew. It wasn't proof but it was positive.

"How do you sell to the kids? Why did Chouck tell me 'Farnsworth' was in Pishkun?"

Flannel sighed mock-sadly but looked like he had decided what to order. He stood up.

"Sit down!" barked Gil.

Flannel furrowed his brow piously. "I know you didn't consider this visit very carefully before you embarked, my dear Gil, so I'm going to offer you a free return ticket. It's time to go home and sleep it off while I consider what action to take against you. You're not a killer. You're just confused about how to pass the time while you wait to die. You've invented some kind of terrible conspiracy in which you can play the hero."

Flannel stepped forward and Gil stepped back, his finger numb against the trigger.

"Are you really ready to write the last entry in your records? You were a good teacher a long time ago. Now you're a criminal and a drunk. I know you've got a record with the police, and I have rather enjoyed authoring your performance appraisals at Porte. You're one step from a sensational headline in the *Garden City Gazette* and life in prison. Because the man you are threatening—excuse me, about to kill—is a paragon of virtue, a pillar of society."

Flannel took another step forward, but his eyes flickered in the opposite direction, toward a rotary phone on the wall. Gil followed the glance. By the phone was a wall-mounted memo pad. A stub of pencil dangled from a string. There appeared to be three words written on the paper, the only sign of human habitation besides the dinner on the table.

Gil tried not to register what he'd seen. He watched Flannel advance and wanted badly to shoot. He stopped Flannel with the shotgun barrel and thumbed back the hammers. He pushed Flannel and snarled, "Sit down!" More off-balance than intimidated, Flannel sat down. He smiled warmly.

"Close your eyes," said Gil.

"No," said Flannel.

Gil raised the twin barrels to Flannel's forehead. "Close them."

"To humor you, then." Flannel shut his eyes. Gil looked at the memo pad. It read: *TUESDAY. 10 P.M. BUCK STOP.*

"Say your prayers," said Gil. At the end of his shotgun was a beatific Buddha. Gil lowered the gun and walked out of the house into the glare of the yard lights.

Behind him, Flannel called, "I'll say them for you!"

Gil drove back down to the valley. He'd sealed his fate at school and he hadn't learned anything. Spotting a scribbled note had been his only accomplishment. Even with a gun, he hadn't intimidated Flannel.

Still, the note was intriguing. The Buck Stop Bar was a roadhouse on the way to Pishkun, a wide spot on the frontage road between specks on the map. A meeting there might be worth observing. It also might be nothing more than a place where a seemingly pious administrator could knock back a few drinks in privacy, far from his own school district.

He drove to Dick's and banged on the door. Sharon answered.

"You look terrible," she said. "What's wrong?"

Gil pushed past her into the house. "I have to see Dick. Now."

She squeezed one of her hands with the other. "He's in his study."

Gil strode through the house and into the study. Dick was at his desk, writing. He swiveled in his chair. "What's up, amigo?"

Gil shut the door. "You were holding out on me," he said. "You know more."

Dick dropped his pen and sighed. "I didn't know you were in the detective business."

"I'm not. I'm in the goodwill business. I'm trying to spread it around."

Dick peered at Gil incredulously. "Jesus. Christ, look at

yourself. You're acting like a, I don't know, some hard-on from a movie."

"You knew there was a connection between Kristen and Flannel," said Gil.

Dick swiveled again, showing Gil his back. "I wasn't happy about it. Talk about a double bind: I was dating a student who I knew went to coke parties at the vice principal's."

"You never went with her?"

Dick paused. "No."

"That's the truth?" Dick said nothing. Gil took that to mean he was lying. "Who did Kristen go with?"

"I don't know. Cheerleaders."

"If you didn't approve, why didn't you do anything about it?"

"You're some detective, Gil," said Dick. "I've got to feed my kids."

"Were you thinking of your family when you fucked a student? Your daughter's the same age, Dick. How would you feel if I or someone else—"

"Okay!" said Dick. "Stop!"

They were both silent for a minute.

"Can I stay here tonight?" Gil asked.

"Why would you need to?"

"I had a talk with Flannel. Tomorrow I'm going to find out who's supplying him."

"You talked to him?"

"I threatened to shoot him."

Dick propped his elbows on his desk and buried his face in his hands. "You're insane," he said.

"Don't worry," said Gil. "I didn't tell Flannel anything about you. How could I? You won't tell me anything worthwhile."

"He knows we're friends," said Dick through his fingers.

"I'll sleep on the couch," said Gil.

★ ★ ★ ★ ★

With nowhere to go and nothing he could do, Gil spent the evening watching TV with Tommy and Katie. Sharon baked cookies and packed sack lunches for her family, at times silently coming to the doorway to watch for a few minutes. Dick remained sequestered in his study.

Gil had never spent any one-on-one time with Dick and Sharon's kids, and had often found himself at a loss for things to say to them. As he drank his way through Dick's beer, however, he kidded them loudly—his way of razzing Dick through the study door. Tommy and Katie responded enthusiastically, surprising Gil with both their intelligence and their irreverence. Both had active minds, and even the sedentary act of watching TV brightened under their inquisitive scrutiny. They liked police dramas, though they viewed the TV cops as hopelessly square and rated the performances on a scale that went from "Yeah, *right*" to "I'm *so* sure." For his part, Gil wished the policemen of the G.C.P.D. had half the wherewithal of their imaginary counterparts.

Dick's living room was a shrine to his achievements as both athlete and coach. Photos and trophies documented his wins in running, basketball, volleyball, and soccer. There was little trace of Tommy and Katie's interests or accomplishments. Neither was athletic, Gil knew, but both were good students and Tommy was a promising artist for being in sixth grade. Katie regularly placed near the top in math and science challenges. Where were their feats showcased?

But it was probably a good thing neither Tommy nor Katie was sports-minded, thought Gil. Dick would have had a hard time with in-house competition.

When the ten o'clock news came on, the kids said goodnight to Gil and Sharon and went up to their rooms. Though she seemed distracted, Sharon sat to watch the news with Gil, then brought sheets and blankets and helped him make up the hide-a-bed. She didn't ask why he was there or what was bothering Dick so much.

When the Simonsens had all retired, Gil turned out the lights in the living room and stretched out on the thin mattress that had unfolded from the couch. He was exhausted. Despite the discomfort of hard metal bars under his back and knees, he fell hard into the pitch-black well of sleep.

Chapter Eleven: Tuesday

Hands grabbed Gil roughly and rolled him over. He flailed but his arms were caught under the blankets. Opening his eyes, all he could see in the purple light was the tweedy couch back.

"What the hell is going on?" he gasped. There was no answer. Two sets of hands were holding him down.

Someone sat on his legs while someone dug under the covers, fighting to pull his hands together behind his back. He heard the high whine of peeling duct tape and felt the adhesive grab as it wound around his wrists. The duct tape was handed over and his feet were taped tightly together. The blankets were tugged up and he was rolled, swaddled, lifted by his feet and shoulders, and trundled out the door. On the porch, one captor lost his grip and Gil started slipping to the ground.

"Goddamnit, put your arms under his shoulders," said one.

"Fuck you," said the other.

They turned Gil over and tried again. He caught his first glimpse of his abductors. They wore navy-blue knit ski masks, with orange piping around the eyes and mouths. Their lips looked somehow silly and soft. They lugged him down the steps and across the yard. Despite the blankets, Gil felt a rush of cold. He was only wearing boxers and a T-shirt. Gil saw Dick's white face staring down from the window under the peak of the roof, disappearing as Gil met his gaze.

"Damn it, Dick!" yelled Gil, his voice cracking in the predawn quiet.

"Shut up," said one of the men. The voice was young, the tone almost petulant.

They carried him to a blue van and dropped him in the back, on a metal floor so cold it burned. The van rumbled to life and lurched off. As Gil rolled first one way, then the other, he began to shiver uncontrollably. His teeth chattered like a wind-up children's toy. When his sore ribs thudded into a wheel well, he wished he had a drink.

They drove for ten minutes with no sounds except the creaking springs of the old van and the whiz and burp of the tires against pavement. When they stopped, Gil was hauled out the back and recognized the warped, red-brick street as a disused avenue by the railroad tracks. They lugged him up onto a loading dock, then into a cold, empty warehouse. Stripping off his blankets, they taped him to a chair.

Gil saw unlined eyes behind the masks, pupils tight with fear. One of the young thugs lifted his foot and poised the sole at Gil's chest. He kicked, and the chair tipped over. Gil tried to keep his head up but it bounced off the wooden floor. A dull wave of pain flooded his body. His vision tunneled, a dancing blackness that tried to overwhelm his sight but slowly receded.

He stared sideways at approaching feet.

"This is your only warning to leave town," said a voice, lower and huskier than the first.

"I get the picture," said Gil. "I'm on my way."

A boot hit him in the stomach and he gasped.

"Let's just make sure," said the higher voice.

They pulled the chair up and one man punched him in the stomach. The other glanced a blow off Gil's temple, then shook his fist in pain. The chair was kicked over again and Gil saw stars. A mask leered into his face. He couldn't tell which one it was.

The lips said: "You know, I had a class from you." It was the higher voice. As they pulled the chair up again it seemed ready to give.

"Really?" Gil wheezed. "You drop out?"

He was punched and the chair broke. He hit the floor. "You flunked me."

As Gil passed out, he heard the high voice say, "That didn't take much."

"He's just a teacher," said the low voice.

Gil woke up in the back of the van. They were moving again. He was wrapped only in a sheet. His body throbbed in a half-dozen places, and he now knew from experience that the pain would only grow worse. He was pretty sure they weren't trying to kill him, but he wasn't sure they wouldn't do it accidentally.

They were playing country music on the radio, which didn't help.

He could see the windshield from where he lay; through it, only light-gray sky and an occasional powerline.

The van stopped. One of the thugs walked hunchbacked into the back. He opened the side cargo door, lifted Gil by his armpits, and pushed him out into a ditch. Gil landed face down in a deep snowdrift. The van door slammed shut and the tires spun and skidded away on the icy road. Gil felt both relieved and alarmed by their departure.

He wriggled onto his back and looked at the ashen sky, trying to blow snow off his face. He lay there a minute, thinking he wasn't that cold and the pain wasn't that bad. *I must be in shock,* he decided. Hearing the whine of an approaching engine, Gil yelled for help. The car whizzed past. If he couldn't see the car, the car's driver probably couldn't see him.

He changed his mind. He was cold. He struggled against the tape that bound his wrists, but the weight of his own body made it difficult. Laboriously, he rolled onto his front again.

The snow melted a little against his wrists and helped reduce the stickiness of the tape, but the thin strips still held tightly. He pulled his wrists at cross directions and managed to loosen the bond. Then, twisting and pulling for all he was worth, he slipped his left arm free. He rolled over and sat upright. The silvery tape was slick as his numb fingers searched for purchase, but finally he unwound the rest from his wrists. The last pull plucked a broad swath of hair from his forearm.

Even with both hands free, it took him five minutes to untape his feet. He realized another reason no driver would have seen him: He was lying in the snow, wrapped in a white sheet. Under the sheet his skin was white, maybe a little blue.

Gil stood up. He fell down backward, then tried again more slowly. This time he remained erect, a battered busybody, swathed in a dirty sheet like a refugee from a toga party. The road was silent. He was still in town, however, at the bottom of a hill, across from Blue Creek Park. There were no houses on the street.

Gil stood and stared stupidly into the trees. *Maybe I should leave town,* he thought. *I could find Lo in California, have everything shipped down and sell the house. We could be warm.* He saw Lo's face against the green plaid blanket in the grass, sunny and happy, startled for a moment as he pushed into her, then her smile widening. She closed her eyes in concentration and then laughed, pushing back, arching against him.

A gust of cold wind opened his eyes again. He staggered a little and decided to start walking.

A maroon station wagon crested the hill and started down. Gil waved his hands. The car slowed, then pulled over. Gil wrenched the passenger door open.

"Mr. Strickland?"

Jerry Feinstein sat at the wheel, mouth agape.

"I didn't know you were old enough to drive," said Gil.

"I'm a senior," Jerry said slowly.

Gil climbed in and shut the door. The blast from the heater was disorienting. "What time is it?"

"Seven. I'm going in early to help Mr. Haddon set up the—"

"That's great," said Gil. "Can you take me to my house?"

"Sure." Jerry checked the rearview and put the car in gear. He looked at Gil out of the corner of his eye and said admiringly, "You must have had some night."

Gil started to snap at his student but stopped. He said, "No. Things didn't go too well."

When they neared Gil's house, Jerry said, "I hate to ask, you know, at a time like this, but you know my recommendation?"

"I haven't forgotten," Gil lied. "But it's not a good time."

"Oh, I know. And I hate to keep bugging you about it. But it's important. I mean, it's not—I can get other teachers to write them, you know. But I really want one from you. You're the only one who really understands me. I guess you're my favorite teacher."

Gil didn't have anything to say to that.

In front of Gil's house, Jerry said, "Do you want me to wait while you get dressed?"

"No," said Gil. "I'm not going to work."

"Does that mean class is canceled?"

"You teach it."

Gil assumed his pants and wallet were still on Dick's floor. He walked barefoot in the snow to the back of his house. Using a soggy log from his half-covered woodpile, he punched a pane of glass out of the back door and let himself in. He had two quick drinks and started a pot of coffee. He ran a hot bath and set the bottle on the edge of the tub. As he eased himself into the steaming water, his numb extremities began to throb and burn, reawakening. He gulped whiskey for relief but even drinking hurt.

The thought of staying conscious hurt. He used both hands to steady the bottle and drank again, ignoring the scald in his throat and stomach.

He'd never believed the mind-over-matter mumbo-jumbo, but he was desperate. Closing his eyes, he tried to visualize himself as sound in body and mind. It wasn't easy. His stomach felt like he'd done a thousand pushups. Knots the size of ping-pong balls were rising on the back of his head, and it felt like someone had taken a cheese grater to his temple. His ribs ached and his skin was on fire. Each pulse of his tired heart made him want to gasp.

He looked down at his pale body, his unweathered skin almost translucent, varicose veins like a road map to middle age. His sad cock was wilted and his balls were still trying to climb up into his body as if they didn't trust the hot water. He was too hairy some places, too bald in others. He saw a yellow, horny toenail and realized he hadn't finished painting the medicine on it.

He chanted silently: *Sound in body, sound in mind.* His closed his eyes to concentrate.

After a while a new image asserted itself. Pulled by invisible chains, his body slowly stretched and tore apart, limbs and organs drifting lazily off into an inky black void.

He opened his eyes. "Fuck this," he said. "And fuck Flannel."

He wasn't leaving. But he wasn't safe. He had to strike back. Who could help him? To the Garden City police, Gil was just a drunk whose patched-together life was falling apart. If he tried to find help from a higher authority, like the FBI, Roger Blanston would be the first person they'd talk to. Allies were in short supply: Dick, his alleged best friend, had betrayed him once already. Gil wasn't beaten yet, but he was alone. Maybe the best he could do, he thought, was to yank on the few threads in his grasp and hope to unclothe the wrongdoers. Flannel had business tonight at the Buck Stop, which was between Stone Creek—the location of the kegger Kristen Swales had supposedly been returning from—and Pishkun. With luck, Flannel had more business to conduct than eating a hamburger and drinking a beer. The pudgy pusher wouldn't be expecting Gil Strickland, crackpot teacher of English and student of the arts of vengeance.

Clean, warm, and anesthetized, Gil risked a look in the mirror. He closed a cut on his temple with a white piece of adhesive. He needed a shave but skipped it. Other than bruises, bags under his eyes, and a haggard demeanor, he didn't look too bad. He got dressed. In the kitchen, he poured bourbon straight into the thermos and topped if off with a little coffee. He filled two suitcases with old newspapers and carried them outside. He didn't see any unfamiliar cars on the street as he loaded the trunk of Lo's vehicle, but hoped someone was watching his performance. For good measure, he returned to the house and grabbed a sleeping bag, two cardboard boxes filled with old tax returns, and a lamp.

Gil turned off all the lights and locked up the house. He lingered on the front sidewalk as if he were silently saying goodbye to his home, then drove straight to the freeway and headed west. The roads were good and he could easily drive eighty miles per hour, the speed of someone with a reason to leave town. Traffic was light and Gil didn't see anyone following him. A few cars were moving at a similar speed, but after a while they pulled ahead or drifted back and disappeared.

After an hour, Gil got off the freeway at the small town of St. Philbin. No one followed him down the exit ramp. He stopped at a gas station to fill up and then drove north on a two-lane highway through forested hills. He turned east and entered the Flatfoot Indian reservation. The name had been given en masse to several local tribes by trappers who believed early—and mistaken—reports that the tribes had practiced a form of foot-binding. Historians later traced the error to the writings of a French missionary whose imagination had been captivated by tales of the Far East before he was called to duty in the Wild West.

Gil drove steadily, if more slowly, passing through tiny towns that seemed buried in snow and which showed little sign of activity other than the pickup-truck traffic that, even moving well under the speed limit, would traverse the town limits in under a minute. Between the towns, pine boughs burdened with snow glittered as prettily as any postcard. An even wind skimmed flakes off the tops; once in a while, a whole branch let go and triggered an avalanche that grew as it cascaded down over the lower branches. He passed the southern edge of the bison range and saw a small herd of the shaggy beasts ambling through the snow, their rumps to the wind, their craggy nostrils blowing steam.

At the town of Reveille, a windmill watched incongruously over a half-closed cluster of businesses and houses with junk-strewn yards. He turned south toward Garden City, about forty miles away. He had enjoyed the drive and the temporary escape, but as he neared town, he drove back into heavy clouds with a sinking feeling. The whole trip had taken less than three hours.

Lo's car, a dark blue Mazda, was nondescript, but to play it safe, he parked a block away from the Cambridge and walked over. It was only a couple of blocks from the police station and a straight mile from school. He ate hash browns and eggs for lunch, pouring his own coffee from his thermos.

After eating, he paid the check and walked to the back. He paid again and pushed through the green curtain. Sitar music played quietly. Missy was on stage, contorting her body in what appeared to be a yoga position. She was wearing a leotard and, in place of the curly red wig, sporting her own short, brown hair. The burly bartender had his face buried in the sports page. Gil sat down by the stage.

Missy looked up. "Oh, hi, Mr. Strickland," she said brightly. She snapped her gum.

"Hi, Missy, how are you doing?"

"Better than you, I guess. Did some kid punch you out over a bad grade?"

"I suppose so." He touched his temple gingerly. "Actually, that's what I want to talk to you about."

"Getting punched?"

Gil glanced at the bartender, who hadn't looked up. "Can we talk somewhere else?"

Missy looked guardedly curious. "I'm working," she said. "I'm supposed to be on stage."

"Working? There's no one here."

She looked around the room and giggled. "Yeah, I know, but the ad in the paper says, 'Live girls from eleven A.M. to two A.M.,' so someone has to be onstage until the next girl gets here. We kind of take longer shifts during the day."

Gil looked at her striped leotard. "That's not exactly Frederick's of Hollywood. What do you do if someone actually comes in?"

"I just take it off!" She laughed and slipped a strap off her shoulder. "I'm sorry, I guess you want me to—"

"No, no," said Gil. "Thank you, but I'll just use my imagination." He pulled a five out of his pocket, cash from Lo's grocery fund. Placing the bill on the edge of the stage, he said, "Pretend you're entertaining me while we talk."

She smiled at him and snapped the strap back into place. "But I still don't know what you want to talk about, Mr. Strickland."

"I have to ask you something that you probably won't want to tell me," said Gil. "But I desperately need any information you have. I'll leave in a minute and no one will ever know that I was here except the bartender."

"Oh, that's my fiancé, Teddy." Missy called to him. "Ted, honey, this is Mr. Strickland, my old high school teacher!"

Ted Honey looked up, nodded, and resumed reading.

"We're getting married in May," said Missy happily. "We're going to Reno for our honeymoon."

"I'm happy for you," said Gil.

"Now what did you want to know?"

"Were you ever a cheerleader?"

"I was a Sparklerette freshman year, I cheered sophomore, and then I dropped out junior year," she said wistfully.

"Did you ever do coke when you were in high school?"

Her face darkened. "Why are you asking me something like that now?"

"Did you ever buy from Tim Flannel?"

She looked nervously around the empty room. "I think you should keep putting money on the bar while we talk so it doesn't look suspicious," she said.

Gil put a ten dollar bill up.

Missy unwound her legs from the yoga position and did the splits. She leaned forward, closer to Gil. "How do you know about that stuff?"

"Things have gotten out of hand. Someone seems to have hooked half the cheering squad. One died in a drug-related accident and another nearly overdosed in my class yesterday. Someone gave me Flannel's name and last night I confronted him. He told me I was crazy, but this morning two guys in masks beat me up and told me to leave town."

Missy looked at him with real concern, then switched her lead leg. She put her cheek on one knee. "That's terrible," she said.

"I think you know something, Missy."

"So do you, and look at you."

"No one saw me come here. No one knows we're talking except Ted. I won't reveal your name to anyone."

"Can you promise that?"

Gil thought of how he'd felt taped to the chair that very morning and knew it could have gone much worse. "No, I can't," he said. "But they'd have to just about kill me."

Missy sat up and folded her legs lotus-style. She was thinking hard.

"I just want to keep them from killing anyone else," said Gil.

Missy suddenly looked very tired. "Flannel sells," she said. "But he's more of a middleman. He finds girls who like to party and gets them high. He has little parties in his basement and hangs out with them. They start buying the product, and then he kind of hands them over to the Senator."

Gil froze. "This goes that high up?"

"It's just a nickname—he's not an actual Senator. His real name is Mike Sennett. Get it? 'The Sennettor'?"

"What does he do?"

Missy's voice had been getting quieter and Gil found he was almost holding his breath in order to hear her.

"Strippers," she said. "When the girls owe him money—and they're like high school kids, I mean, they can't buy much coke working at Dairy Queen—he locks them into the stripping circuit and starts sending them around the country. Some of them hook, and most move drugs for him."

"Did you, I mean, how do you—"

Missy laughed mirthlessly. "Kind of obvious, isn't it? But I kicked last year. I still dance, because it's all I'm really good at. But I don't do drugs anymore, or . . . the other stuff." Her voice almost disappeared.

"So you still work for him?"

"It's like he's my manager, except he's got an exclusive

contract and he gets fifty percent of everything I make."

"Can you tell me where he lives?"

"I don't even know what town he lives in. No one knows anything about him. He just shows up sometimes."

Gil realized the danger he'd put her in. "I'm sorry," he said.

"You don't have anything to be sorry about," Missy said. "I hope you can bust the fucker. After we get married, Teddy and me aren't coming back. I can't tell you where we're going, but Teddy knows a place where we can work."

"Aren't you afraid Sennett will follow you?"

"I'm not worth as much as I used to be now that I'm clean. But I think Teddy can be pretty persuasive, too."

"I'd better leave," said Gil. He stood up and put a small stack of twenties on the stage. "Thank you, and congratulations on your engagement. Please consider this a wedding present."

"Thanks, Mr. Strickland. But be careful. The Senator is pretty scary. And you don't exactly look like you're winning so far."

Gil grinned, which made his face hurt. "I suppose I don't."

He drove home. Just to be safe, he parked a block away, walked up the alley, and entered through the back door. He'd locked it that morning despite the missing pane of glass; when he reached through to turn the button on the cheap handle-lock, he nicked his thumb on a shard that stuck up like a tooth.

He didn't turn on any lights. The drapes were still heaped on the floor, and anyone watching would have been able to see right through the house. In the gray winter gloom, he looked for a clue to the date of Lo's return: a circle on the calendar, an airline receipt, a Post-It note. There was nothing in the obvious places, and his memory was filled with maddening gaps. He could picture her telling him, but couldn't remember the word that had come out of her mouth. Was it Friday? Thursday? Saturday?

Rifling her desk, he found a scribbled list of hotel phone numbers: Morro Bay, Big Sur, Carmel, Monterey. There were no annotations, but he knew he could cross the first one off the list—that was where she was when they had spoken on Sunday. He called Big Sur, got the usual name disbelief from the clerk, convinced her he wasn't a prank caller, then learned that Lolita Gudmundsdottir-Strickland had been there but wasn't any longer. They had no further information. Gil called the next place on the list, in Carmel, but Lo hadn't shown up there yet. He tried to think of a message he could leave her—*Don't worry, I'm not dead yet?*—but hung up without leaving his name.

But maybe it was better he couldn't talk to her. She would have tried to talk sense into him.

Gil set his alarm for four o'clock and took a nap. When the plastic bleats jolted him awake, he got up and sat down in his shadowy living room to eat a dinner of cold cereal and bourbon. Fortified, he grabbed a bottle of Karo syrup from the cupboard and headed out.

He stopped by Mr. D's first. Sean O'Donnell looked at Gil and pursed his lips. "Looks like you asked for a rematch when you should have thrown in the towel."

"It's part of my strategy," said Gil. "I'm wearing him down."

"I think you need a lesson or two from Dad."

"I could use some help with my footwork but I think my hands are hopeless."

Sean poured his drink. "Furthermore, you're half an hour late. We used to set the clock by you. We'd hate to think you're falling off your game."

"Is that the royal 'we,' Sean?"

"I think I speak for the community. Reliable timetables are the cornerstone of modern society. When any one of us stops holding up our end of the bargain, it puts a crack in the foundation."

Gil chuckled. "You're just worried about your bottom line."

"You've got me there." Sean smiled, but Gil could see pity in his eyes and it angered him.

"You're too educated for this, Sean," he said.

Sean smiled again. "That makes two of us." He moved away down the bar.

Gil couldn't even injure someone with words.

A few stools away, a group of secretaries were having a farewell drink with a coworker. The soft darkness normally had a quieting effect on patrons, but the women's animated chatter seemed brittle and too fast. Mr. D's lack of windows had been a key factor when Gil decided to adopt the establishment. Gil felt time should stop for drinkers. In the same way suspension in isopropyl alcohol would preserve them outwardly, ingestion of ethyl should preserve what they looked out on. There was no need to drink in a bar with a window, watching the sun go down and the cars pass. There was no point in watching things fade. In a bar without windows, the magic moment of the drink lingered longer.

But no delay would be long enough to make what he had to do easier. When Sean came back to refill Gil's glass, Gil put his hand over the top of it, thanked him, and left.

He drove to Dick's, watching the mirror carefully for police cars or any other tag-alongs. He reached the house safely and walked in the front door, interrupting the family at dinner. Gil said, "Hi, everybody," and started looking around the couch for his pants.

Sharon covered her mouth with her hands and stood up, knocking over her chair. She stumbled into the kitchen. Dick dropped his napkin on his plate and came into the living room.

He was visibly shaken by Gil's appearance. "I'm sorry, Gil," he whispered.

Gil lifted the cushions, found nothing, then got down on all fours and reached under the couch. "Not as sorry as I am, *friend.*"

"It's not just my job now, it's my family," Dick hissed. "Flannel knows people, dangerous people. And once you threatened him—"

Gil stood up. "Just give me my pants. I need my wallet."

"I didn't know what they'd do, Gil."

Gil's angry stare sent Dick into the kitchen, where Gil could hear him asking Sharon about the pants. The kids looked at Gil curiously. "Why'd you stay over last night?" asked Tommy. "Are you fighting with Lolita?"

"No," said Gil. "She's out of town."

"You look like you've been fighting with someone," said Katie.

Dick came back in, bearing Gil's neatly stacked shirt, trousers, shoes, and wallet like an offering. The clothes were crisply folded, though they were salted with white. "Sharon washed them for you," he said. "There was a Kleenex in your pocket, so they're—"

Gil slid the wallet into his pocket. "Don't worry about it." He walked out the door.

Dick followed him onto the porch, still holding the clothes. "Gil, it was for my family. I was worried about my family. You don't have kids, so you can't know."

Gil turned around, balling his fists. He thought about leading with his left and slamming a right into Dick's face.

He said: "I have kids. Classrooms full of them."

He stalked to Lolita's car and got in, leaving his Datsun still at the curb. He drove up the Copperhead, to Flannel's place. Parking at the bottom of the hill, he put the bottle of corn syrup in his pocket and walked the rest of the way, keeping to the darker side of the street.

At Flannel's house, he walked hunchbacked to the blue Jeep in the driveway, keeping the vehicle between him and the line of sight from the house windows. The bright yard lights made him feel like he was filming a scene in a spy movie. Fumbling in his thick gloves, he unscrewed the gas cap and then the cap on the bottle. He upended it into the tank, poured until it was empty, then replaced the gas cap. No explosion this time.

A door slammed and Gil's heartbeat stuttered. Behind him and across the cul-de-sac, Flannel's neighbors had come out their front door. Gil dropped to his stomach and crawled under the Wagoneer. His vinyl gloves scrabbled on the concrete; when he sucked in his gut, trying to fit into the short space under the chassis, the pain in his ribcage made his eyes water.

Thirty or forty yards away, the couple crossed their lawn and got into their car. They started it and sat idling for a few minutes before they pulled out. The cold of the cement reminded Gil of his morning ride on the floor of the van. It was too bad he couldn't do Flannel in himself.

The neighbors drove away, and Gil squeezed out of his hiding place and sneaked back to his car. He had plenty of time. Flannel's car would seize well before he reached the meeting place.

Gil drove east, keeping an eye on the speedometer. It would be a particularly bad time to get stopped by the police.

He'd been to the Buck Stop before. It was a log-cabin roadhouse that drew its regular clientele from a half-dozen small settlements with just enough population to have their own rural school district. He remembered hearing that all the students, from kindergarten through high school, were crammed into four classrooms. An hour and a half out of Garden City and it was like frontier times. Social life could be isolating for such young residents, thought Gil, although by way of compensation the Buck Stop had a reputation for serving anyone who could see over the bar with one foot touching the ground.

He arrived early, at ten minutes after nine, and parked on the dark side of the small building. The parking lot was crowded with pickup trucks and large American sedans. A few were new but most were of considerable vintage. A mud-spattered Willys jeep went topless; there was snow on the passenger seat and a butt-sculpted basin on the driver's side.

Gil walked into a smokey warm din. There were old ranchers at the bar, families at the tables, and kids fighting over the lone video game. The animated customers seemed to treat the place as an extension of their living rooms, albeit with the added attraction of electronic gambling machines and an endless supply of cold beer.

Gil headed for a row of dark booths with very high backs at the back of the room. In the most secluded one, he sat down with his back to the wall and his eyes on the door.

A waitress his age came over, scratching her head with a ballpoint pen through a hairdo that she must have settled on shortly out of high school. She smiled apologetically.

"I'm sorry, hon, you can't sit in that booth."

"Why not?" said Gil.

"Party of four. They called ahead."

"I didn't know you took reservations."

"Well, not officially," she said patiently. "But there's this well-to-do fella comes in once in a while and he likes this booth. He's not local, but he tips everybody, even the cook."

Gil was pretty sure he was being bumped for Flannel's dining partners. All three of them. He smiled weakly and got up. He gestured at the adjoining booth. "This one all right?"

"Great," she said. "I appreciate it. Now what can I get you?"

"How about a double bourbon with a beer chaser. What's good to eat?"

"Special's a buffalo cheeseburger with tater tots."

"Sounds good."

"Hope you like 'em crispy," she cautioned as she walked off.

Cheeseburgers? Gil wondered. *Or tater tots?*

When she brought the drinks, Gil gulped the bourbon and sipped the beer, thinking he should do it the other way around. He had another beer when the food came. The tater tots were nice and crispy, and the burger was pink and juicy, but after a few bites he couldn't taste anything. Flannel had planned to meet three men. For some naïve reason Gil had thought it would be only one, hopefully Sennett himself.

He ordered another whiskey.

"What's wrong with the food?" the waitress kidded him.

"It's great," said Gil. "I'm just . . . savoring it."

She rolled her eyes as she walked away. Country women. She was probably used to truckers and ranch hands who ate their weight—or Gil's weight—daily.

Three men.

The hands on the clock swept toward ten and went past. Bar time: The clock was set a quarter-hour ahead. A half-dozen damp rings on the lacquered wood table in front of Gil marked the resting places of short-lived whiskeys. The remains of the burger and tater tots lay, bloody with ketchup, on their round ceramic bier. Gil held yet another glass in his hand and ran his index finger around its rim as he tried miserably to adapt his original game plan to accommodate a greater number of players. At least Flannel wasn't likely to show up.

At ten-thirty, bar time, a trio of burly men walked in the front door and headed straight for the booth behind Gil. Two of them wore unzipped parkas over expensive-looking sweaters and the third wore a tweed overcoat over a dark suit. Given that no one else in the bar was even wearing a tie—unless you counted the bolo variety—they sure didn't look like locals.

The men in sweaters looked like they'd been recruited from the Australian mafia, if such a thing existed. Tall, blond, and tanned, they were built like farmhands but wore the blank expressions of combat-hardened soldiers. One of them, incongruously, wore round, silver-framed glasses. The man in the suit was shorter—which made him about normal human height—with curly, sand-colored hair and a bemused expression. He walked a step ahead, carrying a calfskin briefcase that might have cost more than Gil's car. Not wanting to gawk, Gil turned away and sipped his drink, staring at nothing. When the men sat down behind him, the back of his seat lurched forward. Is this what they mean by *heavies?* he wondered.

Gil signaled the waitress for another drink and strained to hear the men's conversation over the bar noise.

"We should stop meeting here," one was saying. "Even these yokels might get suspicious."

"Or, I don't know, dress like farmers or something."

The third voice spoke with authority. "If you boys walk in here with boots and hats on, the shitkickers are going to laugh so loud they'll hear it in Garden City. Hell, you'd probably wear *chaps.* No, everything's fine as is. Far as they know, we're businessmen driving through, but nobody's looking anyway. We're out here at our guest's request. He has more to fear from the Garden City Police Department than we do. Personally, I wouldn't care if we met at City Hall, but you know me, always eager to please."

The other two guffawed. It must be "The Senator" talking, thought Gil.

"No, fellas," he continued, "what we have to watch out for is Federal involvement. But if I keep good books and make nice with the locals, we can eat dinner wherever we like. *And* deduct it on my taxes."

The men guffawed again.

The waitress brought Gil's drink. "Maybe I should bring you a dog bowl so you can just lap it up," she joked. "Make sure you got a pocketful of Certs if you're drivin'."

Gil smiled blearily and toasted her.

He heard someone else sit down behind him. Was it Flannel? Could he have found a ride already? Gil cursed himself for not paying attention.

"Gentlemen," said the new arrival. The voice rang a gong in the subterranean vaults of Gil's brain.

"Hello, Lieutenant. Nice of you to join us for dinner," said Sennett. Gil could practically see the two goons smirking as the chief criminal continued. "We don't often get to dine with a member of the law enforcement community—at least in such nice surroundings. When you host us, it's usually a buffet-style setup."

"Very amusing," said Blanston. "But save the standup comedy for someone else. I do not want to sit here any longer than I have to."

"Strictly business," said Sennett amiably. "Fair enough."

"Where's Flannel?"

"He's running late, apparently. Maybe he had lesson plans to approve. I'm sure he'll be here any minute."

"I would rather not wait."

"It's your call. What's on your mind?"

"You know why I am here."

"Well, I can't be certain, but I'm guessing it has something to do with a late-night boondoggle two weeks ago. I'm sorry if I forgot to send a thank-you card."

"I want money, Sennett."

"And again, straight to the point. How much money are you hoping for?"

"Twenty-five percent of the street value should be about eighteen thousand."

"Lieutenant, I do appreciate your help. I do. It was an unfortunate turn of events and you rode in on your white horse and straightened it all out. But it's a little bothersome to have you laying claim to our proceeds."

Blanston bit off his words even more cleanly than usual. "If it were not for my help, you would not have any proceeds to share. I went out on a limb and I want fair compensation."

"It wasn't even that much, really," sighed Sennett. "Enough to goose the starters on the football team, but not enough to chalk a goal line on the field."

"It was a full kilogram."

"That's not what Flannel said when he got it. He said it was a little light."

Blanston sounded startled. "I delivered every gram that my man pulled from the car."

"And you trust him?"

"He is a devout Christian."

"So's Flannel," said Sennett dryly.

"Whitaker is an evangelical who attends church five times a week," said Blanston.

"Well, if this saint is out of the running, maybe we should wait to hear what Flannel has to say."

"I would like to hear what he has to say. He was too lazy to make the drive himself, so he sent a teenaged girl in his place. She stopped off at a party, shared some of the buy with her friends, drank a quart of whiskey and ran her parents' car into a billboard. I recovered the cocaine for him and kept it out of the papers—and he accuses me of doing something wrong?"

"You're right," said Sennett. "If a few flakes swirled away, there are a number of ways it could have happened."

"So you will pay me."

Sennett laughed. "In the interest of goodwill, I'll give you a finder's fee for it. I'll be more than generous. Let's say seven hundred dollars."

"You must be joking. That is—"

"My final offer," said Sennett. "I have expenses, you know."

"I am putting my career and good name in danger, and you are offering me one percent? I owe a certain press officer considerably more than that already. A finder's fee is at least ten percent."

"I'd like to remind you, police lieutenant Roger Blanston, that you've been risking your career and good name for some years now. When I first started doing business in your particular neck of the woods, you were more than happy to offer me protection. But can you remember me complaining even once? You can't, because I didn't. You set your price, and I paid it, month after month after month. I paid you so much and so often that we are even. In fact, you may even owe me a few favors. Because all I have to do is make a phone call to the district attorney and suggest that he reexamine the bag of cocaine that was seized from that dead bitch's car. Not only do I know that it is now foot powder, I know who took the real coke: the man with the key to the evidence room."

"Who would listen to you?" said Blanston.

"You may also have some documentation incriminating me, it's true," continued Sennett. "But consider who has more to lose if we, as they say, go to court. I'm already a criminal with a rap sheet and a very expensive, very experienced lawyer. You, on the other hand, are a bastion of the Garden City community, a war hero, a crusader against crime—and a pinched, moralizing little prig who is a fucking hair's breadth from having his pants pulled down in public. Those blue-haired ladies love you now,

Rog, but they'll be the first ones screaming for them to hang you when they find out what you did to their granddaughters. Crooked cops don't have any friends. You're gonna get run out of town on a rail, and when you get to jail, they're gonna bust your teeth out so you can't bite 'em when they want to pretend they're with Maisy Sue back home."

Sennett had been warming to his subject but paused, perhaps to sip water from the plastic tumbler in front of him. "Lieutenant, these are the ties that bind. Let's not endanger our friendship by quibbling over a few pennies."

After a moment, Blanston stood up and released a single, strangled word: "Fine."

Gil hunched into his seat and held his glass in front of his face.

"Pay him outside, boys," said Sennett. "We flash a roll like that in here and we'll have to buy a round for the house."

Chuckling, the two heavies stood up and followed Blanston as he stalked outside.

Sennett called the waitress over. "I'd like a glass of single-malt Scotch whiskey, please, and your twenty-ounce T-bone steak, rare."

"You want anything else with that?"

"What do you recommend?"

"Tater tots?"

"Sounds delightful."

When the waitress left, Gil guzzled the rest of his drink and then moved to the next booth. He sat down across from Sennett. Belying his bluff demeanor, the man looked like a waxwork. His ruddy cheeks seemed rouged and the skin on his hands had the bloodless pallor of a corpse. His curly hair and small mustache were neatly groomed, his nails carefully buffed, and he regarded Gil with the disdain of a dandy who's found a biscuit-sized gravy stain on his favorite silk tie.

He raised an eyebrow. "Yes?"

"Mr. Sennett?"

"And who are you?"

"Christopher Grouse," said Gil. He noticed that he was breathing heavily. "I'm with the *Garden City Gazette*. I was wondering if you'd answer a few questions for me."

Sennett put his fingertips together. "A reporter? That's interesting. What are you reporting?"

"Sponsors of . . . erotic dancing. You know the controversy: Is it art? Is it porn? It's a really hot topic right now. I was wondering if you, as a, um, sponsor or promoter of stripping throughout the Northwest, could, you know, just give me a sound bite or something."

Sennett tapped his fingertips together. His pale blue eyes seemed to penetrate Gil's boozy skin and see right through to his trembling core. "Who gave you my name?"

"Strangely enough," said Gil, "it was an administrator at one of the Garden City high schools. I was covering the school board meeting and we got to talking afterward. Big fellow. I think his name was Flannel. Maybe Tom Flannel?"

"I see. Off the record, Mr.—ahem—Grouse?"

Gil was so surprised his plan was working he forgot to be afraid for a moment. "Certainly."

Sennett leaned forward. "Any time I see a woman without her clothes on, I call that art. On the record, I don't know what the hell you're talking about. The only people I sponsor are Jerry's kids."

"I apologize for the misunderstanding," said Gil. As he slid out of his seat and stood up, he thought he had done pretty well, all things considered. He thanked Sennett for his time and turned to go.

"Mr. Souse," said Sennett, looking at the table top.

Gil paused.

"Who are you really? Even a cut-rate actor would have brought a steno pad."

The waitress stepped past Gil to serve Sennett. "Here's your drink, sir. Sorry it took so long, but we couldn't find the exact thing you asked for—"

Gil bolted for the door.

"—is butterscotch schnapps okay?"

The front door opened when Gil was halfway there. Sennett's men were walking back in.

"Mr. Grouse," said Sennett behind him. "Don't leave just yet."

Panicking, Gil saw a set of bat-wing doors behind the bar. He tried vaulting over the pitted pinewood barricade but banged his knee on the front and tumbled onto the beer-soaked rubber mat behind it. As shotglasses clattered to the floor around him, patrons applauded and the bartender bellowed a curse. Gil crawled under the doors and climbed to his feet. He stumbled through the kitchen, pulling a giant bag of frozen tater tots off a counter as he went by. A cook in a baseball cap stared at him.

Above the din, he heard the bartender yelling: "No, you can't go in there!" Gil ran into the storeroom and bumped a tower of empty beer kegs. They began falling, bouncing off the concrete floor with high, cavernous booms. The room had a walk-in cooler on one wall, stacked kegs against the other, and a door right in front of him.

Gil hesitated, wondering why his pursuers weren't right behind him. Shielding himself behind the doorjamb, he peeked out into the kitchen. The gray-haired barman was standing halfway through the swinging doors, a sawed-off shotgun in his hands. The thugs stood at bay, glaring.

"I don't care what you say that feller did," said the man with the gun. He was shaking with fear or anger. "This is my bar and you can't go back there."

"Look, old-timer," began one of them.

"Don't you 'old-timer' me," fumed the barman.

In an instant, one of the goons grabbed the barrel of the gun and forced it down while the other punched the old man in the face. The shotgun discharged into the floor and was answered by shouts and screams from the room beyond. Looking excited, the goon wrenched the gun away from Gil's defender and racked a new shell into the chamber.

Gil charged for the back door. Someone yelled, "There he goes!" Outside, he ran around the corner to his car, struggling to keep his balance on the icy, packed snow of the parking lot. Frightened patrons were running out the front door, and as Gil got in his car and slammed the door, another driver gunned it out of the lot, spattering his windshield with dirty snow and road sand.

Instead of starting the car, Gil ducked. He lay across the passenger seat and turned his face into the upholstery, panting.

Heavy footsteps ran by his car.

"You see that?"

"Yeah, a shit-brown Crown Vicky. Let's go."

They ran on. Gil peeked over the dashboard and saw them climb into a dark Cadillac. Sennett strolled out of the building, carrying his shotglass of schnapps. A tinted window rolled down on the Caddy and an arm gestured frantically. Sennett sniffed the glass, took a sip, grimaced, and dropped the glass in the snow. He climbed into the back seat. The car rolled away smoothly with its lights off.

Gil sat up and started his car. He waited a few minutes and then drove in the opposite direction, toward town.

The road was dark and had more curves than he remembered. Reflectors and mileposts were drifting out into the dark. Gil eased the wheel toward them until suddenly white diamonds were riding up the passenger side of the hood. He corrected quickly and then started over. He hoped no one had been hurt. It was a victory of sorts. So what if he'd been a little sloppy, if his alias hadn't lasted a minute. Sennett would know Flannel had talked to someone. Gil knew where matters stood with a high-ranking member of the G.C.P.D. And best of all, Gil was still alive. He'd been bruised but had been hurt no further. With luck, "The Senator" would silence Flannel and shut down his dealings in Garden City.

A semi thundered by on his left, chains clanking from the underside of the trailer. Its enormous wheels seemed dangerously close. Gil glanced over irritably. Why were the damn things always so brazen, even in the worst weather? Facing front again, he saw a Volkswagen Beetle crawling along immediately ahead. His foot felt like it was strapped into a snowshoe. He struggled, lifted it, and stomped on the brake. He swerved left. The taillights of the semi passed before his hood like red wolf's eyes. He kept going left. Wrenching the wheel right only steepened the wrongness of his angle to the road. Pointing south on the westbound lanes of the freeway, he left the shoulder.

The snow looked soft, but the impact was harder than anything he could have imagined. He felt a cold lead weight drop from his gut to his groin, then right down to his feet. His lungs froze and every tendon in his body hardened. He was immobile behind the wheel. With brilliant clarity, he saw his rooster plume of snow catch the disappearing red lights of other cars, saw smooth sheets of snow rushing at his side window. He felt a series of quick, sickening thumps as the car's suspension smashed into rocks and uneven ground under the snow. Then, with a grace he would not have expected of so much steel and rubber, his side of the car lifted in the air and climbed over the other. He dropped across the seat, slamming into the passenger door, then fell back to his original side, breaking an ear open against the steering wheel. The car righted on its wheels again, carved a quick slew in the bottom of the median ditch, and slammed nose first into the upward slope. Gil, too, slammed nose first into something.

He wished he would have been knocked out. He would have enjoyed a brief respite and a chance to "come to"; in books, people in accidents were always getting knocked out and then "coming to." Instead, he sat, listening to the horrible metallic grinding of the still-running engine. He felt warmth flooding his face and neck. Drunk as he was, he knew he hadn't drunk enough.

Discomfort stabbed him in the back. Reaching for the source, he dislodged the rearview mirror and tossed it on the floor. Breathing was wet, sticky, and difficult. *I should turn the car off,* he thought, but he was too tired to raise his hand.

"I should turn the car off," he said aloud. He saw his hand moving up. What it did instead, for reasons unbeknownst to him, was turn the radio on. Santo and Johnny's "Sleepwalk" sang out. Gil's hand moved to the steering column and turned the key toward him. The grinding stopped, and Johnny Farina's guitar chimed with a beautiful perfection Gil had never heard the dozen other times he'd listened to the song. He heard the wires on the drummer's brushes tapping softly against the snare head, heard the great empty spaces that opened between the glissandoing notes like brilliant rays from a mirrored ball. He wanted to crawl inside the song, into the radio. On the other side, surely, there was a beach party, a 1950s TV show, warm under spotlights, everyone wearing obscenely modest swimwear, pantomiming conviviality against seashore cutouts, drinking from hollowed-out pineapple shells festooned with umbrellas. Unfortunately, the pineapple shells were empty.

He came to. The short song was winding down on the radio, so he knew he had only been out for a few handfuls of seconds; he also knew it was a bad sign to lose consciousness for any length of time.

Gil turned off the headlights and the radio. His door was crumpled shut, so he crawled across the seat and climbed out the passenger door, carefully locking it behind him. He pocketed his keys and patted the pocket to make sure he had them. Struggling in the knee-deep snow, he wasn't sure which direction was which. The wallows and swerving wheel ruts in the snow seemed to offer a clue, but he couldn't string together enough thoughts to decipher it. He walked away from the tracks, up the opposite bank, falling once. At the top, the road was clear. He stood swaying, his breath making brisk clouds in the cold darkness. He knew it was important to keep his feet, but didn't feel certain he could.

"I have to stand," he said.

Far down the road, twin lights appeared. Dozens of white reflectors on posts winked on, first farther away, then nearer, flickering fitfully as the lights trembled over uneven roadway. Gil watched the lights grow brighter and brighter. They began to slow. He squinted into them as the car pulled to the shoulder and stopped. A door opened and a man stepped out.

"I have for so long wanted to play Good Samaritan," said Tim Flannel.

Even before he saw the ugly steel maw of Flannel's long pistol, Gil had begun to get into the car. He didn't feel beaten. He just couldn't think of any sensible alternative to sliding into the plush, heated interior before him. At least it was running better than Lolita's car.

"You slowed me down a bit, Gil, I'll grant you that. But you should have looked in my garage. When my Jeep seized up, all I had to do was hitch a ride back home to fetch my trusty Pontiac." He chuckled. "It's true that, until a few moments ago, I was feeling a bit miffed. But, I assure you, this serendipitous encounter has lifted my spirits right back into their usual jolly sphere."

Gil lifted his aching right leg into the car and closed the door. "Missed your meeting," he said hoarsely.

Flannel buckled his seatbelt, put the car in gear, and steered them back onto the road. "Yes, I did, Gil. I'll simply reschedule. My partner passes through the area quite often, and we can transact our business the next time. It's a momentary inconvenience. Did you meet him?"

"The Senator? As a matter of fact I did," said Gil.

"Did he find your manners wanting? Perhaps that's why you found yourself snowbound."

"It's not his fault I'm a lousy driver. We had an informative conversation."

A frown darkened Flannel's face. "No doubt you spoke ill of me. But still, it's no more than a momentary inconvenience. Your quick and, unfortunately, permanent exit from the developing scenario will no doubt allow me to mend fences with that gentleman, and should also serve to prevent any future winds from ruffling the feathers of his heretofore doe-like disposition." Flannel ended his oratorical flourish with a self-satisfied smile.

"You mixed your metaphors," said Gil. "But other than that, you're actually one of the better-spoken administrators I've worked with."

Flannel crossed over to the westbound lanes at a highway patrol turnoff. Soon they were in Porte l'Enfer Canyon, passing the trailer homes of East Garden City, a bedroom community for service industry workers. They rounded a broad flank of mountain and Flannel took the first exit to Garden City proper. He drove two blocks to a small shopping center that adjoined the river. Turning off his lights, he piloted the car behind the building to a narrow paved strip above a steep riverbank twenty feet high.

Flannel put the car in park but left it running. "I wonder which little goddess whispered in your ear."

"I had a vision," said Gil. "A divine revelation."

"It was Maria, right?"

Gil fought off a twitch and stayed frozen. Out of the corner of his eye, he could see Flannel studying him carefully.

"No matter. I'll catch up with her soon for a friendly chat."

Gil imagined a long row of tombstones, his only the second.

Flannel pressed a button and his seatbelt slithered across his belly. "Shall we," he said, "look at the moon, you and I?"

Dully, Gil got out of the car and shut the door. A whipping canyon wind almost made him lose his balance, and he leaned against the car. The air lashed through his clothing and made his wounds pulse and throb.

"A fitting night, isn't it?" Flannel said over the whine of the wind.

Gil looked up the dark, forbidding canyon, its jagged south wall spiny with burnt trees. He looked up, higher, and saw ragged clouds streaming across the sky, obscuring and then revealing the bright moon. A gust of wind shook him, and, as he steadied himself against the car's steaming hood, he saw he cast two shadows on the snow-streaked asphalt: one stark and well-defined, cast by a security light behind them; the other dim and dying, cast by the moon.

Flannel was still there, unfortunately. "Gil, you seem unsteady. Would you like a drink? I'd be a hard-hearted man to deny you a last slug of that which you love so dearly."

Flannel's gloved hand offered a half-pint of Old Forester. Gil took it, fumbled the cap off, and drank greedily. Flannel's other hand, the one with the gun in it, motioned him toward the riverbank. Between delightfully warm mouthfuls of bourbon, Gil edged closer to the bank. Past his booted toes, ragged weeds and jagged rocks rumpled the snow all the way down to a snow-crusted skirt of river ice. Beyond the ice the river ran dark and wild toward the center of town.

"Gil, my boy, I think you'd better give that bottle back to me," laughed Flannel. "It's empty."

Gil handed it back.

"I wouldn't want you to cut yourself," said Flannel, "or to take it into the water with you and hide a carefully contrived piece of evidence."

Gil couldn't take his eyes off the dark water. He was almost anxious to feel it seeping into his clothes. Steam was boiling off the top—surely it was warmer under the river than above it.

"What could be plainer than a fingerprinted flask at a river-bank, especially at the top of your impromptu toboggan run? Try to flail a lot on the way down."

Hurry up, thought Gil.

"I feel I ought to say something eloquent." Flannel paused for thought. "It's a most satisfying end to a very unsatisfying relationship."

The gloved hand came at him and Gil dipped a shoulder, trying weakly to lunge under it and take the burly man off guard, but the hand still caught his shoulder for a solid push. His left leg collapsed under him and he fell to his side on the brink. A large foot raised before him and readied itself for the final push, but Gil lost his balance on his own and slipped over the edge.

He fell fast, grabbing frantically at anything, catching nothing. He hit bottom, sprawled onto the ice, and stopped with the black channel of rushing water scant inches from his head. The tumble of water was loud now, louder than the wind, than the idling car above, than the laughter that trickled down to him. On his belly, he thought he should turn over to better perceive the situation. He carefully extended one hand and began to raise himself and the ice cracked with the sound of a large tree limb coming loose from the trunk.

Frigid water sucked him down and held him, wouldn't tell him which way was up, banged him against rocks and ice and whirled him around. Then the current subsided, and he knew he had gone deeper. He paddled his arms and kicked his legs but felt nothing and didn't know if he'd moved. He half expected to see King Neptune on a seahorse, come to lead Gil into a hidden grotto from which he'd never return. He closed his eyes against the cold and wished for air, even a single subzero gust, just a chance to fill his lungs. How he missed the blast of the wind. His lungs burned and his chest heaved as if by reflex; he had to clamp his mouth shut to keep from sucking in water. Then, as acrid bile was rising in his throat as if to force his jaws open to swallow the river, his foot struck a rock.

He stalled in the current; the rock was ahead of him. He pushed against it. Water pushed from behind and began to raise him. He knew which way was up. His head popped into the air and he began to inhale but couldn't move his feet and the water pushed him back under again, face first. His feet came loose and he was moving with the water, near the surface. He could feel cold air on the back of his head. It was hard for Gil to move his sodden limbs but with a weak flop of one arm he rolled over in the water, coughed mouthfuls of puke onto his cheeks, and convulsively sucked in air with panting, shallow breaths. He was sure he'd never fill his chest.

Rocks dragged across his back and stopped him from moving. The rushing water dizzied him. He raised himself to a sitting position and belched and puked until he was empty. Tears squeezed out of his eyes and turned slushy on his cheeks.

Gil tried to stand, slipped on the smooth river rocks, and fell down with a splash. Dragging himself forward, he reached a shelf of ice and crawled onto it. He crawled until he reached a rocky bank and crawled up it until he reached the top. He looked around and recognized nothing, as if he had been dropped out of the sky into a foreign city. Then, slowly, he began to recognize landmarks he'd known his whole life: a bridge, a park, the tower of a defunct railroad depot. He had come a long way in the water.

With no confidence that one step would lead to another, Gil rose to his feet and walked away from the river. He wanted to lie down more than he had ever wanted anything in his life.

Two slow blocks brought him to a motel across from the courthouse. The night clerk stared open-mouthed when Gil hobbled in, his clothes frozen hard as boards.

"I need a room," Gil whispered.

"You need to go to the hospital, is what you need."

Amazingly, Gil's wallet was still in the back pocket of his pants. It was difficult to retrieve with a shaking hand, however. He dropped it on the floor, picked it up, and struggled to pull the credit card from its plastic sleeve. When the wallet hit the floor again, the clerk came around the desk and picked it up. He set it on the desk. In the warmth of the motel office, Gil began to drip.

"I'm serious, buddy," said the clerk, an owl-faced young man with long hair and large, round glasses. "I check you in, you're liable to die on me."

"I'm in the polar bear club," said Gil, trying to control his chattering teeth. "I do this all the time. Hot bath and I'll be as good as new."

The clerk regarded Gil for a long moment, then shook his head and swore softly. He snapped Gil's credit card into the imprinter and ratcheted the machine back and forth. Gil was shaking so hard he could barely hold the pen; when he tried to sign his name, he tore the paper and the carbons. The clerk folded Gil's receipt and tucked it into his pocket, then walked him to his room, unlocked the door, and threw the key on the bed. Gil shuffled through the door and thanked the clerk, who slammed the door angrily.

With numb, swollen fingers, Gil turned the thermostat all the way up. When he opened the hot water tap over the bathtub, a pencil-thin trickle began lightly drumming the rusty tub enamel. Gil pushed in the rubber drain stopper and returned to the bedroom. With all the agility of a 110-year-old man, he dragged the desk chair over to the radiator and sat down. As the electric heater warmed up, its metal bands glowed orange and coaxed popping sounds from the chrome reflector behind them. It smelled of burning dust.

In the next room, the tub filled with a slow burbling sound. Gil's clothes were limp and steaming. His head was heavy, and it was hard to hold it up.

Chapter Twelve: Wednesday

When Gil woke, his tongue felt like a sweatsock, his eyelids like shoe treads. But he was warm and mostly comfortable, with a blanket pulled up to his chin. He had no idea what time it was, and the feeble line of gray that showed through a crack in the curtains offered no help. There was something on his right arm, and when he tried to brush it off with his left hand, he felt tape. The tape was holding a needle into his arm, and a plastic tube snaked out from under the covers. Gil saw white-painted walls instead of cheap wood paneling. He was in the hospital.

He had lost time like this before, and each time his mind raced backward to his last remembered thought, trying to map the unknown terrain in between. He had been at the motel and now he was here; the clerk had called the hospital. At least he hadn't called the police. Or had he?

Gil wasn't handcuffed, and he saw no guard outside his open door, just a quiet nurses' station where a white-hatted head faced the opposite direction. Dopily, Gil roused himself and struggled out of bed, taking pains to be quiet. Using the IV stand as a walking stick, he inched his way into the bathroom. He dropped his flimsy hospital gown so he could assess his injuries in the angled mirror over the sink. Bruises polka-dotted his body, and a half-dozen silver-dollar-sized scrapes had already begun to scab over. An insistent pain in his side—under broad swaths of an ACE bandage—made him wonder if one of his lower ribs was broken. Two of the fingers he tried to probe it with were badly sprained, but splinted and taped. His nose, once proudly Roman, had a sad, new outline, crooked and broad as porch steps. Fortunately, it didn't hurt too badly if he didn't touch it or breathe through it. Unfortunately, when he breathed through his mouth it made a terrible wheezing sound and allowed him to smell his reeking breath, a mixture of sour booze, old food, and vomit. They hadn't brushed his teeth or washed his hair, which was stringy with grease, but someone had worked his skin over with a washcloth and he was otherwise clean.

Turning around to check his back in the mirror, he saw stitches over an ugly gash where he'd landed on the rearview mirror, and a bruise on his shoulder that neatly mapped a car door armrest and window crank. He knew his body should be screaming with pain, but he didn't feel too badly. In fact, he felt as mellow as a man who's just drained his third martini after work. He scrutinized the medical jargon on the IV bag that dripped into his arm and wondered what comforting chemical cocktail he was sipping.

He decided to go see Thad and Maria, if they were both still in the hospital. He needed to warn them about Tim Flannel. He had passed the nurses' station undetected when a wheel on the IV stand stopped rolling and instead quietly skidded along the floor. Gil prodded it loose with his toe, only to have it start squeaking instead. The nurse rounded the corner with a curious look that quickly turned to professional concern—although Gil thought he saw a humorous sparkle in her eye.

"Mr. Strickland," she said. "You're not supposed to be on your feet."

"I have a feeling I'm not supposed to be alive," he said, "and look at me now." His voice sounded funny to his own ears, indistinct, as if he were having a hard time with his lips.

The nurse smiled warmly as she took his elbow and began guiding him back toward his room. "You'll live even longer if you rest up a bit. Let's at least get your gown on so you don't catch cold."

Gil looked down and realized he'd left his gown on the bathroom floor. "Fair enough," he said.

As the nurse dressed him and helped him back into bed, he told her he needed to know how Maria DiNizio and Thad Chouck were doing. She promised to check and report back right away.

Gil fell asleep before she'd taken ten steps.

When he woke again in the afternoon he didn't feel as mellow as he had at dawn. His head was clearer, but it was hard to think with pain coming from every part of his body. He was ravenously hungry, but when the nurse brought food, the smell of steamed fish and macaroni made him nauseous. He asked for more of the marvelous pain medication, but the nurse insisted he eat first. It was the same woman who had caught him streaking that morning, now near the end of her shift. Her name tag read: *RENEE LAHAYE.*

Under Nurse LaHaye's watchful eye, Gil began carving a cube of green Jell-O matted with grated carrot. He tried to make a good show of enjoying it.

"I checked on those two patients," said Nurse LaHaye.

"And?" Gil said through Jell-O.

"You're their uncle?"

"I am?"

"That's what you told me this morning."

"I did?"

Nurse LaHaye nodded. She was friendly, but clearly had a few reservations about Gil.

"I wasn't feeling very well. I'm just a teacher at Porte. They both go there and I'm worried about them."

"Well, I guess it's all right to tell you that Maria is doing fine.

She stabilized yesterday and she's already taking solids. First thing tomorrow, her parents are flying her to California to an excellent treatment center. If it makes you feel any better, she hasn't been alone for a minute. Her mother has been staying in the room with her."

Gil forked a piece of fish as a bargaining chip, then asked: "What about Thad?"

"He's going to be with us a while longer, and then of course he has some legal troubles."

"But he's going to be all right physically?"

LaHaye sighed. "After he recovers from his—after his bones knit, I doubt he'll have any serious disability. But he isn't likely to play football again."

"Is he still under guard?"

"Off and on. I think they realized he's not going to be able to tie the sheets together and climb out the window."

"Do you think I could see him?"

She shook her head. "You're not getting out of bed either." Looking at Gil's half-eaten food, she stood up. "I'll ask the doctor about your pain medication, Mr. Strickland."

After Nurse LaHaye left, Gil pushed the tray to one side and lay back on his pillow. He used a gizmo with three buttons on it to adjust the bed until it was in the shape of a W and he was comfortable.

It occurred to him that he couldn't stay long. He wouldn't have minded lying in bed until he became a very old man. In fact, he thought, refusing to leave might be the only way he would survive that long. But there was just as much chaos outside as there was peace in here. And the longer he waited to venture out, the more his opponents would have found their footing. But what weapons did he have? What weapons had he ever had? As a young man, Gil had taken judo lessons for one year, until his abject lack of physical grace convinced him to drop out. He hadn't been able to execute any of the throws his instructor had wowed the class with, although he had grasped the simplicity of thinking behind the then-exotic martial art. It wasn't necessary to be strong or fast if you could anticipate your opponent's moves. If you watched carefully the direction in which he was about to shift his weight, the gentlest trip and the slightest tug might send him sprawling to the mat. In fact, the more violence and fury he attacked with, the more power you had at your disposal: Your opponent provided all the momentum necessary for his own downfall. And the larger he was, the harder he fell.

Gil had witnessed the dislike and distrust that existed between Blanston and Sennett, and it was possible Sennett and Flannel loved each other just as much. Although his clumsy ruse at the Buck Stop had been seen through instantly, Gil might still have accomplished his goal: Even if it was apparent that the closest Gil had come to journalism was serving as advisor to the *Beatrice*, Porte's yearbook, Sennett still had to wonder if Flannel had been talking out of school. Certainly Sennett would pursue it, and if Gil was in luck, things would go badly for Flannel, Sennett, or both. He would need a lot of luck. But maybe if he stirred the pot more vigorously, he wouldn't need quite as much good fortune to season it.

There was a phone next to his bed. He punched *0* and got the hospital switchboard. He asked for Chouck's room and heard the operator pause.

"I'll put you through to the nurses' station," she said.

The nurse who answered called a policeman to the phone. Fortunately, it was Benton, who recalled Reverend Bolan and agreed to put him through to Chouck for a quick telephone ministry.

Chouck picked up the phone but didn't speak.

"Thad? This is Mr. Strickland—Gil Strickland. Do you

remember me?"

"Yeah." Chouck's voice sounded stronger and just as belligerent as before.

"Can I ask you a few questions?"

"You can ask."

"I think you knew about Tim Flannel."

"That a question?"

"Did you?"

There was a pause. "Yeah."

"Why did you send me after Farnsworth instead of telling me about Flannel?"

"You asked where we got the coke." Gil heard anger in Chouck's voice, maybe even hatred, and wondered where it was coming from.

"So you bought it from Farnsworth, not Flannel."

Chouck's breathing was labored. He might have been crying. "Fuck you," he said. "Fuck you, taking everything."

"I don't understand," said Gil.

Chouck *was* crying. "She's dead. You can't have her anymore."

Gil was lost. Two sick men in the same hospital, he thought, and neither understood the other.

"I told you about Farnsworth because I hoped he'd kick your ass."

"He did," said Gil.

"Good."

"And then Flannel did. I'm in the hospital, too."

"Good."

"But"—it was becoming clear—"I didn't have an affair with Kristen, Thad. I know she was seeing a teacher, but it wasn't me."

Silence.

"You were in love with her, weren't you?"

"Yeah." It was a simple word teenagers said hundreds of

times every day, but there was a world of confusion and suffering in it now.

"Tell me what happened the night Kristen died."

The teen started slowly. "I just, you know, people told me she was going out with a teacher. I didn't believe them, so I asked her. She was all weird about it, so I knew she was. And then you showed up."

Gil waited.

"We were partying at Flannel's house and he kept saying how he had to go out and do something, so everyone would have to leave. There were like five or six kids there, and everyone was bummed to have to go home. So Mr. Flannel asked Kristen if she wanted to do him a favor, if he could *trust* her. He wanted her to drive to Pishkun and pick up a shipment."

"From Farnsworth," said Gil.

"Yeah. I said I'd go to keep her company, and I could tell Flannel didn't like it, but I was thinking, 'Fuck you, man.' So we drove out to Pishkun and that Farnsworth dude made us do a couple lines with him. Then on the way back we stopped at that party, and I guess we were a little high, 'cause Kristen's like, 'Well if he doesn't trust me, then I guess this won't surprise him.' So she shared a bunch of it."

Chouck paused, then went on, choking up again. "And I didn't drive back with her. We had this weird conversation in the car, and I was thinking—I was thinking maybe Flannel was the one. And I didn't want to be around her. So I let her drive and then . . ." He broke down in wrenching sobs.

Gil didn't know what to tell him, but he didn't have long to think about it.

"That cop's coming back in," said Chouck suddenly. "Thanks, sir."

The line went dead.

Even if the "sir" had been for Benton's benefit, it reminded

Gil that it was men like him who were supposed to show the young how to balance life's burdens.

And it made him acutely sorry he was a drunk.

After a while, Nurse LaHaye returned and put a fresh bag on Gil's drip. The bare hospital room suddenly felt as cheerful as a crowded house on Christmas morning. As his pain dulled, Gil smiled and felt his brain go soft and buttery. He tried hard to hold onto his plan. Had he had a plan?

He waited until Nurse LaHaye went off duty and then took off his hospital gown and put on his filthy clothes, which were hanging in the closet. Leaving the IV needle taped into his forearm, he unhooked the bag from the stand and stuffed it in his coat pocket. He stopped at the nurses' station and announced his imminent departure.

They told him no five times before they allowed him to sign a waiver stating he took full responsibility for checking out against doctors' orders. Gil hadn't yet seen a doctor but agreed a good one wouldn't have approved. Before they let him go, they double-checked Gil's insurance information. As a teacher, he had excellent benefits.

Gil accepted a wheelchair ride to the front door and then waved goodbye to the nurse and orderly who'd accompanied him. They stood, shaking their heads, as Gil tottered through the sliding doors of the front airlock. The frigid wind howling down the barren street made him exceedingly grateful for the tube in his arm.

Jaywalking through the sluggish trains of cars that passed for rush hour traffic, he made his way to a credit union next to the state liquor store. In a heated foyer, he stuck his credit card in a cash machine, keyed in Lo's birthday, and received two hundred dollars in return. He bought two bottles of whiskey and doubled back to the motel. On the western mountains, the sunset lingered like the red rim of a bloodshot eye.

The clerk was surprised but not shocked to see him. Gil wondered if the cheap lodgings had cultivated a particularly dogged clientele.

"Thanks for calling the ambulance last night," Gil said.

"I guess they kicked you out," said the clerk. "No insurance, huh?"

"The drinks are terrible," said Gil. "Can I get a room with hot water this time?"

"Put it on the same card?" asked the clerk.

"Why not?" said Gil.

He checked into an identical room with an identically bad hot water tap. While he waited for the sink to fill, he unwrapped a sanitized glass and filled it with whiskey. With the painkiller in his veins, his head felt like a helium balloon tethered to his neck by a long, thin rubber band. He wrapped himself in a blanket and used a tiny bar of soap to wash his clothes in the sink, then hung them on the radiator to dry. He turned on the TV and had another glass of whiskey before he fell asleep.

When he woke, the ten o'clock news was just ending. The Porte l'Enfer hoops squad looked like a lock to go to state, he learned. His clothes were dry, although the shirt was scorched and smoking. Fortunately, it was plaid. He got dressed and walked to a bar he'd never used before. He downed a shot and then borrowed the phone book. When he found the number he was looking for, he carried the tattered directory over to the pay phone and fumbled for a quarter. He dialed and then covered his left ear against the noise from the bar.

"Blanston residence, Roger speaking."

"You have a very nice phone manner," said Gil.

"Who is this?"

"I'm sure you remember me. I have a *wild* imagination."

"Is that you, Strickland?"

"It's no wonder they made you lieutenant."

"You really must want to dig your hole deeper," said Blanston. "I am hanging up."

"Wait until I tell you what the Senator said after you left the Buck Stop Bar last night," said Gil. He couldn't hear very well over the racket in the bar, but he was pretty sure Blanston didn't hang up. "Lieutenant?"

"I have no idea what you're talking about."

A row of keno machines bubbled with steady *bloop bloop* sounds. The jukebox played a soft-rock tune from the seventies, some long-haired sensitive guy backed by a steel guitar and four-part harmonies. Gil's thoughts felt like a handful of marbles dropped on a staircase. He struggled on.

"It's just painful, as a taxpayer, to witness a negotiation in which the criminal element has such an upper hand over law enforcement. I mean, it sounded to me as if the pitiful kickbacks you're getting don't even make it worth worrying about the threat of exposure. In fact, you've probably spent the last twenty-four hours thinking about that yourself."

"Get to your point, Strickland."

"I'm already there. I imagine your decision-making processes would be helped along if only you knew what a certain curly-haired coke dealer said about you after you went out into the parking lot to receive your tip."

"If any of this were true, how would you know about it?"

"I'll quote you to you: 'These are the ties that bind.' "

He listened to a whole chorus of the Eagles song before Blanston said: "What do you want?"

Gil suddenly felt sick of having the phone against his ear. He wanted to hammer the plastic handset against the wall until it broke and severed his link to Blanston's corrupt world. "Peace and quiet," he said, so quietly that Blanston asked him to repeat himself. "I just want to be left alone, and I want Sennett and

Flannel and Farnsworth to leave my kids alone. I know Potter is Farnsworth. And I'm the only one—the only regular person—who knows what you did. I can make sure all Garden City knows, but if you leave us alone, I'll never breathe a word. So do you want to know what Sennett said or not?" Gil was ready to scream his line into the phone.

"I am very interested," said Blanston. "But I would rather not say any more over the phone. Let's meet and discuss this further. Where are you? It sounds like you are in a bar."

"Let's meet at the Cambridge. It's close to your work, so I'm sure you'll feel comfortable."

"I will be there in half an hour," said Blanston.

Gil hung up. On his way back to the bar, a drunk accidentally elbowed him in the ribs and the pain made him clench his teeth. He felt his gorge rising even as he ordered a last drink.

He hobbled over to the Cambridge, running a little late. He didn't mind if Blanston had to wait a little. He just hoped the trees he was chopping down would fall the right way, away from him and not on top of him. Gil was willing to have blood on his hands, to hold dark secrets, to do anything to stop the shadows growing overhead. He wasn't so naïve as to think his life would return to what it had been, but maybe that wasn't such a bad thing, either. Maybe something new would grow between the tree stumps.

He rehearsed his line, afraid he'd forget it when he sat across the table from Blanston: *Sennett said you were the one who stole some of the coke, and that he was going to teach you a lesson.*

As he approached the bar, Gil passed a police cruiser sitting in the alley with its lights off. Turning the corner to the entrance, he saw two more cop cars on the street, both with their lights off and their engines running. They were parked on separate streets but pointed toward the Cambridge, so quick taps on their accelerators would allow them to block off the front and side entrances. The car in the alley would cover the emergency exit.

Gil lowered his head, walked past the entrance and kept going. It took him five minutes to reach a convenience store, where he called the Cambridge and asked for Blanston. The waitress who answered the phone bellowed "Branson" several times before the policeman came to the phone.

"Blanston speaking."

"What the hell's going on?" said Gil.

"I came to meet you as you asked."

"And you brought the night shift with you."

"I never said I would be alone."

"I guess you don't want to hear what Sennett said."

"I am curious, but I'll listen once you're in custody. That way I can get the whole story."

"What are you going to charge me with?"

"Perhaps I should remind you that conditions of your release on bail mandated that you not leave town," said Blanston. "Since a wrecked car registered in your name was abandoned on the freeway last night, well out of city limits, I think it is reasonable for the City of Garden City to assume you have jumped bail. Therefore, an all points bulletin has been issued for the apprehension of one Gilbert Strickland, white male."

"I'm sure a jury would be interested in learning the real identity of Farnsworth," said Gil. "Or the real identity of Potter."

"I'm sure you would, too." Blanston chuckled. "If you plan on resisting arrest, I would like to say that it has been a pleasure knowing you."

"Sennett said you were the one who stole the coke—" said Gil, but the line was already dead.

Gil walked slowly back to the motel. Even his words were worthless. His enemies didn't care to listen, and didn't seem to care who else did. They'd take care of him when they could, but in the meantime he could go to the newspapers or even the governor—Gil knew as well anyone that his name and position carried no weight with anyone. Not now. Sennett might still remove Flannel from the picture, but Sennett and Blanston had declared open season on meddlesome English teachers. A few drinks in a warm bed seemed like the most appealing course of action.

Back in his room, he gingerly stretched out on the bed and dug in his pocket for Lo's list of hotels. She must have used her fancy fountain pen instead of a practical ballpoint, he thought with a groan; the ink was smeared beyond legibility. He pulled the phone over anyway. It was covered with grubby foil stickers.

LONG DISTANCE RATES APPLY.
NO LOCAL CALLS.
ROOM SERVICE DIAL BELL CAPTAIN.

He was pretty sure the motel, with twelve units crooked in an L-shape around the parking lot, had never had a bell captain. Perhaps the phones had come from a luxury hotel's fire sale. He dialed *O*.

"Yeah?" said an unfamiliar voice. A new clerk seemed to be on duty at the desk.

"How do I call long distance?"

"There is no long distance." It sounded to Gil like the man needed to cough up some phlegm that was making his voice buzz.

"I guess you don't have room service, either."

"It depends on what you want."

"A sandwich?"

"I can make you a two-girl sandwich, but I don't have peanut butter."

Gil lowered the phone, stared at it, then set it on the cradle.

He wasn't sure he was in Garden City anymore.

Getting up, he looked out the window and saw a phone on the street. Dreading the cold, he put his shoes and coat back on and went outside again. The phone was hung inside a flimsy plastic shield that did a fine job keeping snow from falling on the buttons. With the wind cutting into his legs, Gil found himself wondering where he'd last seen a full-sized phone booth.

He made a collect call to Lo's mother, Charlotte, waking the kindly gray-haired lady in her Florida home. She woke quickly, and concern turned to irritation when she learned Gil was not calling to inform her someone had died.

"You should think twice, calling morning people in the middle of the night. What time *is* it?"

"Charlotte, I'm sorry to wake you, I really am," chattered Gil. "I need to know if Lo has called you from California."

"You've lost track of your wife, I see."

"I've lost track of her phone numbers."

"Yes, I've talked to her. Call me back at a reasonable hour, and maybe I'll be able to find the phone number with the help of daylight."

"I need to talk to her now," said Gil. "I'll explain why later, but you've got to help me."

With a deep sigh that registered as static, Charlotte clunked the phone onto the nightstand. Gil heard her muttering about his absent-mindedness as she rummaged around in the background. She came back. "Well, I can't find it. I'm sorry," she said defiantly.

"Do you remember the name of her hotel?" asked Gil.

"I don't. Seabreeze, maybe, or Sea Horse. It was in Monterey, but I don't know how long she was staying there."

"Thanks," said Gil. "Go back to sleep."

"Easy for you to say," said Charlotte.

Gil hung up. He reached a long-distance operator and

convinced her to charge his home phone, then ran *Sea*-words by an information operator until she suggested the Seafoam Inn in Monterey. He asked to be connected. A sleepy desk clerk answered, and said "I'll connect you" when Gil said his wife's name. It was too easy.

After Herb Alpert had tooted his horn for a few minutes the clerk came back. "Sir? There's a no-calls request for that party."

"I know she'd want you to make an exception. She's my wife, and this is very urgent."

"I'm sure it is, sir, but it is our policy to respect the guest's wishes."

"Even if I tell you that, given my emergency situation, your guest would wish to be disturbed."

"She didn't know you'd be calling when she asked for no calls."

"Precisely." The exchange was making Gil a little dizzy, but he was determined to get through.

"But unless she has asked for an exception to be made, I can't make an exception. Perhaps she has to wake very early in the morning. I'm sure you understand."

"I understand that you've got all the initiative and imagination of a mushroom!" shouted Gil.

"Sir, shouting won't help."

Gil let out a strangled, inarticulate screech and thumped the handset repeatedly against the Plexiglas bubble. He kicked the metal post that supported the phone, stubbing his toe and dropping the phone in his paroxysm. Why on earth had Lo asked for no calls? Was she making love to a ponytailed twenty-year-old photographer at this very moment? Was she simply sleeping, warm and relaxed? He cursed her for shutting herself off, for not anticipating his need to call in the middle of the night.

A police cruiser rolled up to the motel office. Gil turned away as a patrolman got out of the car and walked inside. Gil picked up the handset. He didn't hear a dial tone or the relentless Morse-code alarm that usually warned of an off-the-hook phone.

"Hello?" he said.

"Sir, are you all right?" asked the clerk.

Gil looked over his shoulder. In the office, the clerk sullenly showed the cop the registration book that Gil had never been asked to sign. "I'm really not," he said into the phone. "Listen, you have to put me through to that woman."

"I thought she was your wife."

"She is."

"Then why did you say 'that woman'?"

The clerk was handing over a short stack of credit card receipts.

"For fuck's sake," Gil hissed. "She is my wife and I have to talk to her now, you little fucker—"

There was a click and the phone went dead. His heart sank, but Gil kept the handset to his ear and looked once more toward the motel office. The clerk was pointing toward Gil's room, and the cop was speaking into his radio.

Gil hung up the phone and walked casually down the empty sidewalk, toward the river and away from the police station. His steps were short and awkward, and his side felt tight, but he moved as quickly as casual would allow. As he passed the motel office, the cop came out of the door and his eyes scanned Gil's face. Gil nodded hello. The cop nodded back, then turned his eyes toward Gil's room. Gil kept walking.

In his coat pockets, his hands clenched and unclenched. The plastic IV bag was almost empty. His booze was in the room. The bars were closed. He had his wallet and his keys. That was all.

When he had walked little more than a block, flashing lights brightened the street like fireworks as squad cars converged on the motel. Gil cast staggered, strobing shadows as he hurried away.

Another block brought Gil to the last street before the river. Slipping down an icy incline, he crossed a parking lot and reached a park that ran alongside the river. He floundered hastily into the snow, trying to escape the glare of security lights that illuminated the empty but well-plowed lot. A siren broke the silence with a few loud whoops. He climbed up the diked riverbank, crossed a footpath, and climbed partway down the other side, his hand seeking tree trunks for support. It was dark. He could hear the river flowing but couldn't see exactly where it began.

Sitting on a large, flat rock, Gil pulled his knees to his chest and rested his forehead on them. His few minutes of exertion had warmed him but the flush wouldn't last. He couldn't walk around all night, and he couldn't show his face at any motel or coffee shop. His house would be watched, and Dick couldn't be trusted.

On his key ring were keys to his house, his garage, his car, Lo's car, school, and the filing cabinet in his room at school.

He stood up and started walking to work.

Porte l'Enfer High was on the other side of the river. The closest bridges would be as hard to escape as dead-end streets if a patrol car caught him halfway across. Following the footpath, Gil walked east toward the canyon, passing under the first bridge where its steel girders thrust out of the earth-and-concrete embankment. The path petered out and he detoured through a short street and another park until he picked up the next segment of footpath. He passed under the second bridge and again walked on a dark, narrow street for a while. He was almost in the mouth of the Porte l'Enfer Canyon, almost to the place where Flannel had pushed him into the river. Just before the shopping center, he turned right on a wooden footbridge. He crossed over the cold water, numbed by the stinging wind.

He turned back west, following a dark path along the opposite riverbank. After walking through the shadow of one bridge, he trudged across a football field and up a short hill into the tree-lined neighborhood near the school. Two short blocks brought him to a rear entrance where he fitted his key to the lock and pulled the door open.

It was warm inside, blissfully, steamily warm. Radiators hissed and banged as Gil navigated the halls by the dim red glow of exit lights and the occasional soft white flutter of a streetlight. He hoped he wouldn't stumble on a janitor working the graveyard shift; he assumed no one worked past midnight, but he'd never stayed late enough to find out.

He went to his room and retrieved a bottle. Cradling it like a baby, he walked down the hall to the teachers' lounge. He was very hungry. The several plastic containers in the fridge smelled bad; Gil wasn't entirely sure if they were abandoned lunches or if a biology class was borrowing space. On the counter, however, was an open box of candy for some teacher's child's fundraiser. Gil filled his pockets with the heaviest candy bars and put a ten dollar bill in the adjacent coffee can.

As he closed the door to the lounge, a dim glint caught his eye: The trophy case with his Teacher of the Year plaque. With the halls quiet as a morgue, Gil was sorely tempted to break the glass and remove the taunting eyesore. He glanced around for a tool—a window rod, a fire extinguisher—but saw nothing at hand. He was just too tired.

Thinking of a little-used dressing room behind the stage, he walked back downstairs and made his way to the auditorium. On the first floor, headlights from the street outside passed over him like myopic searchlights.

With no windows, the auditorium was nearly pitch dark. Four exit lights illuminated the doors and little else. Gil had to feel his way down an aisle to the stage, stooping to touch wooden armrests in each row. Climbing stairs at the edge of the proscenium, he walked carefully upstage, his hands stretching for the back wall, thinking how it always seemed, when he walked in the dark, that the ceiling above was sloping down like the roof of a cave.

Something hit his face. He dropped the bottle and, as he stood disoriented, listened to it roll buzzing on the wooden stage and then clink to a stop against the wall. He reached cautiously into the dark but found nothing for a moment. Then his fingers closed around a large iron hook on a pulley, which he presumed was used for raising and lowering drops. His forehead throbbed, but he'd been shuffling too slowly to be hurt.

Getting down on his knees, Gil swept the floor with his hands, looking for the bottle. He worked methodically, laboring, breathing heavily. It could have been one minute or ten before he found it. When he did, he followed the back wall of the stage to the right, to a small passageway leading to a flight of stairs. Here, deep in a windowless tunnel, he felt safe enough to flip a light switch. Blinking even under a sixty-watt bulb, he walked up peeling, gray-painted cement steps to a dusty dressing room. There was a dirty couch there, a counter with a couple of sinks cut into it, and a pile of broken desks. Old, warped floorboards creaked under his feet as he walked to the couch.

He lay down, and the couch welcomed him to its stale, understuffed bosom. He took a few pulls on the bottle and ate half a candy bar and then fell asleep.

Chapter Thirteen: Thursday

Gil woke up. He was cold. The light bulb in the ceiling was still burning, but, without a window, he had no idea what time it was. He heard high, laughing voices far away that flickered like a ghost station on an AM radio. The day had begun, anyway. He sat up with a groan, wincing at a sudden pain. The tape holding the IV into his forearm had loosened and the needle was digging in at the wrong angle. Blood oozed out where the silver shaft lanced an eggplant-colored bruise.

He pulled the needle out, gingerly removed the flaccid bag from his pocket, and hid them behind the couch. He held the palm of his left hand against the small wound until it stopped bleeding.

The taps in the sinks ran only cold water. Shivering, he splashed his face and finger-combed his hair into submission. In the long, corroding mirror, ringed by empty light sockets, Gil was gaunt and pale as Max Schreck in *Nosferatu*—except for his swollen, purple nose. That was more Bozo than bloodsucker. Gil looked away. He hid the bottle under the couch.

When he limped into the hallway, a clock told him it was halfway through first period. His clothes, which he'd worn for three days, had survived with only a few torn seams but were beginning to acquire a stiff greasiness that Gil had recognized before in the clothes of transients. He stopped at Whitehead's office on the way to his classroom, inventing excuses for the two days he'd missed and the reason he looked like shit now. But

Whitehead wasn't there. His secretary gaped at Gil but managed to utter: "Go to your room."

He peeked around the open door into his freshman class. Whitehead was standing at the front, telling a story about wartime rationing. Half the students were asleep, and the others were doodling in their notebooks or gossiping.

Gil took a deep breath and walked in. "Sorry I'm late," he said.

Whitehead turned to him with a look of concern but forced a smile. "You'll be glad to see your teacher's back," he told the class.

"Better late than never, I hope," Gil said to Whitehead.

"Certainly," said Whitehead. "Especially in light of . . . events."

Gil felt a pang of fear. Was Whitehead crooked, too? Had he been debriefed by Flannel or even Blanston?

Whitehead stepped closer and lowered his voice. "That red-haired student, Jerry something, passed your note on yesterday morning. About your auto accident. He must be such a dedicated student, stopping by your house to help you grade assignments."

"Oh, he is," said Gil, relieved.

Whitehead stepped even closer and turned his back to the class. He barely whispered. "The accident, it wasn't a—relapse?"

"No," said Gil. "Just some random thing. The other guy's fault." Behind the principal's back, students were staring at Gil and whispering to each other. Even the nappers were stirring, their ears pricked by the atmospheric change.

Whitehead patted Gil on the shoulder and gave a small smile. "I'm glad to hear it. And I'm glad you're feeling better. We couldn't reach a substitute today, which is why I was sitting in for you. Forgotten how much I like being in the classroom, although I'm afraid I would have run out of material by this afternoon."

Gil tried to laugh politely, but coughed instead. The cough triggered a pain in his side and he felt suddenly dizzy. He needed to sit down.

"Thank you," he croaked.

Whitehead was clearly not sure he should go, but Gil waved him on and stumbled to his desk. He sat down and turned to face the sea of freshman faces. He looked at the clock above them. Only twenty-five minutes. Then they'd all leave and he could have a drink.

A hand shot up and Gil nodded at it.

"What happened to you, Mr. Strickland?" asked the kid.

"Never," he said solemnly. "*Never* tell your wife she looks like her mother."

They didn't get it.

Another hand shot up. "Are we going to have a reading day?" asked another kid sarcastically.

"No, actually. Pop quiz on the reading."

The sea groaned and Gil smiled. He wasn't going to run from all challenges.

"And then I'm going to lecture until the bell," he added for good measure.

At the end of the period, Gil pulled an oversized map off his wall, rolled it up, and tucked it under his arm. He returned to the auditorium and found that Larry Haddon, the drama coach, had a class hard at work building a set for the next school play. Haddon was a dreamer who inspired his classes by his total commitment to their projects; he was also often the recipient of behind-the-back snickers for his legendary absentmindedness. Gil had once seen Larry with his tie zipped into the fly of his pants.

When Gil climbed the stage, Larry didn't seem surprised to see him. He didn't react to Gil's battered appearance, either.

"Gil, I'm glad to see you," said Larry. "There's been a problem."

Gil was afraid to ask what it was. Maybe a drama queen had sneezed her septum across the proscenium.

"I need a faculty member to do a bit part in the play. Coach Van Axle was going to do it, but I had to let him go. It's only a dozen lines, but frankly, you'd fall asleep in the time it took him to read his driver's license. I asked Flannel, but he read the script and decided the play's message was too secular."

"What's the play?"

"*The Diary of Anne Frank.*"

Gil shook his head.

"What do you say—can you help me out?"

"I'm sorry, Larry, but I can't act."

"I'll coach you," pleaded Haddon. "You've got a whole week."

"I'm flattered to be asked, Gary, but I have to say no. I think I'd make Van Axle look like Gielgud."

Haddon looked crestfallen. "We're doomed," he moaned. "Doomed."

The kids had just attached two flats together for the walls of a room. One wall, however, was painted to resemble a brick exterior, complete with window shutters and a flowerpot. Gil couldn't suppress a smile and nodded toward it.

"Guys," said Haddon. "Wrong wall."

As the kids groaned at their mistake, Gil headed for the passage at the back of the stage.

"So what are you doing down here, if you haven't come to save the play?" asked Haddon.

Gil held the map up. "I'm looking for an old map, similar to this one."

"Boy, is this place disorganized," said Haddon. He moved

toward the mismatched scenery.

Gil climbed the stairs to the dressing room. He slid the bottle into the center of the rolled-up map and held it carefully. As he crossed the stage again, he told Haddon to break a leg. Haddon waved vaguely, his brow furrowed and his lips pursed, already solving the next problem of his production.

Back in his room, Gil locked the door and doctored his coffee. He stood by the window, drinking deep, feeling warmth kindling in his belly.

Down on the street, a black-and-white crawled along the curb. Gil felt his adrenaline surge and was surprised that, instead of parking, the car continued on out of sight. Blanston was planning to kill him, then. If he wanted to arrest Gil, he could simply walk in the door and take him. There was more than enough of a paper trail. But if he wanted Gil to be shot supposedly resisting arrest, he couldn't do it at a public high school where witnesses could testify that Gil was not inciting violence but peacefully teaching class. The very surroundings would make the police the aggressors, no matter what Gil's record said. He was safe unless he left. The question was, how long could he stay?

Someone knocked on the door and Gil flinched hard, spilling coffee on his shirt. He set the mug down shakily, hid the bottle, and answered the door. An office aide, a scrawny kid with a frog face and an enormous Stetson hat, handed him a memo.

Gil thanked him and closed the door, locking it again. He scanned the page. The single salient point was a seventh-period pep assembly, with mandatory attendance by both students and teachers. Gil poured another drink, emptying the bottle. He put it in a paper bag and pushed it to the bottom of the trash can, carefully piling paper on top of it.

Outside, the prowl car made another drive-by. He had to remember to thank Jerry, much as he hated to do so, for smoothing things with the school authorities.

It seemed as if there were extra faces in his next few classes. Gil thought he was just being paranoid until he realized that word was out he'd shown up looking like Jake LaMotta. The kids were just curious.

Seventh period. The seal was broken on Gil's last bottle and it was more than half empty. He walked slowly through the deserted third-floor hallway, past rows of red metal lockers, and turned a corner near the gym. Blaring horns, stamping feet, and muffled roars burrowed through the thick walls of the old building. Outside, the clouds were thin and a fair gray light came through the windows. Motes of dust drifted slowly from the ceiling.

He climbed down the stairs, his hand gliding lightly over the pitted wood of the bannister. Different eras of initials and slogans were layered with varnish, like pictographs preserved under tree sap. The marble steps were warped from nearly a hundred years of pounding teenage feet.

It was just drums now, and some sort of chant. The different classes would take turns, each trying to be the loudest. After the first round, the kids erupted into utter pandemonium, yelling and screaming while the pep band instruments forsook melody for volume. It was like the soundtrack to a Brueghel painting.

And then order was restored, and another chant began. As Gil made his way down the stairs, resting both feet on each tread before stepping down again, he heard all four classes proclaim their bragging rights. When he reached the gym's main entrance on the second-floor landing, two kids burst out the doors, laughing. They froze for a moment when they saw Gil, then laughed again and kept running, down the stairs and out the door.

The noise subsided and one voice rang out. Flannel. Gil

walked toward the doors and stopped just outside. He listened.

"Well, all your class rivalries aside, it's time now to make a lot of noise together, to proclaim that we at Porte l'Enfer High are the Class AA champs of anything we want to be!"

Enthusiastic cheers. A flourish from the band.

A more sober tone: "But, as you know, before the awards, before the accolades and the cheers of the crowd, there's a lot of hard work to be done. Don't think that Michael Jackson was born with a god-given ability to dunk the ball."

Someone yelled something and the kids tittered.

"Thanks for raising your hand," said Flannel with a crowd-pleasing warmth in his voice. "But no, Michael *Jordan* wasn't born with the ability to fly from the top of the key to the basket and slam that ball home. And don't think that Ronald Reagan was born a political mastermind. Even he had to work for that knowledge. And do you know what? Knowledge is power. I know that sounds like a saying on a bumper sticker or a T-shirt, but it's true. Knowledge is more powerful than the ability to kick a football through the uprights, or to hit a baseball into the bleachers. No one is born strong. But with enough work, anyone can be powerful, even some little guy in a wheelchair. Do you kids want to be powerful?"

More cheers.

"Do you?"

Louder cheers.

"You kids are hard workers in school and on the field. You're smart and you're strong. You've got the talent and you're learning the skills to be champs for your whole lives, not just in high school!"

Wild cheers.

"Now, let's have a big hand for the Sparklerettes!"

Music and cheering. Gil pushed through the doors. Two columns of girls, spangled with sequins and holding red and yellow flags at attention, were marching briskly from the far corners of the gym toward center court. Flannel, Whitehead, and a few other administrators sat in folding chairs on a platform directly opposite Gil. Flannel's gaze was rapt on the bare legs of the marching troupe. To Gil's right and left the bleachers were packed with animated kids.

Gil stepped out onto the floor and walked straight ahead. The Sparklerettes were forming an X at center court as one line of girls seamlessly passed through the other. Questioning eyes caught his as he proceeded toward them, but broad smiles stayed plastered on every mouth. A pitch change rippled through the crowd.

The nexus of the X disappeared as the lines parted. The girls continued past on either side of Gil, and he was fully visible to the administrative platform. He kept walking toward it. Flannel saw him and rose from his chair with a slack jaw that tightened into a hard grin. Whitehead looked like a man who had been proven right in predicting a friend's death. The students were laughing now, and the pep band sounded like deflating bagpipes.

Gil reached the two-foot-high platform, put one hand on the podium, and pulled himself up. He nodded to Flannel and Whitehead, then bent over the microphone, making the PA screech loudly. The pep band had quit and the Sparklerettes stood in disarray at the far end of the gym. The cavernous hall fell silent.

Flannel and Whitehead appeared at his elbows and gently pulled him away. He shook them off with a convulsive flail and almost fell down.

Whitehead stood back. "Gil," he said quietly.

Flannel sat down and settled back in his chair, smiling.

Gil tried to adjust the metal gooseneck that held the microphone and it creaked and groaned as the speakers screeched again. A few kids laughed. The perforations on the head of the microphone were like giant, heaving black pores. The speakers squealed again, the sound reverberating as if the room were empty, just hard seats and blank walls. He looked up and the kids were still there. They hadn't run out. They were doing the wave, a giant swell coursing around the bleachers. They wanted to hear him. Once they heard Gil's words Flannel would have lost. He would be blown away like a puff of smoke.

"Kids," he began, his voice sounding dull and compressed. "This man has been lying to you."

Silence. He looked back at Flannel and hated his smugness, hated him for being confident enough to sit down while Gil told the truth about him.

Gil continued: "Not about what you are, or who you are, but about his concern for you. You have to . . ."

He trailed off. The room was too big. There was no way to make his point across that distance. He needed to find a way to say it right. Far away, there was a shout. Flannel was at his shoulder, taking his arm again, still gently. Gil yanked it free and lost his balance, falling against the podium. Laughter. Loud, many-throated, unrestrained laughter. He slipped to the floor of the platform and landed in a sitting position.

"You'll have to excuse us, kids," Flannel said into the microphone. As he bent to Gil, he said, "Even I couldn't have made you look this bad."

He tried to take Gil's arm again and Gil flailed madly, trying to stay out of his soft, paternal grasp. Swinging his legs off the platform to the gym floor, he stumbled forward. His shirt sleeve ripped and Flannel's fingers slipped off his arm.

Flannel played to the crowd: "It looks like Mr. Strickland got up on the wrong side of the bed this morning."

Gil limped quickly to the nearest exit door and pushed it open, stumbling outside with the students' catcalls ringing out behind him.

"Sleep it off!"

"Go home, you loser!"

Fresh air. Tears stung his cheeks. He reentered the building through another door and went back into the auditorium, up the stairs, and into his hiding place. Outside, the kids were streaming toward their cars, toward their homes.

He woke hungry in pitch-black darkness. It was silent. For a moment Gil wasn't sure where he was, but when he shifted on the couch, the musty smell of the cushions reminded him that he was in the old dressing room. His mouth was dry and his forehead pulsed painfully. He felt his way to the sinks, ran some water, and slurped it out of his cupped hand. Without turning on the light, he worked his way along the wall to the doorway and then down the stairs. There were no voices on the stage, no banging hammers.

He flicked the hall light on and followed his shadow through a pale rectangle and across the stage. He cracked a door to the first-floor hallway and looked out, checking for janitors. He saw no one. He walked to the cafeteria. It was locked, but his room key fit the lock and he got in. White Formica tables had been folded and stacked against the far wall, and checkerboard floor tile was dimly lit by a trio of glowing snack machines. Gil felt in his pocket for coins but found only a nickel and several pennies.

The serving counters were shuttered and the door between them was locked. His key worked again, however, and he entered, locking the door behind him. The large kitchen was even darker, illuminated only by a window facing a lightwell. The glass was old, striated, and reinforced with chicken wire. He clicked on the hood lamp of an industrial stove and looked around. Several large refrigerators hummed throatily. Yards of stainless steel counters and sinks shone dully, as did a clutter of industrial-size mixers and pots. Spoons, spatulas, knives, and other implements hung above the counters, below shelves of smaller skillets and pans. Two doors led out, one to a walk-in freezer, one to a pantry. Rubber mats covered the tile floor beneath his feet.

Gil tried the refrigerator doors but they were all locked and his key didn't fit. He took a huge ladle from a rack and wedged its thick handle through the rubber insulation of the refrigerator door. Bracing his leg, he pulled back with both hands. The door gave a little but held. The ladle handle bent double and Gil nearly fell backward. He gripped the door handle in both hands and shook it as hard as he could, but it held fast.

Suddenly, Gil stopped and listened. Had he heard voices? It was hard to tell over the hum of the equipment. He stood frozen, straining, wondering if he was picking up phantom radio stations because his own wires were crossed. In the deserted building, against the pulsing murmur of the refrigerators, it was easy to imagine things. He relaxed his breathing and pulled the pantry's heavy latch-handle. It opened. A dangling string brushed against his cheek and he pulled it. Fluorescent tubes fluttered and winked on. In the cold light, he saw shelves lined with giant bags of onions and potatoes, pioneer-sized sacks of flour and sugar, and comically large cans of everything from tomatoes to lima beans to teriyaki sauce. Gil grabbed a five-pound can of tuna, took an onion out of a fifty-pound bag, and went back into the kitchen.

There was an oversized can opener that worked on the second try; he had to push a spike into the lid and turn a crank that forced the can to cut itself against the dull edge of the spike. The can opened like a jagged smile and he upended it, disgorging tuna into a bowl. He diced the onion with a cleaver and scooped it into the bowl, then added some hot sauce from a bottle he found lying out. After a search, he found a garbage bag full of crusty rolls under a prep table. Ripping a couple of rolls open, he stuffed them with tuna and prepared to leave.

Gil was holding one roll in his hand, had just taken a bite, when he pulled the string on the light in the pantry. He heard the rattle of a key in a lock. He stopped chewing. It was the lock to the kitchen. He dropped to a crouch. Holding the food in his mouth, breathing through his nose, he peeked around the pantry door. Someone entered the kitchen and pulled the door shut. Gil's view was obstructed by a wide table. The hood light, which he'd left on, seemed as bright as a searchlight. He expected sirens to blare at any moment.

The new arrival crossed to one of the refrigerators, fitted a key to the lock, and opened it. Gil inched forward, craning to see. Two feet extended below the open stainless steel door. Then the door closed, the refrigerator light momentarily illuminating the features of Tim Flannel.

Gil nearly spit out his food. What was Flannel doing there? The big man moved away and Gil stood up slowly to see better. His mouth was dry, but he quietly ground the hard roll of his improvised tuna sandwich between his teeth, swallowing a little bit at a time. He watched as Flannel put two corn dogs in a paper boat and placed them in a giant microwave. A few push-button beeps and it started, its fan blowing like a car's. Smiling, Flannel retrieved ketchup, mustard, and a small carton of milk from the refrigerator. When the microwave beeped again, he began his snack.

Gil's stomach knotted as Flannel, slowly munching a corn dog, began to pace. If he completed a full circuit of the kitchen, he would see Gil's second sandwich and the mess he hadn't bothered to clean up.

Flannel sauntered away from Gil, the paper boat in his left hand, a battered, fried, and impaled hot dog in his right. He moved down the long row of countertops and prep tables, rounded the far end, and stopped. Nibbling the hard, crunchy part off the corn dog stick, he placed the stick in the boat, removed the other corn dog, and resumed walking. Gil tried to think what he could use as a weapon. His clammy hands gripped his roll tightly, smashing it flat.

Smacking his lips, Flannel came closer. When he reached Gil's dirty dishes, he stopped and looked down. He took another bite of his corn dog and chewed it thoughtfully, then set his food down. He lifted Gil's roll and squinted at it, then exchanged it for the cleaver. A small cube of onion had clung to the side of the blade and Flannel plucked it off, rubbed it between his thumb and forefinger, and then sniffed it. He flicked it aside, glanced around the room, and moved quickly to a bank of light switches near the door. A series of clicks brought tube lights trembling to life across the whole ceiling. Gil stepped back behind the pantry door.

Flannel's footsteps again circled the room, more quickly this time, but pausing, presumably, to look under counters or behind cabinets. The footfalls began proceeding directly toward Gil, with purpose.

Three more steps and Gil would slam the door into Flannel and run past him and out the door.

Two.

The outer door opened again, letting in voices, the words of a conversation trailing off. Flannel stopped.

"You're working late." Gil recognized Sennett's voice, dripping with sarcasm.

Flannel chuckled. "The work of the righteous is never done. Is this a state visit, Senator?"

"I like to visit with my constituency," said Sennett. "I hope I didn't catch you at a bad time."

Flannel's footsteps retreated. "Not at all. I was just enjoying a midnight repast."

"That explains why your fingerprints are all over the cookie jar."

Flannel seemed uncertain what to say.

"Only kidding—unless there's something you need to tell me," said Sennett.

Flannel laughed feebly. "Of course not."

"It's awfully bright in here," said Sennett, as several lights went off.

"Just enough for a head count. I see you brought your henchmen."

"*Henchmen.* Now there's a word you don't hear that much anymore. But you always did have a way with words, Flannel. Or a gift of gab."

"You have me at a disadvantage," said Flannel. "I'm not sure I know what you're referring to."

"What's with the chopper?" said Sennett abruptly. "You punishing a rowdy student? Or cutting up a big line of blow?"

"Just chopping some onions."

"Or do Jimmy and Clay threaten you?"

"Of course not." After an inordinately long pause, Gil heard the steel blade of the cleaver slide against a steel tabletop. The kitchen was again in shadows, so, carefully, he edged his eyes around the door. Flannel faced Sennett and his two smirking men across a long row of prep tables. The cleaver lay between them.

"I suppose you're looking for Strickland," said Flannel.

Sennett smiled blandly and shrugged.

"He surprised me by coming to school today, even after his swim in the river. He's proving himself to be rather hard to kill."

"Maybe you're not very good at killing."

"But at least you know he's in town."

Jimmy and Clay started drifting in opposite directions, toward the ends of the long row of tables. Both acted as if the only thing that interested them was seeing how a high school kitchen was laid out.

"You know," said Sennett. "When I met Strickland, he told me, after a fashion, that you told him I own a bunch of strip clubs."

"I never did," said Flannel.

"That may be true. But appearances are everything in this business."

Flannel seemed to be panicking. "No one will believe him!" he blurted. "He's a drunk. He publicly humiliated himself. I've filled his files with worse things than he's even done, so he'll be totally discredited if anyone listens."

Jimmy and Clay were rounding the corner and moving toward Flannel. Flannel eyed the cleaver in front of him, but Sennett put his hand under his shoulder and showed Flannel a thin black pistol in a holster.

"I can help you find him!" said Flannel.

"But I'm not looking for him," said Sennett. "I'm looking for my cocaine. I'm taking it back."

Flannel's eyes bulged as Jimmy and Clay converged on him, grabbed his arms, and pinned them behind his back. "But I bought it!"

"You're not trustworthy. You use kids to do your job and you blame other people when the delivery is light." Sennett tugged on black leather gloves, speaking as if he were encouraging a misbehaving ten-year-old to confess to a household misdemeanor. "Now, we were just at your house, and the cocaine isn't there. Where is it?"

"It's mine!" shouted Flannel.

"Do something to convince him, Clay."

The goon in the glasses wrinkled his brow, then reached out and grabbed the cleaver. He forced Flannel's hand to the counter, pinned it, and raised the blade above his head. Flannel closed his eyes, barking out the word "No" like a machine gun. Clay brought the cleaver down swiftly, but turned it as he did, smashing it flat against the metal counter with a resounding clang.

Flannel cried out, then opened his eyes and saw a grinning Clay. Shaking, he looked at his hand and saw it was intact.

"It's more fun to make them really scared first," said Clay to Sennett.

"It's in my office," whispered Flannel. "Just take it and get the fuck out."

"Well done, Flannel," said Sennett, coming around the tables. "You're fired."

Clay grabbed Gil's remaining tuna roll and stuffed it in Flannel's mouth. Flannel flailed as they dragged him back to the giant mixing bowl and pinned him against it.

"Look at it this way," said Sennett. "If you were me, who would you rather have working for you? A police lieutenant? Or a high school administrator?"

Flannel, choking, couldn't say a word.

"I thought so."

The blond killers strained as they lifted Flannel and threw him into the shoulder-height bowl. When Flannel's hands came up and grabbed the rim, Jimmy pulled a chrome .45 out of his coat and smashed the fingers until they let go. Sennett cranked a dial to the right and pressed a green button. The huge crooked mixing arm started turning at breakneck pace, but the bowl barely moved. A few strangled cries escaped before Gil heard the sickening crack of snapping bone. The cries stopped. The mixer hummed, churning with quiet efficiency. Its human contents thumped heavily and wetly inside.

Clay picked up the remains of Flannel's corn dog, his glasses flashing. "You know, I bet they made the batter for these things in that bowl."

All three men chuckled.

"Okay, let's find that office," said Sennett. They walked out, leaving the door open behind them.

Trembling, Gil made his way out into the room. He wanted to stop the mixer but when he looked at it, his gorge rose in his throat. His stomach spasmed with his desire to vomit. He needed to get out as quickly as possible. Fighting to hold his jaws closed, he crept to the door and looked out. To his right, Sennett, Clay, and Jimmy were disappearing into a darkened hall.

They were going the wrong way. Flannel's office was to the left and up a flight of stairs, practically at the top. If the three men kept going, they'd wander at least five minutes in the mazy old building before they found their way back. Gil didn't think any more than that. He waited until they were out of sight and beelined for the cafeteria door.

The run up the stairs made him short of breath, but it was only a few steps to Flannel's office. The door was open and light fanned into the hallway. Gil entered and pulled the door shut behind him, locking it. Flannel's office was as bare and sterile as his home. There were few hiding places, and Gil quickly exhausted them. He shook out the five desk drawers and found nothing. He rifled the filing cabinet. He opened a metal wardrobe and put his hands in coat pockets. He became aware that he was gasping. He knew he had overestimated the time it would take for the men to walk one hallway, climb a flight of stairs and return. He knew he had used all of his time. He knew he should run.

Turning to the bookcase, Gil put his hands behind the books and groped for anything solid. After dredging two empty channels, he realized he was face to face with a large, leather-bound

King James Bible. He snatched it off the shelf and wrenched open the covers. There, in a deep rectangle cut into the pages, was a clear plastic bag of white powder. Gil removed the bag, replaced the book, and turned to the door. He was afraid to open it, afraid to see the men he knew were approaching.

There was an interior door that led to the school secretary's office, the room where kids brought their forged excuse notes to bored secretaries or waited in hard chairs for punishment to be doled out. Gil turned the handle; it was unlocked from his side. He closed it behind him and stumbled over a chair, then crawled into a corral of high counters where the secretaries worked. He curled into a ball in the dark and tried not to vomit.

He heard voices, a rattle, and then falling glass. It sounded like they were breaking Flannel's office to matchsticks. He heard cursing. He heard the door open and light stabbed into the room while eyes roved over the contents.

"It's where the fucking secretaries sit," said Sennett. "Fuck!"

"We should of asked him *where* in his office," said Clay or Jimmy.

There was a thick slap and then silence.

Gil didn't move for an hour. When he did, he took the cocaine and returned to his couch. Where else could he go?

His dreams were devoid of light. He was surrounded by writhing, tortured bodies. No one spoke or cried out, but Gil heard bones breaking, knew that organs were tearing and victims were bleeding under the skin. He could see nothing, but he smelled sweat and blood, felt stifling breath and trembling motion, and heard the thumping of bodies tossed by unfeeling machinery. It went on until he was screaming and still didn't stop.

He woke exhausted and couldn't get up. With his eyes open or closed the room looked the same; he hoped it was still night. He was desperate for a drink. He needed the shimmering brown bourbon sluicing up the side of the glass, needed the choking burn to fill his throat and scald out the filth, to steal his breath and seal his sleep.

Sweat crept under his clothes and chilled him. He felt a pain in his jaw and found his teeth clenched vise-tight. Trembling, he opened his eyes and saw the ceiling after all, milky pale and lowering like storm clouds, the wind-whipped vapor boiling angrily. Stars came out in the clouds and fell on him like sparks. He felt them dimple his skin like pinpricks of cool, spring rain.

He slept again, fitfully. Lo lay on the blanket in the grass. He was looking at her from far, far away. The long grass surged toward her and began bearing her away.

Chapter Fourteen: Friday

Gil sat, feeling like a spectre, in the chair in front of Whitehead's desk. Whitehead had his back to Gil and was looking out the window, intent on something happening at the curb. Gil couldn't see down from his position in the second-story office, but he wondered if EMTs were carrying Flannel out in a bag. He was glad he wouldn't have a chance to learn just how little the remains resembled a body.

Just minutes ago, before Whitehead had called him from his classroom to the office, Gil had also been monitoring the activity on the street. There were a half-dozen patrol cars, two ambulances, a fire truck, several dark sedans, and two Subarus painted with the logos of the competing television stations. A steady stream of city employees had made their way in and out of the building over the course of the first period, while Gil—doubtless like other Porte teachers—watched from the window of his empty classroom. The students had been sent home. A young-looking policeman had made the rounds to tell teachers they would be interviewed by the police, but he didn't know when and seemed to be in no particular hurry.

And now Gil sat, pale and trembling, watching Whitehead's back. He'd had several drinks. He needed several more.

Whitehead turned around, his face ashen. He seemed to be fighting to maintain his composure. His expression hardened and he turned back to the window.

"This tragedy has shaken this school to its very foundation," he said. "But I will not let that stop me from carrying out my duties as principal." He grabbed the sides of the window sill and his voice thickened. "I'm not hard to work for, Gil. You know that. I've given you chance after chance to address your problem. We're like a family here, and I've tried to keep the family together."

Whitehead wheeled and leaned over his desk. He sprayed Gil with spittle as he shouted: "And you mock these children's education by showing up falling-down drunk at their spirit assembly! This is it, you goddamn son of a bitch!"

Gil didn't have the energy to rise, to back away, or even lift his head.

Whitehead sat down and lowered his voice. "And to think that, on his last day on this earth, Tim Flannel had to witness the wasting of our Christian charity. I'm placing you on administrative leave for your drinking problem. You'll be required to enroll in a treatment program. If you complete it successfully, we'll be compelled to offer you your job again. But my brother-in-law supervises the drying-out center at St. Ursula and you will fail. The board may elect to give you a pension but fuck you."

Gil stared without blinking, unable to snap his eyes into focus. He felt as if he were in a trance. He rose and moved to the door, willing his hand to close on the doorknob. As he opened the door, Whitehead finished.

"I want your desk cleared out and I want you gone from the building in thirty minutes. Otherwise, I'll have the police come upstairs to throw you out."

The bell rang as Gil dragged his feet through the hall and up the stairs. It sounded too loud in the hall with no students around.

He opened his briefcase on his desk and put in a framed picture of Lo and a couple of pens he liked writing with. His to-do list, always an inky mess, seemed irrelevant. He winced a little as he crumpled it, seeing *Jerry—recommend* scrawled on the bottom. He put the cocaine and his remaining whiskey in the case, snapped it shut, and walked out. His plan was simple enough: go home, call Lolita, pack, and leave town—for real, this time. If he didn't come back to Garden City, he would live. He didn't plan on being found dead and bloated when the snow melted in the spring. He wasn't sure what he'd do with the cocaine, but if he poured it into the river he might feel as if he'd slipped past Sennett's guard to deliver one stinging jab.

At the head of the stairs he saw the trophy case that should have been filled to bursting with the bragging rights of Porte l'Enfer teachers. His stale picture was front and center as it would probably always be—not out of respect, but because no one noticed it and the damn thing was never even dusted.

Gil looked over his shoulder. The halls were empty. Voices carried as murmurs from the first floor, but that was far away. He walked to the trophy case and jiggled the lock. He tried all his keys. Setting his briefcase down, he went into the teachers' lounge and found a butter knife, a piece of someone's flatware that had caught in the trash disposal too many times and been demoted to lunchtime duty. He wedged it behind the sawtooth arm of the lock and pried, but the lock wouldn't bend. He moved the blade between the overlap of the two glass doors and pulled outward. The glass doors bowed until the knife handle was almost perpendicular to them. Gil wrenched it to the side, and with a booming crack, one door broke into several large, jagged pieces. He stumbled out of the way as they guillotined to the floor. The unbroken door thrummed, held in place by aluminum rails.

Gil reached in and grabbed his Teacher of the Year award, shook the broken glass off it, and put it in his briefcase.

He walked down to the first floor. As he passed the cafeteria, he saw a crime scene crowded with a dozen uniformed cops and a few men in suits. Blanston had his back to the doorway. Gil went outside into a courtyard, reentered the building through the shop annex, then crossed the echoing gym and left the building from the northeast corner. The snow was painfully bright and he blinked repeatedly as his eyes adjusted. For a brief moment he forgot his plan. *Concentrate,* he told himself.

He approached his house through the alley and let himself in through the back. It was odd to think he would never fix the broken pane of glass in the back door.

A noise in the living room made him stop. He waited, listening, then crept through the kitchen into the dining area. A light flicked on and Gil cried out involuntarily.

Sennett was sitting in Gil's easy chair. Jimmy stood behind him. Clay was perched on an arm of the couch. On the couch was Lolita, looking terrified.

"Gil, honey," she said.

Sennett seemed amused by the tears in her eyes. "You really have managed to put yourself in the middle of things in the most amazing way, Mr. Strickland. Frankly, I preferred the name 'Grouse,' but it doesn't pay to be nostalgic. We were waiting for you, but guess who came home first?"

Gil leaned heavily on the back of a chair. His legs were losing the strength to stand. The chair tipped and he struggled to remain upright.

"It's a funny thing," said Sennett. "Sometimes you just have a gut feeling. I was pretty mad when I couldn't find my merchandise last night, but then I remembered a certain English teacher who seemed to be following me around. It was Jimmy's idea to look in the phone book for your address."

Jimmy performed a courtly bow.

"I'm sorry, Lo," said Gil. "I tried to call. This is all my fault."

"Yes, it is," said Sennett. "If you had just kept quiet and

stuck to looking down the bottle instead of into our business, none of this would be happening."

Lo was crying silently, the tears streaming down her cheeks and dampening her smart business suit. She looked beautiful, thought Gil. He couldn't remember seeing her so tanned.

"So," said Sennett. "You do have my cocaine, right? I'd hate to think I kept Clay and Jimmy from having a healthy breakfast for no good reason."

The thin plastic case in Gil's hand seemed filled with bricks. Clay slid off the couch and stepped forward, smiling.

"Would you like to trade places with your lovely wife?" said Sennett.

Gil couldn't think to speak or act. When Clay reached out toward him, he ran without deciding to. Lo screamed, but Gil kept running. He jumped off the back porch, landed staggering in the yard but kept his feet and ran into the alley. His feet slipping in the snow, the briefcase flopping like a broken rudder, he crossed the street into the next alley.

Gil ran until he dropped in the snow. He looked back and saw no one. Curling into a ball, he moaned and let go of the case, his limbs shaking with rage. He pulled himself to his knees and punched a trash can. He felt his knuckles split and hit it again. He lifted the can and slammed it into the wall of a garage, scattering garbage. Dogs started barking ahead of him, then behind him. His breath was coming in ragged bursts. Putting his head back, he yelled as loud as he could.

He stood up, wanting to tear off his skin. Picking up the briefcase, he started walking back to his house. By the time he got there, he was running again. A weatherbeaten two-by-four was leaning against the side of his garage. He set the case down in the snow, grabbed the wooden beam, and walked into the house.

No one was there. They'd left, considerately turning out the lights and closing the front door. One of Lo's bags was in the living room; the other was gone. Her scarf was on the arm of the couch. Gil picked it up and held it to his face, smelling her. Closing his eyes, he pictured the two of them in bed, their arms tightly around each other, naked and close.

Gripping the two-by-four tightly, he wheeled and smashed the lamp off the ceiling. He brought the board down on the television set, cracking the glass and releasing a puff of smoke. From the center of the living room he lunged out, swinging hard into anything he could. He shattered an end table lamp, the leaded panes of his bookcases, framed pictures. He swung into the stairway handrail and broke out a baluster. His hands stinging from the impact, he swung again and broke nothing. With a final heave, he launched his weapon through the back window; it punched a hole through the glass, clattered off the back porch, and came to rest in the yard.

Gil went to his liquor cabinet and opened a fresh bottle of bourbon. Upending it, he gulped ferociously, stopped for air, vomited a mouthful back up, then drank some more. He threw the bottle into the face of the TV set, which coughed sparks and erupted in flame.

He wasn't ready to burn the house down—not yet. After yanking the cord out of the wall, he ran to the kitchen and put on two of Lo's oven mitts. Lifting the set, he threw it through the window into the snow.

His nerves felt like they were juiced with lightning. Panting, he climbed the stairs. In his typewriter was a note:

IF YOU CHANGE YOUR MIND, GO TO THE THREE STAR BAR IN REVEILLE TOMORROW. YOUR WIFE SENDS HER BEST.

Gil sat down on the bed. He knew Reveille, and he knew the bar, even though he hadn't given a thought to either when he drove through the other day. What day had it been? He counted back but couldn't believe it was only three days ago. Reveille was less than an hour's drive north, a canyon hamlet clustered at a minor highway junction at the bottom of a hill. At the crest of the hill, the breathtaking crags of the Monk Mountains came into sight. Their windmill notwithstanding, the people of Reveille lacked a view. The Three Star was a broken-down roadhouse, an establishment with an intermittent past and a dubious future. At one point it had even been slated for demolition. Gil didn't know why it had been saved. It had caught the eyes of many trailer-park entrepreneurs over the years, all of them hungry for tourist dollars, not realizing their marks would forever stop for gas, lunch, and postcards in the next town, five miles up the road, where they had an unobstructed view of the Monks and an honest-to-god historic church besides. After a few lean months or years, the acumen-lacking entrepreneur would sell the place to another, equally dim speculator. It wasn't likely to be open in the winter. What was Sennett's connection? Did he now own it and use it as a front for his criminal dealings?

Gil would be finding out soon enough.

After dark, he knocked on the Simonsens' door. Dick opened it.

"I didn't expect you," he said. "After yesterday at the pep assembly, I thought they'd hospitalize you."

"You were there?"

"We all were, Gil. All of your colleagues, all of your students."

"Can I come in?" asked Gil.

Dick stepped aside. Gil walked past him and stopped. They stood in the entryway; behind them, Dick's family was sprawled out in front of the TV.

"You need to take a hard look at things," said Dick quietly.

"I need your help," said Gil.

"All right."

"We're going to kill someone. Maybe three people."

Dick nodded vaguely.

"Does the name Sennett ring a bell? 'The Senator'?"

Dick shook his head.

"He's the one who killed Flannel."

Dick repeated the word "killed" but it seemed to catch in his throat.

"You thought Flannel got hungry for a midnight snack and drove to school to lick out the bowl?"

"But, Gil—even if you're right—what would this guy want with you?"

"He wants to trade my wife for his cocaine. He has Lo. But if I give him what he wants, he'll kill us both."

Dick stepped back as if evading a punch. "My god, Gil."

"You owe me, and you owe Kristen. In a way you gave us both up."

"But Kristen—I never—"

"You never helped her, which is what an adult should have done."

"Gil, just go to the police."

"They'd like their cocaine back, too, but for the wrong reasons."

"How did you get it?"

"I took it from Flannel's office so I could keep it off the street. Do you have a gun?"

"Yes, but—"

"Get it. Pack an overnight bag."

Dick looked at his shoes. "I can't, Gil. I'm sorry about Lolita, but I can't."

Gil saw the worry on Dick's face and almost felt he could forgive him. The very features—the sun-pinkened, balding head; the push-broom mustache—that had become such bludgeoning eyesores to Gil over the years now seemed to have hidden fragility and fear. He wanted to reach out but froze his muscles.

"I see," he said. "Well, I have to go now. I hope you sleep well."

"You don't have a family, Gil. You don't know what it's like."

"I have nothing."

He left.

Out front, Gil unlocked the hatch of the Datsun and felt under the blanket for his shotgun. It was still there. He climbed behind the wheel and started the car.

Hands thumped against the glass. Dick. Gil rolled down the window.

"I'm sorry," Dick gulped. "I'm scared. But I'll come with you."

"I don't want to die, either. I'm scared to death."

They looked at each other while it sunk in and the car idled arrhythmically.

"Get your things," said Gil. "I'll wait here." He rolled the window back up.

When Dick came out fifteen minutes later, the car was as warm as it was going to get. They had driven for a mile or two when Dick said, "The other morning, I had no idea what I was doing to you."

"We never know what we're getting into. You kiss the kids goodbye?"

"Yeah."

"That's good."

He could see Dick swallow hard.

They filled up the car and drove north, stopping at a liquor store for a bottle. With one hand on the wheel, Gil uncapped it and had a pull. He passed it to Dick.

"I don't drink much, usually," said Dick. "It kills my running times."

Gil waved the bottle in front of his friend's face, splashing him. "You can't run every day of your life."

Dick took the bottle and swallowed a little, then drank again.

They took the Interstate ten miles out of town, then took the turnoff for Flatfoot Lake, a popular summer recreation spot that lay beyond Reveille. As the road carried them along, they could still dimly see the glow of Garden City in the rearview for a few miles. Then the road climbed into the hills and Garden City disappeared.

Traffic was almost nonexistent and they made good time on the highway, which was rough and pitted but free of snow. They entered the Indian reservation—"the rez"—and saw the perennial signs for fireworks and cheap cartons of no-name cigarettes. Because it was scenic and home to tourist destinations, the Flatfoot Reservation was less poverty-stricken than those in more isolated parts of the state. But still, jobs were scarce, social problems were many, and mobile homes more common than those with permanent foundations. The mobile home seemed a bad tradeoff for the tipi, thought Gil.

Approaching the small burg of Arles, they saw a sign that was painted:

PREPARE TO MEET THY GOD

As they drove past, the other side read:

THE WAGES OF SIN IS DEATH

"That doesn't sound right," said Dick.

"The wage of sin is death?" said Gil.

"Clearly it's not, 'The wages of sin *are* death,' " said Dick.

They chuckled and Gil wished his problems could be solved by parsing; that was one challenge he could meet.

The streets of Arles were empty except for blowing trash and a rangy, lupine dog that crossed the road in front of the car, unafraid. As Gil slowed, the dog stopped and looked at them, its breath steaming and its eyes glowing like sapphires in the headlights. One store was open, a twenty-four-hour gas mart, its brilliantly lit concrete pad blazing in the night. As they drove out the other side of town, Gil saw a half-dozen deer darting across a lawn.

They reached Reveille. The town wasn't more than a half-mile from end to end, and the Three Star Bar was at the midpoint. They saw lights in the windows of several houses, but there were no other signs of life. Gil pulled into the unplowed parking lot of the Three Star and parked. He and Dick got out of the car and looked around. Up on a pole, an unlit sign still had plastic letters spelling out *WELCOME STOCKMEN.* They peered through a picture window that shivered in the wind and saw broken chairs piled on tables, empty coolers, and a cash register with its drawer hanging open. The front door was locked tight, so they circled the building, looking for a way in.

In the back, a fire door was padlocked from the outside, but the hasp looked as if it could be pried off. There were no footprints on the ground but theirs. Gil wanted to break in right away but Dick voted for eating first.

"You want a last meal?" said Gil with false bravado.

Dick tried to lift the corners of his mouth.

They got back in the car and drove north again, cresting the hill to a nighttime view of the Monks. The snowy peaks almost glowed in the dark blue night.

"You ever hike them?" asked Dick.

"Never once," said Gil. "The last time I put on a backpack, I was nineteen."

Dick wasn't listening. "I was up there, I think, six or seven years ago."

As they passed St. Paul, a new wooden sign advertised the historic mission with rustic, faux-primitive lettering. The belfry of the church, which they could see in dim silhouette, seemed frail against the looming mass of the mountains beyond. After another twenty minutes, they stopped at Trudy's Truck Stop

Diner. Inside it was warm and bright but empty. They sat at a booth with a view of the highway and ordered full meals: soup, hot turkey sandwiches with mashed potatoes, and coffee. They ate ravenously.

Gil kept his eyes on the road. A few semis passed, and a few pickup trucks, but no Cadillacs.

He wanted to thank Dick for coming but kept quiet. They'd both made their decisions. Broaching the subject again would remind them what was at stake, and Gil didn't want to spook Dick or to think too much about the danger he'd asked Dick to share. He didn't want them to both dwell on the absurdity of two teachers confronting armed criminals.

They paid for the meal and then drove back down to the Three Star. On the way, they made a plan. By arriving in the middle of the night, they were sure to be first on the scene. When the time came, Gil would stand behind the bar with his shotgun at the ready. Dick would hide outside. If Sennett and his men left Lo in the car, Gil would be able to get the drop on one or two men, while Dick could take care of a guard outside. If they brought Lo in with them, Dick was to come in the door behind them, put his gun barrel to Sennett's head, and tell him to order the others away. The thugs wouldn't necessarily expect Gil to be armed; he was sure they wouldn't expect him to have backup. And just for added measure, he'd try to surprise them.

A few hundred yards from the bar, Gil took a side road that crossed the railroad tracks and descended the grade. He parked out of view of the highway. They slung their guns over their shoulders and Dick grabbed his small duffel bag. Gil put the bottle in his briefcase, next to the cocaine, his plaque, and a tire iron, then tucked the case under his arm. As they made their way back to the bar, they saw their earlier tire tracks and footprints breaking the snow like a hunter's dream. Dick nodded, then pulled heavy boughs off a nearby pine and used them to sweep the snow more or less smooth.

"It's not perfect, but those guys sound like city slickers," he said. "They won't notice if it's not obvious."

Gil hoped he was right. They walked to the back door again, Dick sweeping behind them as they went. Using the handle of Gil's tire jack, they pulled the hasp off and let themselves in. The building was unheated, but the four walls made it warmer than outside. Half the room was a bar and half of it was a restaurant. There were a few booths left, their vinyl upholstery spilling yellow foam rubber like fat from a slashed carcass. Taped to a long mirror behind the bar, a few curling flyers advertised now-defunct bar bands. Mouse turds were scattered everywhere.

The only problem with the layout was that the front door faced the narrow end of the bar, not its broad front. Still, the bar was solidly built and would offer good cover. Dick wouldn't be able to find a hiding place until it grew light out, so they climbed into booths and huddled into their jackets to wait for dawn. Gil took a few draws on the bottle and capped it. He checked the time: one-fifteen. They had a long wait ahead of them.

After an hour, Dick's breathing grew deep and steady. Gil couldn't sleep. He watched the dusty front window for the infrequent sweep of headlights. When big trucks passed, the whole building shuddered.

He'd thought he hadn't even looked back at Lo when he ran, but he could see the terror on her face as clearly as if he were staring at a photograph. The look in her eyes was something he couldn't blink away. And when he remembered her scream, he knew he had hurt himself worse than Sennett ever could have. Somewhere, Lo was still terrified, still knowing her husband had run away to save himself. Even if Gil was able to rescue Lolita, he knew something had severed that would never be reattached. If he still had to leave Garden City, he wasn't sure she would come with him. He ran through every outcome, but no matter how he calculated the equation, he still came up with nothing. He had robbed his wife of her safety and shown himself to be a coward.

He rested his head on his arm and closed his eyes. But sleep was far away.

Chapter Fifteen: Saturday

Gil woke, cold to the bone, and saw a dull gray light in the window. Dick was standing in shadow, holding his gun across his chest and looking out at the raw day.

"You sleep much?" he asked Gil.

Gil rubbed his eyes and reached for the bottle. "Some."

"You think you can shoot someone?"

"I think so."

"If you know you will kill them?"

Gil took a drink. "I never thought so before, but I guess I will if I have to."

"Maybe you can never know until the moment it happens," said Dick.

They were silent for several minutes.

"I'd better hide now," said Dick. "You don't know when they're coming?"

"No," said Gil.

Dick headed for the back door. "I saw a shed out there with a window. I don't think anyone will see me there."

"Okay," said Gil. "Just watch carefully."

"Do you think I'd go to sleep?" snapped Dick.

"Sorry." Gil got up and looked out the window. The door closed behind him. Gil unlocked the front door. On the off chance that Sennett didn't have keys, Gil didn't want him making his way around the back to get in the same way Gil and Dick had. He walked behind the bar. There was a shelf just below the bar top that was the right width and depth for the shotgun. He could keep his hands in sight but still pull the gun up in a second. He practiced several times to be sure he had the motion right. He wondered if that was the purpose of the shelf, to hold a gun. It was strange to think that someone who poured drinks would also need to aim a gun at his customers. But he had seen it happen. He saw the briefcase in a booth and brought it back behind the bar, setting it on the floor.

He broke the gun open and checked the shells, even though he knew it was loaded. Two shots. With a shotgun, that would be enough, but there was no margin of error. Even a warning shot could be a mistake if it forced him to reload. Gil had seen Jimmy's pistol and knew he wouldn't hesitate to use it. Sennett, Jimmy, and Clay would have at least three guns between them and they would be comfortable using them. Gil imagined pulling the trigger and seeing another man fall down. His stomach corkscrewed.

He tried not to think of where Lo might be, or who might be with her.

The day waned. Gil felt like a sleepwalker. His eyelids were drooping and his stomach was complaining, growling for food and irritated by the infusions of bourbon. He was afraid he'd pass out if he moved too quickly. Out on the road, traffic was slow but steady. Everyone seemed to be passing through.

Keeping an eye on the window, Gil checked coolers, cabinets, and shelves for some forgotten morsel of food, a rock-hard candy bar or a can of chili. There was nothing.

He opened his briefcase. He saw the cocaine and thought about using it. Was it wrong? Would it help? The only drugs he'd ever tried were pot and mushrooms. Cocaine was a rich man's drug he'd found easy to disdain because it had never been offered to him. He knew it was a stimulant.

Poking a hole in the thick, cloudy plastic with his car key, he sawed it open a little wider and stuck his pinkie inside. His fingertip came back sugared with cocaine and he dabbed it onto his tongue. It didn't taste like much and didn't make his tongue go numb, although there was a slight deadening of sensation. He scooped some onto the corner of his driver's license and looked at it, comparing it to powders he'd seen before: baby powder, baking soda, powdered sugar, foot powder. He couldn't decide which one it looked like.

Gil had seen enough movies to know how it was done. The bar was filthy, so he used the only clean, flat surface at hand—his Teacher of the Year plaque. He scooped with his license and drew ragged lines, then rolled up a dollar bill.

Covering one nostril he inhaled with a snort. The drug scoured his nose like the spray he used for his hay fever. For a moment he felt frighteningly lightheaded—and then he felt good. Damn good. Without even a reason, he smiled.

He put more up the other nostril. It was like waking after ten hours' sleep in fresh country air. He was sharp-eyed, alert, raring to go.

He wanted to talk.

He settled for muttering under his breath, a narrative of possible scenarios for the end of the day. Periodically, he interspersed a song, half humming and half singing while he drummed on the bar top.

A figure passed in front of the window and he jumped. He needed to remember to watch for Sennett. Was that Sennett? Or had a bird just flown by? Grabbing his gun, he ran and looked but saw no one. His nerves stretched. He really wanted to talk to Dick, just to reassure himself that his partner was still there, still watchful. Maybe Dick's voice would calm his nerves. But he couldn't leave the building.

He snorted more cocaine and then put the bag back in his

briefcase, wishing he had tape to cover the hole he'd made. Maybe he was a hypocrite now, but he was a wide-awake hypocrite, which was vital.

Trying again to wait, he felt the sterile room was chirping with life. It seemed as if he had grown hair to his shoulders; *something* was behind him, but when he looked, it moved with his head.

A car cruised slowly by on the shoulder of the road but kept going.

What time was it? Three? His bladder weakening, Gil went into the men's room. The frozen trough still reeked of piss. Gil held his breath. In the silence, the rattle of his urine onto the metal seemed deafening. He pulled his zipper up as he hurried back into the bar.

The dark Caddy was outside the window. Gil's head swam—were they inside? He scanned the room as he stumbled toward the bar. He had just reached the pass-through, its hinged piece of bar top raised like a drawbridge, when the door opened and Sennett and Jimmy walked in.

Gil froze. He was outside the bar, fifteen feet from his gun. He'd been a step too slow to hide.

Sennett and Jimmy had been talking, but stopped in surprise. Sennett recovered quickly; Jimmy's eyes raked Gil for potential weapons.

"I didn't think we'd see you today," said Sennett. "Did you go to the wizard for your cup of courage?"

"Where's Lo?" said Gil. "Is she in the car?"

"No, she's safely hidden away."

Gil faltered. "But . . . I brought the cocaine."

"Great!" said Sennett. He clapped his hands and then rubbed them together.

"That was the deal," said Gil. "That's why you took her. To trade." He looked at the bulge under Jimmy's jacket and thought of the huge gun that had broken Flannel's grasping fingers.

"Deal? I don't remember signing my name to anything. Did I sign my name to anything, Jimmy?"

Jimmy laughed, revealing teeth square and white as Chiclets. "You never sign anything," he said. He reached inside his jacket.

Gil wondered how many steps it would take to reach his shotgun.

"Besides," said Sennett. "Your wife is awfully attractive for an older gal. I might be able to find work for her. We could have seniors' night—of course, it would have to start early."

Jimmy's gun was out. Gil stepped to the right and dropped just as Jimmy began firing. The first shot chunked a hole out of the hinged bartop and slammed it closed. Gil crabwalked forward with his knees and elbows as thunderous gunfire created a maelstrom of debris. Wood splintered off the bar and the mirror shattered. Large chunks of glass fell around him like hail. Something tore his calf.

Gil thought he heard a click through the ringing in his ears. Maybe the click of Jimmy's hammer falling on an empty chamber. The firing had stopped. A spent shell rolled buzzing across the floor.

"Should we quit playing with him, boss?"

Gil stood up as quickly as he could and pulled the shotgun off the shelf. The barrel banged on the bar as he raised it but he had it aimed at Jimmy before the tall man could slide a fresh clip into his big Colt .45. Jimmy froze with the ammunition just inches away from the slotted handle of his gun.

"Put it down," said Gil.

A gun fired and blood spurted forward out of Jimmy's left shoulder.

"Fuck!" he screamed, dropping the clip. Outside the window, Dick drew back the bolt of his rifle and drove it forward again, taking aim as Jimmy crouched down and clawed for his clip with a rebellious left hand. Dick's next shot thudded into the floor behind Jimmy who, after shoving his clip home, unleashed a burst of fire toward Dick. Gil knew he should shoot Jimmy but couldn't summon the will to pull the thin, curving trigger. Dick flashed out of sight. Gil didn't think he'd been hit.

Sennett was smiling at Gil. Gil wondered why, looked down, and saw Sennett aiming a .32 at him. Sennett fired. Gil pulled the trigger of the shotgun as he ducked behind the bar. He saw a sudden hole open in the ceiling.

"Let's waste these fuckers," snarled Jimmy.

Gil crawled toward the back of the room. The briefcase was next to him. He grabbed it and rolled over just as Sennett poked his head over the bar. Gil squirmed into the gap of the pass-through, then wheeled out and shot blindly with one hand, the recoil nearly shaking the gun loose from his grasp. He turned and ran out the back door. He heard more shots and the high whine of a ricochet.

He set the briefcase in the snow and broke open his gun, pulling the spent shells out with shaking fingers. He fumbled new ones from his pocket, dropped them in the snow, then loaded them one at a time. Dick came around the corner as he was snapping the gun shut.

"I thought they were slaughtering you," Dick panted.

"Where's Clay?" said Gil.

"Who?"

"The third one."

"There is no third one. Just the two guys who went in."

Gil couldn't think of any plan except to keep the bad guys from getting out of the building. "Go back around front," he told Dick. "Keep them inside."

Dick nodded and ran off. Gil wedged the barrel of his gun inside the back door and fired blindly. They'd need to follow Sennett and Jimmy if they were going to find Lolita. He changed the plan. He tucked the briefcase under his left arm, crooked the gun in his right, and ran after Dick.

Cars were passing on the highway, some oblivious, some slowing in disbelief when they saw a man using a Cadillac for cover and pointing a rifle toward the broken window of a bar.

"They won't shoot," yelled Dick. "I think they don't want to hit their car."

Gil tried to stay out of the line of sight of the bar window. "I'll be right back," he said. Then he veered right and stumbled toward the highway, timing a break in the traffic. Seeing signs of normal life was even more disorienting to Gil than the fact that he was in a gunfight. He remembered a time in college, when, high on mushrooms, he'd spent a whole night walking the streets comfortably thinking trees had faces and the sidewalk was moving. And then, at dawn, he saw a family friend walking her dog and was terrified when he realized she wasn't high, too.

His lungs burning, his arms too laden to pump, he lumbered down the road. Drivers stared. Two cowboys pointed, laughed, and slapped each other five. Gil felt as if his temples would explode. *How long can a minute be?* he wondered. He felt a ragged pain in his chest but didn't notice his feet hitting the ground.

He turned, crossed the tracks, and reached his car. He threw his things in the back seat and turned the key. It cranked but didn't turn over. It had been out in the cold all night. Worse, it had gone without the bright orange umbilical cord that fed its block heater from an outlet on the side of Gil's house. He cranked again. Again. Each time there was less spark in the battery, and the starter's cough grew quieter. He stomped the gas, punched the horn, and swore. The car started. There was no time for a three-point turn on the narrow road. Gil ground it into reverse and accelerated. The car fishtailed but he guided it up the grade. He thumped across the tracks and squirted into traffic, spinning the wheel right, then left to correct. A horn Dopplered as a speeding car swerved around him. He shifted to first, then second, redlining the engine for a couple hundred yards until he cut a hard left and slewed into the Three Star Bar's parking lot.

Dick started running as Gil flung the flimsy passenger door open. Sennett and Jimmy started shooting again. From inside the building their guns sounded like hammers on an air duct. A small crater appeared in the hood as Dick climbed in the car. Gil was already rolling. With a pop, the back-seat windows suddenly spiderwebbed. They pulled away.

Dick looked behind them and then at the road ahead. "You're going north," he said.

"Let's see if they follow," said Gil. "Maybe we can trap them."

"Trap them," echoed Dick. He closed his eyes.

Gil's Datsun was whining in second gear. He shifted to third and pushed the gas pedal to the floor. They were nearing the bottom of the hill.

"Do you see them?" he asked Dick.

Dick looked over the seat back. "I think they're getting in the car."

They started up the hill. The road curved right and they lost sight of the bar. On the speedometer, the needle had pointed to 50 but began to slip as the small car labored up the steep slope. Gil passed around a slow-moving station wagon, praying for more speed. The Datsun's four cylinders would be no match for the Caddy's eight. They were going 40. He couldn't see the Caddy in his rearview. He prayed for them to follow, but not too soon.

When the needle touched 35, Gil shifted to second and ignored the tortured sound of the tiny engine. They maintained speed. When they were halfway up the hill, the Cadillac appeared behind them.

Gil glanced at Dick. His eyes were glassy and he was biting his lower lip.

"Load your gun," said Gil.

Entranced, Dick complied.

The body of the dark car behind them surged on its struts like a speedboat on choppy water. It was closing fast. Gil's needle dipped again, but they were nearing the top. Another car, even more underpowered, filled the lane ahead. Gil crossed the centerline to pass and saw a pickup heading straight toward him. Horns blared as Gil edged right, straddling the solid double line. The pickup swerved to its right and blew past; Gil was holding pace with the blue sedan on his right. He met the frightened eyes of the driver, a woman with two kids in the back. She pulled onto the shoulder and slowed, and he took the lane again.

They crested the hill. As they rolled down a slight dip, Gil geared up again. The Caddy was only sixty yards back, but he lost sight of it for a moment. When it reappeared, barreling over the rise, Gil was going 50 again and picking up speed.

He saw the sign for the mission a few hundred yards ahead. The Caddy was still closing. Gil lifted his foot from the accelerator but didn't brake. When they neared the turnoff, he braked suddenly and pulled the wheel to the right. The Caddy, almost on top of him, overshot and skidded to a halt just past the turn. The Datsun bucked on the potholed side road. Directly ahead, the church caught a last feeble ray of sunlight in the gathering dusk.

They lurched to a halt in front of the church. Gil ran up the walk and climbed the steps to the front doors. Dick was lagging behind, his stolid frame looking soft as a scarecrow. Gil saw the Caddy a couple of blocks away. It was closing fast, fishtailing on the snowpacked street.

"Run, damn it!" he yelled to Dick before bursting through

the doors himself.

A lone winter tourist turned and saw Gil. He dropped out of sight between the pews.

"Get out!" said Gil.

The man poked his head up, hesitated, and then ran for a side exit. Gil tried the door to his right. It was locked but looked like hollow-core. He raised his gun butt and broke the handle right out of the wood. There were stairs behind; he climbed them and reached the gallery.

Below, Dick was wandering up the aisle toward the altar, dragging his rifle like an afterthought.

"Dick!" shouted Gil. "Come up here!"

Dick turned and squinted at him, but kept walking. Gil scrambled to the top row and looked out the window. The black car skidded to a halt. Dick had turned right and was climbing over a low, white, wooden railing. Above a side altar, against a whitewashed wall, a painting showed Joseph carrying an infant Jesus. There was a small tipi on the altar. Leaning his rifle against the altar, Dick picked up the delicate model and stared at it.

Gil ran down to the front of the balcony and readied his shotgun. "Hide, Dick!" he shouted. Dick didn't seem to hear him.

The front door slammed open and Dick turned, dropping the tipi. He grabbed his rifle and stumbled across the sanctuary toward the main altar.

"You must be the one on Jimmy's bad side," called Sennett. "Where's your friend?"

Beside the altar, Dick froze, facing them. His gun barrel pointed to the floor.

Gil craned to see over the railing, but Sennett and Jimmy had stopped just out of sight.

"Please," said Dick softly. The word carried clear as a bell.

Gil frantically motioned for Dick to take cover, but Dick's eyes were fixed on the killers in front of him.

A gun fired and a bullet splintered wood near Dick's leg.

"Whoops," said Jimmy. Sennett laughed.

With agonizing slowness, Dick began raising his gun barrel while hunkering down behind the altar. There were five or six shots and Dick disappeared, his rifle rising up and then tipping, like a ship's mast keeling over.

Gil's cries had been lost in the gunfire. They trailed away with the echoes that rebounded from the vaulted ceiling. Gil gripped the railing, frozen. He couldn't see Dick. Bullet holes pocked the altar.

In the distance, a siren whined.

Someone said, "Come on," and Sennett and Jimmy ran heavily out the door.

Gil ran downstairs and opened the front door. The dark car spat snow from under its tires as it pulled out of the parking lot. The sirens were louder. Putting the shotgun to his shoulder, Gil fired twice at the car. A taillight went out, and he saw sparks as the side mirror was blown free of the door.

He ran back inside.

Behind the altar, Dick was still alive, but his breath was ragged and his eyes blinked like camera shutters as he lolled his head, trying to focus on his surroundings.

Gil dropped his gun and knelt beside Dick, his knees in a sticky puddle of blood. Blood was pumping from Dick's chest with a wet whistling sound. Gil put his hand over the hole and tried to think what to do. Dick's entire torso was crimson and there was a dark stain at his crotch. One knee was bent wrong.

He thought he should say something reassuring—*You're going to be all right*—but he couldn't speak.

Dick met his gaze. His jaw worked up and down, his tongue struggled, but no sound came out.

Gil smelled shit and piss. He knew Dick's body was not going to be mended. His stomach roiled and he turned his head away and puked. He heaved and coughed and spat, convulsing until he was trembling helplessly on the floor.

He felt a cold draft. The front doors were open. A bullhorn gave a compressed, tin-can squeal: "If anyone is inside the church, come out with your hands on your head!"

Gil turned his head and saw Dick gurgle blood onto his cheek. He struggled to his feet, steadied himself on the altar, and then started walking up the aisle, his arms crooked like goalposts. The brown wood of the pews gleamed with polish, and the racks on the backs were neatly filled with bibles, hymnals, envelopes, and pencils. Gil squinted into the bright light that was shining through the doors.

"Stop right there! Turn around!"

Gil did.

"Get down on your knees, keeping your hands on your head!"

My hands aren't on my head, Gil thought, but he did try to keep them in the air while he knelt down. He heard someone rushing up and suddenly his hands were wrenched down and cuffed together behind him. The steel of the handcuffs was ice-cold.

"Behind the altar," said Gil. "My friend is still alive."

A hand gripped his shoulder while a deputy in a brown uniform pushed past and cautiously approached the altar, gun at the ready. He looked down, then knelt. After a few moments he straightened up again and holstered his sidearm.

"This one's gone," he called out.

Gil was hoisted to his feet. "You stink," said his deputy.

"Go after them," said Gil. "They're in a black car."

The two deputies pushed him toward the door. "Our guys are chasing the other car. Why'd you boys decide to shoot it out in a church?"

"I didn't think we'd hurt anyone here," said Gil.

They stopped on the steps. The deputies looked at each other, then at Gil. They took him up the walk and put him in the back of their car. One of them spoke into his radio. "Sue, we're gonna need the coroner down here at the mission. We had some gunslingers down here."

After several other vehicles had arrived, they drove Gil to a small brick building with a sign that said *TRIBAL POLICE*. Inside, Gil scrutinized his captors for Indian features. One of them looked white. The other was light-skinned but had an aquiline nose and braids held under his hat by a rubber band.

He saw Gil looking. "Looks like you got outgunned," he said. "You should leave the pros alone."

Gil nodded. "I'm a teacher."

The other deputy shook his head.

Gil went along easily, almost glad not to have to make any more decisions. They took his belt, shoelaces, keys, and wallet. They took his picture and fingerprinted him, then locked him in the station's lone cell. Gil tried to tell them about Lo, but they brushed him off and told him they would question him later. Right now, they said, they had to return to the crime scene.

He saw someone peering at him through the window in the door to the front of the station and guessed it was the dispatcher, curious to see a gunslinger. Because she looked again from time to time, Gil wondered if she didn't quite believe her colleagues had hauled in the right man.

After a while she propped the door open. She was pretty, a little chunky, wearing a St. Paul Warriors sweatshirt. The team mascot, apparently, was a war-bonneted Indian chief.

"If you promise not to yell? I'll leave the door open," she said. "It gets kinda cold in here otherwise."

Gil said thank you and she left. It was cold in the cell, he realized, and he was grateful to her. From her crackling radio he learned that Sennett and Jimmy had evaded the other car and that the tribal police were concentrating on the church, recording the crime scene before forensics work began. They referred to Dick as "the dead guy."

Gil tested the bars of the cell and ran through escape scenarios. The steel bars were unyielding, the cinder-block wall was hard, and it only took a minute to realize that, short of injuring or killing someone, he wasn't going to get free. What would happen to Lo? Maybe Sennett would just kill her. Gil felt short of breath. He wondered if he should tear his clothes into strips and hang himself from the bars.

He washed his face and then lay down on the lower bunk. It was a chilly, flat piece of metal. They hadn't given him a mattress or a blanket yet.

There was graffiti in the cell: *KILL THE WHITE MAN* and *DIE, FUCK ASS.* Other scribbles worried the peeling, lime green paint, but they were too small to read while lying down.

Gil passed out.

He woke to a terrible clanging. Someone was using a nightstick to bang the bars like a dinner bell. "Wake up, Strickland," a voice said, wearily and repeatedly.

Gil sat up and the noise stopped. A young-looking, uniformed Indian with copper skin and jet-black hair was looking at him.

"Can I have a drink?" Gil asked. He was trembling.

"Nope," said the man.

"Please."

The lawman slid his baton through a ring on his belt and dragged a molded plastic chair closer to the bars. He sat down. "You gotta be kidding. I don't drink and there's no booze in my station. Although it is sorta interesting to listen to a white guy begging for a shot for a change. Usually it's some guy I went to high school with."

Gil felt like his pores were burning. He rubbed his temples and tried to think about something else.

"I'm Captain Bear Don't Walk, tribal police," said the man. "You can call me Matt."

"I'm Gil—"

"Strickland. I know. We have your wallet, remember?"

"Sort of."

"The dead man is Dick Simonsen."

"Yes," said Gil. "My friend."

"So you two weren't shooting at each other."

"No."

Bear Don't Walk leaned in, his eyes boring into Gil but his voice friendly. "So who were you shooting at?"

Gil wasn't sure how much to reveal. If Garden City's police were corrupt, who knew how things stood in this tiny station?

"Well, let me tell you what I know," sighed the Indian policeman. "Maybe it'll jog something in your memory, yeah? We ran your plates through the computer. You live at 324 Marcus Avenue in Garden City, you have two DUIs under your belt, one drunk and disorderly, and a few other booze-related screwups. You're currently charged with criminal mischief in Pishkun. Your trial date hasn't been set yet, but you sure weren't supposed to leave town." He shook his head slightly, as if he couldn't believe what he was going to say next. "Your occupation is listed as high school teacher, and in your car we found a kilo of coke and a teaching award. Now why did you drive up to the rez and start a gunfight?"

Gil was suspicious of the man's brown-and-tan uniform and his shiny black gunbelt, but his searching eyes told Gil he didn't know the whole score. Besides, Gil could do nothing for Lolita alone.

"It's not my cocaine," he began.

"All right," said Bear Don't Walk.

"The guys in the car kidnapped my wife," said Gil.

"You didn't feel like calling the police?"

"The first time I called them, they told me to shut up. The last time I called them, they told me they were going to kill me."

Matt Bear Don't Walk nodded pleasantly. "Have you been seeing a psychologist, or a therapist, or anyone?"

"It's true," said Gil. "I stole the cocaine from them so I could trade for—ransom—my wife."

"Where were they keeping the cocaine?"

"At the school where I teach. In the vice principal's office."

"That the guy who got chewed up in the kitchen, by any chance?"

Gil nodded.

"But you didn't do that."

"No."

Bear Don't Walk raised one eyebrow.

"They were fighting." Gil suddenly wondered if he was being secretly tape-recorded. Everything he said seemed to incriminate him. His head wasn't clear and he couldn't explain himself properly. "I know how it looks," he said. "But all I can tell you is that I'm a teacher and I wouldn't do anything like this unless I had to. And now my friend is dead, and if you can find my wife to prove she hasn't been kidnapped, I beg you to."

Bear Don't Walk puckered his lips and then puffed out a sigh. "You're gonna have to forgive me if I don't just take your word and turn you loose, dude. This is pretty messy stuff you're talking about. I talked to Lieutenant Blanston and he was very interested to hear that we have you. Says they've got dibs since you jumped bail. And I don't even technically have charges for you, since, as far as I can tell, you guys didn't hit anyone and the complainants ran away. I could do something for vandalism, or illegal discharge of firearms, but that kinda seems ridiculous under the circumstances. I told Blanston, come on up."

"You can't give me to Blanston," said Gil. "He's the one who wants me dead."

Bear Don't Walk pushed his chair back and stood up. "I reckon you might just be feeling the first twinges of the D.T.s. Drunks always feel persecuted, and they're good storytellers."

"Take me to Garden City yourself," Gil begged. "Call the FBI. Turn me over to anyone but Blanston."

The captain regarded him coolly. "Put yourself in my shoes. It's the most farfetched shit I've heard since my daddy told me some crazy stories about how crows and coyotes created the world. Listen: Tribal police get no respect. If I fuck with this guy on your behalf, and you're lying to me, it's gonna set me back about twenty years." He turned and walked out.

Gil lay back on the bed. His chest felt tight and his pulse was racing. His armpits and crotch were damp. He couldn't think straight: It was as if his body were screaming down the asphalt while his mind was locked in the bathroom behind the starting line. He was exhausted and jumpy. His saliva felt like rubber cement.

This was it, then. And he didn't even have a clock to count off the minutes it would take for Lt. Roger Blanston of the Garden City Police Department to wind his way up Highway 93 to the St. Paul pokey.

He stood up and called out hoarsely. After a minute, the dispatcher looked in.

"Can I get a pen and paper?" Gil asked. "I need to write a letter."

"They're gonna wanna read it," she said. "You know, before they mail it?"

"That's fine," said Gil.

She disappeared and returned a moment later with a small

pad of paper and a two-inch-long pencil. The paper was stationery that read: *FLATFEET TRIBAL POLICE.*

"Do you have any paper without the letterhead?" Gil asked.

She shook her head apologetically.

Gil eased himself onto his knees on the floor. He thought for a moment and then started writing, using the lower bunk for a desk:

To Whom It May Concern:

I am writing to enthusiastically recommend Jerry Feinstein for admission into your freshman class this fall. It has been my pleasure to have him in class three of the four years he's been a student at Porte l'Enfer High School. I have watched him grow from an eager but undisciplined freshman into a hard-working senior who is ready to chart a more challenging educational course in college.

I'm sure you've noticed my unusual stationery; I apologize for not using the form you provided for Jerry's recommendation. I'd also like to apologize for my poor penmanship. No doubt you'll learn the details of my situation shortly, and as my time and space are limited, I'll allow someone else to fill you in.

I know something about failure, and this is what gives me the authority to make a worthwhile recommendation to you. For more than ten years, I've failed as an educator. I am also an alcoholic. Those two traits combined to make me a miserable, bitter man who pretended to be blind to my students' talents. By my caustic remarks I tried to make them fail; when they did I took secret pleasure.

Jerry Feinstein refused to be poisoned by my vitriol. He found the few nuggets of wisdom in my rambling, infrequent lectures, melted them down, and fashioned them into something useful. He learned in spite of me, not because of me. If I have learned in class, it was because of him.

It may be cold comfort to my other students, but it is some salve to me to envision Jerry's future success.

Very sincerely,
Gil Strickland

He'd covered three of the undersized pages with his crooked letters. He folded them in half and addressed the outside to Jerry in care of the school. When the dispatcher came back, she agreed to stamp and mail the letter as soon as Bear Don't Walk had made sure Gil wasn't communicating directives to his drug cartel.

Gil's heartbeat slowed a tiny bit. He'd settled one score properly.

It seemed as if several hours had passed before Blanston arrived. As Bear Don't Walk showed the graying lieutenant in, Gil squinted to read the gold wristwatch nestled in the hairs of the white man's wrist. It was just minutes before midnight.

Bear Don't Walk unlocked the cell and stood aside for Blanston. Blanston told Gil to turn around. Gil obeyed, and felt the cold cuffs grab his wrists again.

They walked Gil through the station to the front door. The dispatcher gave him a small, hidden wave. Outside, Blanston put Gil in the back seat of his unmarked car and shook hands with Bear Don't Walk. Bear Don't Walk stood in the parking lot and watched them pull away.

Blanston's eyes roved from the road ahead to the rearview. When he seemed satisfied with what he saw in the mirror, he angled it so he could see Gil.

"I would almost be amused if you hadn't complicated things so much," he said.

Gil just stared back. He'd thought he might be beyond feeling scared, but he wasn't.

"Still, you surprised everyone in your desperation. No one expected you to bring guns and reinforcements."

Gil turned his head and looked out the side window. They weren't driving to the highway. Instead, Blanston piloted his Dodge through the dark streets of the town and stopped at a run-down house. Its roof and walls were shingled with the same dilapidated asphalt tile, which was blistered and peeling like a burn victim's skin. A pillar in front had collapsed, and the porch roof sagged like an eyelid ready to close for good. The front steps rose at conflicting angles.

"I will just be a moment," said Blanston, smiling. "Stay put."

As soon as Blanston was in the house, Gil tried to put a foot under the door handle, but there wasn't one. He should have known; he'd been in cop cars before. He began to feel claustrophobic. He kicked the door and the molded plastic liner thudded and flexed but gave nothing. He kicked the window and it shimmered tightly but didn't crack. On his back, with one foot on the floor, he couldn't kick very hard. He sat up again.

In the front seat, the police radio hissed and clicked. Unintelligible phrases mingled with number codes he didn't understand.

Looking at the house, all he could see were dim shadows that wavered against the yellowing shades. Probably the bad guys trying to figure out how to dispose of him. Was Lo inside?

The front doors of the car were unlocked. Gil put his chest against the front seat and pulled his legs up onto the back seat. He pushed himself over and his head slid into the passenger's footwell. His feet dropped by the steering wheel.

Gil tried to pull his body back on the seat but couldn't. Blood was rushing to his head. His knees hit the car horn and it blared loudly.

He heard a door slam. Blanston wrenched the car door open.

"You are not a contortionist, Gil." Blanston pulled him out of the car by his legs, dragging his face in the snow. Gil coughed and spit as the ice scraped his cheeks and lips. When the cartilage in his nose popped out of place again, he yelped gutterally.

Blanston hoisted him to his feet, then walked him around the car and pushed him into the passenger seat.

"If you want to ride in the front, please, be my guest."

The lieutenant got behind the wheel and gave the horn two short taps. Someone in the house pulled back the curtain and looked out. It was the other goon, Clay. Gil wondered if Sennett and Jimmy were taking a long drive, waiting for things to cool down.

Blanston drove to the highway and headed back to Garden City.

When Gil spoke, he tasted blood on his lips. "Are you going to let Lolita go?" he asked.

"I have nothing to do with that," said Blanston. "That is—*was*—between you and Sennett. I will venture a guess, however, that the Senator feels she is too well-acquainted with his face."

Gil stared at the road. Blanston pulled over at a turnout after only a few miles, coasting down a slight grade and stopping the car by a fence. He turned the lights off.

"Have you ever been to the bison range?" he asked Gil. "This is just an edge of it, a little spot where the shaggy beasts will show themselves to the tourists once in a while. They are amazing animals, don't you think?"

Gil said nothing. A car roared by, heading down the hill. Its headlights swept past the top of Blanston's car, missing it.

"Just yards from the road, and so private. Here, give me your hands, I'll relax those a little."

Gil turned his back so Blanston could get at the cuffs. To his surprise, Blanston took them off entirely and put them in his coat pocket.

"Put on your coat," Blanston said, reaching behind the seat and grabbing Gil's parka.

Unable to extend his arms in the car, Gil struggled to put it on.

"You know, Gil, this may surprise you, but this whole affair has left an unpleasant taste in my mouth. Usually my dealings are with the scum of society, whether they are men like Sennett or penny-ante punks who sell their grandmothers' televisions to pawn shops. But you, despite your problem with alcohol, are an anomaly. You're actually an important part of the fabric of Garden City. My own son once had a class from you and spoke favorably of the experience."

If it was true, Gil didn't remember. "The kid was a little shit," he growled. "I gave him a mercy grade."

Blanston turned his head, surprised, then laughed. "Not dead yet, are you? Would you like a drink?" He reached under his seat, found a pint bottle, and offered it to Gil.

Before his body could contradict him, Gil shook his head no. The last time he'd been offered a bottle it hadn't gone very well.

"Suit yourself," said Blanston. He set it on the dashboard. "I will just leave it here in case you change your mind. You see, I didn't pull off the road to spoon with you. I have an offer: If I let you get out of the car, will you disappear? It would have to be instant and permanent. Walk into the night, hitch-hike your way out of the state. I don't want to go through with this if I don't have to."

"What about Lolita?" Gil asked.

Blanston spread his hands and shrugged. "It's one of you or

both of you. I can't do everything. Sennett has her."

"Your boss," said Gil.

Blanston stared at him coldly. "I will pretend I have bad hearing as well as a soft heart. Get out of the car."

Gil's eyes went to the bottle. In his peripheral vision he saw Blanston's fingers creeping into his open coat.

"Let me take a drink first," said Gil.

"Take it with you," said Blanston.

"Just a quick one," said Gil. He unscrewed the cap and raised the bottle to his lips. He swallowed twice, tightened his grip, and swung the flat glass flask at Blanston's face as hard as he could.

Blanston grunted as it hit; it broke and Gil's hand came away with just the neck and a jagged-edged third. He leaned closer, grabbing the back of Blanston's head with his swollen left hand, shoving the broken bottle at Blanston's face again. The policeman, screaming, pulled the gun out of his shoulder holster and fired, the deafening shot starring the windshield. The noise and flash dazed Gil. His wrist burned. Blood soaked his hands.

Leaning over, Gil opened the door and pushed Blanston out onto the ground, then crawled on top of him. He saw the gun, grabbed it, and wrenched it free.

Blanston grimaced, his face a welter of blood. He spat feebly. "You dumb fuck!"

Gil yanked the keys out of the ignition, staggered to the rear of the car, and opened the trunk. He dragged Blanston back by his armpits, lifted, and heaved him in. Gil fought the trunk lid down against the kicking legs until it latched. Headlights flashed overhead but the passing car didn't even slow. Blanston yelled and beat on the inside of the trunk. Picking the gun out of the snow, Gil stood for a moment by the open car door, looking at the keys in his hand. The seatbelt alarm buzzed like a wasp caught in a screen.

Getting in the car, Gil started it again and pulled up onto the shoulder of the road. He aimed the hood down the long hill toward Reveille, then put the car in neutral. He got out and slammed the door, and the car began to coast away.

Gil crossed the road and climbed a snowy rise. The car gathered speed and crossed the dividing line into the wrong lane. His right hand throbbed but he could barely see it in the darkness. He probed it with the stiff fingers of his left hand and thought he felt a deep gouge. In the cold the blood was like raspberry jam. He balled his right hand and made a fist. Jagged granules of glass ground into the tissue and he gritted his teeth.

Far below, the car drifted around a corner and was gone.

Gil turned back toward the little town with the church. It was only a few miles away if he cut through fields and pasture. He started walking, holding the gun in his jacket pocket with his left hand.

The choppy ground was icy in some places, drifted with snow in others. Starlight and snow gave him something to see by, the white background rendering trees and shrubs like shadows. He struggled over sagging fences and stumbled short distances on pitted tracks before they turned the wrong direction and forced him into the snow again. A small hill left him winded by the time he reached the top. His torso was warm but his arms, legs, and head were freezing. The small cut on his thigh, the slash on his hand, the burn, his nose—all ached.

He floundered through a drift, fell, and climbed slowly to his feet. The quick swallows of whiskey had been a godsend. They'd bought him another hour.

He came to the edge of town, where a few dark trailer homes sat at odd angles to one another. A dog scared him, breaking the quiet with a sudden volley of barks. It reared on its hind legs, slobbering, growling in its throat on each suck of breath, pulling against its chain like a cart ox. But no lights came on.

Either the dog's owner wasn't home, or it barked madly every night, at deer, other dogs, the wind.

Gil wasn't sure where the run-down house was, so he went to the police station first. Through the front window, he could see Bear Don't Walk drinking coffee and talking to the dispatcher. Gil's car had been brought there and was parked around the side of the building. He skirted the outdoor lights and left, knowing the way from here.

He stalked woodenly through town until he reached the green-shingled house. White light glowed from most of the windows. The black car still wasn't there.

Trying to see inside, Gil circled the house carefully, but all the windows were covered with drawn, ratty shades. He couldn't see any shadows or movement.

In back was a small utility room, an add-on that looked as if it were sinking into the junk-filled yard. Quietly, he opened the outermost door and stepped inside. The cold boards creaked under his weight, and it seemed suddenly silent as he came out of the night into the tiny porch. Gil held his breath and listened. He heard nothing at first, then, at the edge of his hearing, a radio. It was as tinny and distant as if it played down ten stories of ventilation shaft.

Thin blue curtains covered the window of the door to the house, but there was a slight gap where the curtains met. He peeked through. The back of the guard's head stuck up above an armchair in the living room, about five yards away and through the kitchen. The kitchen was dirty, with pizza boxes, chicken buckets, and Styrofoam clamshells piled high on the counters.

They were keeping Lo there. The question now was whether she was in the living room or somewhere else in the house.

The man's head turned and Gil pulled his face away from the window. It was definitely Clay. Hopefully he and Jimmy were Sennett's only helpers.

Gil could barely use his right hand. He could pull a trigger with his left, but he would miss anything that moved. Quietly, he backed out of the cold porch.

It only took him a few minutes to get back to the police station. Bear Don't Walk stared as Gil walked through the door. One of the deputies dropped his coffee and drew down on Gil. Gil raised his arms weakly and Bear Don't Walk told the deputy to holster his gun.

"You look like shit, teacher," he said slowly. "What'd you do, knock off the lieutenant?"

"He tried to kill me," said Gil. "He told me to get out of the car. He was going to shoot me when I did."

"And you stopped him?"

"Somehow."

"Where is he now?"

"In the trunk of his car, in Reveille, at the bottom of the hill."

Bear Don't Walk nodded to the deputy. "Check it out, Eddie."

Eddie grabbed his hat and coat and walked out the door.

Bear Don't Walk shook his head. "You know, you're about the strangest person I've ever seen."

"Come with me," Gil said. "I know where they're keeping my wife. It's only a few blocks from here."

"How do you know?"

"Blanston stopped there on the way out of town. He went in and talked to them. But I think there's only one man there right now."

The captain stood up, then looked down at the floor. Blood was dripping out of Gil's coat pocket and tapping onto the tiles. "Step over to the sink," said Bear Don't Walk.

He washed Gil's hand with warm water and used a tweezers to pick out the larger pieces of glass. After gently drying it, he closed the wound with butterfly bandages and wrapped gauze around Gil's palm.

"That's called triage, teacher. What you really need is an emergency room and a treatment program, but you're okay for now, I guess."

Gil looked at his hand. Faint drops of crimson were already freckling the gauze.

Bear Don't Walk shrugged his jacket on. "I'm going to check this out with you, but if you're pulling some kind of a fast one, I'll kick your fucking ass and lock you up until you dry out for good." He grabbed a shotgun from a rack. "I'll put a bottle of top-shelf shit within staring distance."

They got into a Jeep with an insignia painted on the door. Inside a circle reading *Flatfoot Indian Nation,* a white buffalo stood in front of a blue lake. Following Gil's instructions, Bear Don't Walk drove to the house and parked down the street. He put the car keys in his pocket.

"Stay here," he told Gil.

"Let me come."

"You?" he chuckled. "What will you do?"

"You need backup," said Gil.

Bear Don't Walk looked toward the house. He drummed his fingers on the steering wheel, thinking. "You want a gun, I suppose?"

Gil showed him Blanston's .38.

"Oh, goody," said Bear Don't Walk. "Let's go."

They closed the car doors quietly. Bear Don't Walk spoke in a whisper: "If this doesn't get me killed or fired, I'm gonna buy a lottery ticket tomorrow. You go around back. Don't do anything unless something happens. I'm gonna knock on the front door and the old lady who lives there's gonna let me in to look around."

"The old lady's name is Clay," said Gil. "And she's got a gun."

"Don't even take the gun out of your pocket unless she tries to shoot me," said Bear Don't Walk.

They split up and approached the house. Bear Don't Walk hung back, giving Gil time to get in position. Gil crept into the back porch again and peeked through the gap in the curtains. He felt three heavy thumps vibrate through the floorboards. He saw Clay jump up, grab a pistol from a TV tray, and chamber a round.

Gil switched Blanston's gun to his right hand and winced as he tried to crimp his gauze-swaddled hand around it. He took it back with his left.

Clay advanced carefully toward the front door and disappeared from view. Gil heard a thud and the boom of a gun. Clay staggered back into the living room, firing toward the door. He fell into his chair and Bear Don't Walk fired again. There was a splash of red and Clay's gun fell from his hand.

Gil tried the door handle, then put his shoulder to the door. He bumped it three times before the bolt broke the strike plate out of the tinder-dry wood. He rushed through the kitchen into the living room. Bear Don't Walk was surveying the room warily, his gun at the ready.

"Looks like you might be right," he said. "This is one mean old lady, to shoot without even asking if I'm a salesman."

He used his foot to slide the gun on the floor farther from the motionless body in the chair. With two fingers, he checked Clay's neck for a pulse. He shook his head.

Gil found a short hall off the living room and started trying doors. The first led to a bathroom. The second opened on a closet. It was dark beyond the third door. He switched on the light. Lo lay on an unmade bed, blindfolded, her hands and feet taped together. Dropping his gun, Gil slipped off the blindfold and, holding Lo's head in his hands, began feverishly kissing her hair. He saw fear and confusion in her eyes and moved back so she could see him.

"It's me, Lo. I found you."

One of her eyes was bruised and swollen, and the other was red with tears. He started crying, struggling to peel the stiff silver tape from her wrists and ankles.

"Gil," she said softly. "You ran."

He couldn't get his fingernails under the tape. He pinched and pulled frantically, finally freed a long strip and started unwinding it.

"I'm so sorry," he said, choking.

Finally, her hands were free. Bear Don't Walk came to the door. "Your wife? Is she okay?"

"Alive," said Lo sadly.

"Glad to hear it, ma'am. I'm Captain Bear Don't Walk of the tribal police. We'll get you out safe." To Gil, he said: "I searched the house but there's nobody. You said there were more of these guys, right?"

"Two," said Gil, pulling tape from Lo's ankles. "The guys that drove away from the church today. I don't know where they are."

The deputy's radio crackled and he stepped into the living room.

Lolita was free. Gil kissed her face and sat on the bed next to her. They wrapped their arms tightly around each other. Gil ignored the pain that shot through his ribs when she squeezed.

He buried his face in her hair. "Did they—?"

"I thought I was going to die," she said.

"You aren't," Gil gasped between tears.

Bear Don't Walk stepped back in. "Eddie found Blanston's car. You're lucky. He's alive."

"Lucky?" said Gil.

"Cutting his face off in self-defense is one thing. Killing him after the fight is another."

Gil looked toward the wall, holding Lo, wishing Bear Don't Walk would go away, wishing the room would go away and they'd find themselves at home.

"Eddie's calling an ambulance for your wife," said the captain. "And I think you better climb in, too. It'll take you to the clinic here, not Garden City." He removed his hat and scratched the top of his head. "I guess we'll try to start sorting all this out in the morning. I'm gonna look around a little more."

He walked back out of the room. Gil and Lolita stayed on the bed.

"Dick's dead," he told her.

She nodded her head up and down sadly.

"I should have quit when they told me to."

"I don't know," she said.

He held her even more tightly. "Do you remember, when we were first married, we took a blanket to the stream down in Sweetstem Valley? You made a picnic lunch." His voice rasped and he coughed to clear his throat. "We just took off our clothes and made love."

Lo didn't move. "I remember," she whispered. "You got drunk and you passed out."

Gil thought he would never squeeze enough tears from his raw and bleary eyes.

A car pulled up out front. "That'll be Eddie," called Bear Don't Walk from the next room. "Ambulance should be here in about fifteen minutes. They're volunteers."

Gil wiped his eyes and asked Lo if she wanted to get up. She nodded and he helped her to her feet. She was still wearing the same clothes, a pale yellow silk business suit and a white blouse. They were dirty and wrinkled now. She held his arm tightly for balance and looked around the room as if she doubted the solidity of the walls.

They went into the living room.

Bear Don't Walk was walking to the front door. The door opened and a shot punched him backward. He dropped to his knees, fumbling to unsnap his revolver while blood wicked into the belly of his shirt. A second shot knocked him onto his back. His chest heaved and his eyes scanned the ceiling erratically. A third shot made a hole under his chin and he was still.

Lo screamed and ran back into the room where she'd been held hostage. Gil stared dumbly as Jimmy walked in, his shoulder crudely bound with a torn T-shirt. He showed his teeth in a wolflike grin.

"Remember us?" he said.

Sennett came in behind him, watching the street. He closed the door, turned, and shook his head when he saw Clay. Jimmy walked up to Gil and kicked his legs out from under him. Gil hit the floor like a roped calf, grunting as the wind was knocked out of him.

Sennett took the gun out of Bear Don't Walk's holster. He saw Clay's gun on the floor and picked it up, too.

"Looks like you hurt your hand," Jimmy said to Gil. He prodded Gil's palm with the toe of his shoe, then stomped on it. Gil heard a bone crack and a wave of pain rolled up his arm.

Turning his head, Gil saw Lo on the bed, trembling, pulling her legs into a fetal position. Blanston's gun was in the blankets somewhere, wherever he'd set it down, but he couldn't see it.

Jimmy followed Gil's gaze. "See? She likes it here. Wouldn't leave if she could."

Gil grabbed Jimmy's leg and tried to force him down. Jimmy shook it free and kicked him in the jaw. He walked over to Sennett, who had pulled a shade back to peer out the window.

"We can't stay here," said Sennett. "We need to clean it and go."

"Should we burn it?" said Jimmy, eagerly.

Sennett thought, then shook his head. "There's no point in putting an exclamation point on things. Just hide the car until we're done."

"Right." Jimmy headed for the door.

"Not too far," cautioned Sennett.

The door slammed. Sennett turned to face Gil. "So let me guess. The Indians have my coke now."

Gil nodded.

Sennett shook his head, smiling a little. "I never would have figured you for such a pain in the ass, Strickland. Why do you bother?"

"Somebody had to do something," said Gil. "I guess it was my turn."

"Well, strike up the band," said Sennett.

"How could you sell to kids?"

"Everyone else is recruiting them in high school—colleges, the army, the local hardware store—why should I wait? They're old enough to know better, if they choose to remember it. But let's be honest, these girls don't have much of a future anyway. They're just *cheerleaders.* Do you think they're going to make it to the NFL? This state doesn't even have any professional teams. If it wasn't for me, they'd just be taking another kind of drug, drinking wine coolers and watching soap operas. And they'd enter a different kind of prostitution, marrying musclebound jocks that would treat them worse than I would. I'm doing them a favor."

Gil glanced at Lo. Her face was to the wall.

"What, no rebuttal?" said Sennett. "I guess you weren't the debate coach." He pulled his .32 out of his jacket. "This is a small gun, but it does give you something to think about. I'm guessing I can keep you alive for three shots."

He shot Gil's good arm. Gil felt a tug before he heard the

bang. He grabbed his bicep with his fractured hand. It felt like someone had driven an iron bar straight through the muscle. His body flooded with warmth even as he ground his teeth in pain.

Jimmy came in through the back. "Okay, Senator. I moved it to the alley behind the house. We can load it through the back door."

"Good. Let's hurry."

Jimmy walked by Gil, looking with pleasure at his wounds. "That's gotta hurt," he grinned.

As Sennett and Jimmy emptied the house, pulling duffel bags and packages from their hiding places and stacking them by the back door, Gil lay quietly on the floor, wet with blood. He knew he had to concentrate to stay conscious. He couldn't get Lo's attention without making noise. The dead deputy's shotgun was leaning against the wall on the other side of the room, but Gil would be seen before he crawled three feet.

Bear Don't Walk's body was closer. The two crooks had started loading the car. When they went out the back door together, Gil crawled over to the dead captain and grabbed the mouthpiece of his radio with trembling fingers.

He didn't even know if it was turned on. He pressed the plastic button on the side and hoped. "Eddie. Eddie, this is Gil Strickland, we're at a green house about eight blocks from the station. I don't know the street. It's, it's, an old, run-down house. The porch is falling in. Bear Don't Walk is dead, and Sennett and a guy named Jimmy are going to kill us. Get help. Get help." He dropped the mic on the dead man's chest and saw the shotgun. It wasn't that far away.

He was almost there when the back door opened.

"Uh-oh," said Jimmy. He dashed across the room and picked up the gun. He swung the barrel across Gil's back. Gil barely felt it.

"Senator," said Jimmy. "Can I mess up the carpet?"

Gil felt the barrel against his skull. He closed his eyes. He wanted a good thought to take with him when he died. He tried to conjure up Lo on the blanket by the river, but the image flew away like a broken kite in a windstorm.

Sennett walked through the kitchen. "Is everything in the car?"

"Yup."

"Well, let's kill them, then. Let me do this one. I told him I'd go slow."

They laughed.

An explosion rocked the room. Gil felt his bowels let go. The shotgun barrel thumped his head as it fell. Gil turned and saw Jimmy sliding down the wall, painting a bright crimson smear with his shoulder. He looked the other way and saw Lo standing in the doorway, holding Blanston's gun.

Sennett held his gun low but ready. "Well, I'll be," he said. "I am woman, see me shoot."

Lo aimed at Sennett, her hands shaking.

"Lo!" Gil yelled, afraid for her.

She turned to look at him. Sennett rushed forward and grabbed the gun out of her hands. He knocked her down.

"You shouldn't listen to that lamebrain. He'll get you killed."

Gil grabbed the shotgun, aimed at Sennett, and pulled the trigger. It clicked dryly.

"Chamber the round," chided Sennett, taking aim with his pistol.

He hit Gil in the shoulder. The shotgun fell to the floor. Sennett collected it calmly. "That's two," he said. He scanned the room, counting bodies: Clay, Jimmy, Bear Don't Walk, Lo, Gil. "This has really gotten out of hand."

A siren yowled nearby.

Sennett rolled his eyes. He aimed at Gil's chest, thought

again, and walked to the window, leaning the shotgun beside the door. Gil wriggled an inch toward the back of the room. The siren neared and a car skidded to a halt. Sennett peeked out the window. Gil crawled.

Powerful lights hit the window shades. An amplified voice crackled: "Come out with your hands on your head."

Sennett picked up a shotgun, poked it through the glass, and fired. Gil crawled further. A shotgun blast from outside blew the window inward, pocking the far wall with glass and pellets. Gil touched Lo and she looked at him.

More gunfire. Lo crouched and helped Gil into the kitchen.

"Throw your gun out and come out peacefully. We have more cars on the way," barked the voice.

Sennett answered with his gun.

They stepped into the back porch. Gil had to watch his feet and decide where he wanted each one to go. Lo opened the door and helped him down the steps. Threading their way between the twisted hulks of junked cars, they moved into the dark yard. They could just see the police car through the side yard, its spotlight trained on the front of the house. A muzzle flashed over the hood. Gil leaned heavily on Lo and they kept walking.

The dark Cadillac was in the alley, idling with its lights off. Gil wrenched the door open and fell in behind the wheel.

"Don't drive, Gil," said Lo. "I'll drive."

He waved her away and struggled upright. "Get in."

"Don't, Gil," she pleaded.

"I'll take care of us," he said.

She got in the passenger side. Gil turned the lights on and put the car in gear. Carefully, he crept up the alley and turned right.

"Are you sure that's the way to the highway?" said Lo.

The road was flickering like burning paper. Gil had the feeling they were stopped and the parked cars on either side were rolling toward them.

"Gil?"

He stepped on the gas and the car lurched. He braked too quickly and they were thrown forward.

"Let me drive, Gil!"

The rearview pulsed red and blue. Gil looked up. A police car was flying toward them. It rammed them.

Gil put the gas pedal on the floor. He took a wide right and turned left on the next corner, missing it and roaring over a snowy lawn.

"Gil!" cried Lo, petrified.

Gil looked back. The police car was farther back but still coming. He raced up the street and turned again, onto a dirt road by a pasture. The Cadillac surged up and down, each bump sending waves of fire through Gil. They were headed up into the foothills of the mountains.

One tire slipped into snow and weeds. Gil wrenched the wheel, overcorrected, and went up a bank on the other side of the road. Somehow he brought the car back down to the road, still moving forward.

The police car turned on its brights and started honking. The glare from the rearview dazed Gil and he slapped it askew. They sped up and up, around narrower turns, up steeper stretches of road.

"Gil, the road's going to run out any minute."

Snow was in his eyes, making him squint to see. A big ball of fluffy cotton right inside his head, thick, was getting between his thoughts. Gil shook his head slowly.

A candystriped barrier gated the road with a sign reading *ROAD ENDS.* Gil swung the car left. Skidding, they missed the barrier, plunged into a ditch, and stopped hard.

Spitting, Gil looked up. The glass was starred above Lo's

head, a wrinkled halo that sparkled in the headlights. Warm blood filled his mouth. It was hard to breathe. He was at a funny angle, with his legs on Lo's side of the car. Was she breathing? He thought she was, but there was blood on her temple and blood coming from her nose. They needed help.

His door was crumpled shut. Punching the shattered web of glass out of the doorframe, he half slid, half fell out the window.

The sky was lightening. Dawn. Gil saw the police car stopped on the road below, a man holding something to his shoulder.

"Three," he said.

Something knocked Gil over. He tried to get up, crawled, fell on his face. He crawled some more, the hard granules of snow stinging his hands. Tilting his head back, he could see the craggy outlines of the Monk Mountains, dark against the sky like a cardboard cutout.

The snow was really everywhere, and he couldn't do a thing about it. That was the mountains for you. Summer lasted three months. He was cold and tired of it. A drink would warm things up nicely. A fire. He saw a bottle in the snow, wondered what kind it was. He was beginning to warm up a little; it would be all right to stop for a moment.

Falling. He should be more careful. For Lo. A great dark curtain fell as he flew into the mountains.

ABOUT THE AUTHOR

Michael McCulloch is a Montana native. He lives in Chicago.